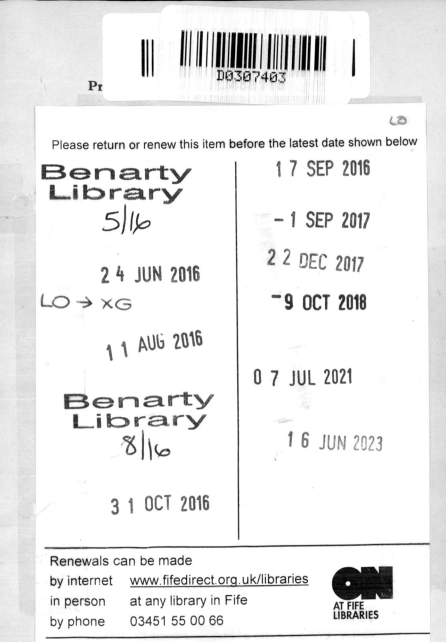

Look for Maggie Shayne's next novel
available soon from Harlequin MIRA

WAKE
TO
DARKNESS

MAGGIE SHAYNE

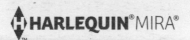

Harlequin MIRA is a registered trademark of Harlequin Enterprises Limited, used under licence.

First Published in Great Britain 2016
By Harlequin Mira, an imprint of HarperCollins*Publishers*
1 London Bridge Street, London, SE1 9GF

© 2013 Margaret Benson

ISBN 978-1-848-45482-8

58-0516

Our policy is to use papers that are natural, renewable and recyclable products and made from wood grown in sustainable forests.The logging and manufacturing processes conform to the legal environmental regulations of the country of origin.

Printed and bound by
CPI group (UK) Ltd, Croydon, CR0 4YY

This book is dedicated to Eileen Fallon, my literary agent and sister-friend. Her keen eye and experience in the business, her ability to tell me gently and tactfully when I'm off track, and to scream loudly and boisterously with me when I nail it, her support and encouragement for more years than either of us will ever admit to, even under torture, are among the most valuable tools in my writer's toolkit. And her friendship is one of the most cherished gifts I've ever received. Thank you, Eileen.

WAKE
TO
DARKNESS

Prologue

Marissa Siorse's new lease on life wasn't supposed to end this way. Lying on her back on the cold ground, unable to move any part of her body. Her mouth was open wide as she tried and tried to breathe, and failed. Her lungs wouldn't obey her brain's commands. Her eyes were open just as wide, as the horror of what was happening played out in front of them. She wished she could close them, but she couldn't, so she tried to focus on the leafless branches of the tree above her, and the sky beyond that. Blue, with soft, puffy clouds.

Then the ski-mask-covered face loomed over her, blocking out the sky. One gloved hand used a scalpel to slice the front of her dress open from hem to collar, laying her bare to the elements. To the cold. To the blade. That same hand had jammed a needle into her neck only minutes earlier, as she'd gotten into her car after a lunch date with her husband. She'd dressed up for him. Things were good between them. Better than ever. They hadn't been. Life had been nothing but fear and struggle, up until her miracle. Back in

August she'd been given a new pancreas. And after that, life had become a dream. She was strong now, maybe back to one hundred percent at this point, and looking forward to spending the rest of her life in the pink of health.

She'd had no idea that would be so short a time.

God, she was cold. Tears blurred her vision as she thought about her two kids. Erin was fourteen, half-way through her freshman year of high school and just now starting to get comfortable there. Cheer-leading had been the ticket that got her through. And Mikey… Mikey was only eight. He needed his mother. And Paul. What the hell was Paul going to do without her?

Black spots started popping in and out of her vi-sion. She wasn't getting any oxygen to her brain. She was suffocating.

And then the hand brought the scalpel sharply across her skin, leaving a path of fiery pain just below her rib cage. Inside her mind, Marissa's screams drowned out every other thought. But on the outside, she just lay there, still and silent. Until she died.

1

Friday, December 15

If the bullshit I wrote was true, I wouldn't have been standing with my back to the man I'd most love to bone, saying "No." Because if the bullshit I wrote was true, the question he'd just asked me would have been an entirely different one, instead of the one he'd asked, which had been, "Will you help me investigate another creepy fucking case that might get us both killed?"

Okay, those weren't his exact words, but they might as well have been.

I was in Manhattan, in a TV station greenroom, getting ready for my live segment, and having him there was throwing me way off my game. Way off. I was tingling in places I shouldn't be tingling, and remembering our one-night stand two months ago.

I should be remembering what happened after. The serial killer who damn near offed us both.

Mason Brown moved his oughtta-be-illegal bod around in front of me so I couldn't not look at him. I knew he knew that. "I shouldn't have sprung it on you like that. Should have started with hello. You look great, Rachel. Really great."

"It's the makeup. They overdo it for TV."

"It's not the makeup." He tried his killer smile on me. A fucking saint would steam up at those dimples. "I've missed you. What's it been, a month?"

Three weeks since I've seen him. Thanksgiving. Two months, nineteen days and around twenty hours since we'd had sex, last time I checked, but I'll be damned if I'll say that out loud. "Something like that."

"Too long, any way you count it."

"We agreed that *we*—" I waved my hand between us "—would be a bad idea."

"Yeah, but I thought that meant we wouldn't date." *And by* date *he meant* screw. "Not that we wouldn't ever see each other again."

Except that seeing him made me want to jump his bones. Hence the not-seeing-each-other part. But I couldn't tell him *that,* either.

"Look, Mason, I have five minutes before I have to be on that stage, in front of a live studio audience, hawking my new book, and you're really throwing me off my Zen."

"You have Zen?"

I closed my eyes. "No, but I fake it beautifully when I'm not..." *Don't finish that sentence.* "What makes you think I'd be any help, anyway? I only connected with the Wraith because he had your brother's heart, along with his penchant for murder, and I have your brother's eyes, and we connected in some woo-woo way I'm still not sure I believe. It was a fluke, and it's over. I'm no crime fighter."

He put both hands on my shoulders. *Yeah, that's right, touch me and make it even harder for me not to rip your shirt off, you clever SOB.* "Just give me a chance to tell you about the case. Come on, please?"

I closed my eyes, sighed hard and dropped my head to one side. When I opened my eyes again, he was flashing those damned dimples. He knew he had me. Hell, he'd had me at hello. The bastard.

"Buy me lunch after I finish up here and I'll let you bend my ear, but that's it, Mason."

The door opened. "Two minutes, Ms. de Luca," said the curly head that poked through.

I nodded and looked at Mason. His hands were still on my shoulders, and his smile had faded into an "I want to kiss your face off" sort of look.

I licked my lips, then wished I hadn't. I reminded myself of all the reasons we'd decided not to "date." I'd been blind for twenty years. Now I wanted to live my life as a sighted adult for a while before sharing it with anyone else. That made sense, didn't it?

I couldn't look at him. "I've gotta go."

"Okay."

"Fine." I turned away from him and tried to school my face into that of a spiritually enlightened guru who could change every viewer's life for a mere $17.99 in hardcover or $22.99 for the audiobook, plus tax where applicable. Only a fool would wait for the paperback or ebook versions, though they would be cheaper.

Mason sighed. *Maybe in disappointment that I didn't seem as glad to see him as he'd seemed to see me. A lot he knew. My inner idiot was doing cartwheels.*

The door opened again. Polly-Production-Assistant came all the way in this time. "Ready?"

"Sure am." *Not even close.*

She took my arm and led me out the door and through a maze of hallways. Mason was following right along behind us.

I turned to shoot him down over my shoulder. "I thought you were gonna wait in the greenroom?"

"I want to watch the taping. That's all right, isn't it?"

"Oh, sure, it's fine," said Polly or whatever the hell her real name was. "We're in a commercial break, on in thirty seconds."

She dragged me through a set of big double doors, and then we high-stepped over masses of writhing cables onto the set, stopping along the way so someone could run a mike up my back, under my dressy black jacket, over my shoulder and clip it to my flouncy lapel.

"Say something."

"Mike check," I said, looking through the window

to where the sound guys wore headsets suitable for a firing range. "How's it sound?"

They gave me unanimous thumbs-up, and I headed for the sofa. The show's host, failed comedienne Mindy Becker, got up to shake my hand, then I sat down in the most flattering manner, uncomfortably on the edge of the sofa, legs crossed at the ankles, one hand resting lightly atop the other on my thigh. I wet my lips and plastered a great big smile on my face. I tried with everything in me to forget that Detective Mason Brown was standing a few yards away, watching my every move and hopefully wanting me as much as I was wanting him. He'd better be.

He knew my deepest secret, too, I thought. The secret only those closest to me knew. That I didn't really believe in what I wrote. That I was a skeptic, feeding the gullible a steady diet of what they most wanted to hear—that the power to change their lives was in their hands—and laughing all the way to the bank.

And then the director said, "In three, two..." and pointed a finger at us.

"We're back!" Mindy told the camera. "Joining us now is the bestselling author of *Wish Yourself Rich,* the book that's sweeping the nation and changing lives, while spending its fifth week on the *New York Times* bestseller list. After going blind at the age of twelve, Rachel de Luca, the author who's been teaching us how to make our own miracles for five years now, experienced one of her own when her eyesight was restored by a cornea transplant this past August." She swung her head my way. "Welcome to the show, Rachel. I'm so glad to have you."

"Thanks, Mindy. It's great to be here."

"I want you to know that I have read this…" Mindy picked up a copy from the arm of her chair. "…this *gem,*" she said, "from cover to cover, and I loved it so much I got copies for every single member of today's studio audience as an early Christmas present."

Applause, applause.

"I can't tell you how deeply this book touched me."

"Thanks, and thanks for saying that."

"While the title is *Wish Yourself Rich,* this book is about so much more. About creating our own experiences, and actually having the lives we dream of. A lot of spiritual leaders today are saying many of the same things that you say in these pages, but, Rachel, you are the only one who is living, breathing, undeniable proof that it's true."

More applause.

"Why don't we start at the beginning? You went blind at the age of twelve."

I nodded. "It was a gradual process, but yes, eventually, I woke up one morning completely unable to see."

"What was the last thing you remember seeing?"

Oh, good question. "It was my brother Tommy's face."

She made a sympathetic sound. "This is the brother you lost earlier this year?"

"Yes, just before I got my transplant. He was the victim of a serial killer."

She set the book on her lap and, frowning, put her hands over mine. "How do you manage to have something like that happen and not let it rock your faith? You are so positive, so certain that we create what we focus on. How did you come to terms with your brother's murder?"

It was not the first time I'd had this question. Thankfully, I was prepared for it. I wrote this crap for a living, after all. "Tommy's journey was his own. I can't know what his higher self intended for him, or why his life had to end the way it did. I only know that I have two choices. I can be at peace with knowing that *he* is at peace, trusting that everything happens for a reason and that I will know what those reasons are when my own time comes to cross to the other side, or I can wallow in misery and ask 'why me' and 'why him' and resent the universe for being so cruel. My brother is going to be just as dead, either way."

"That is so *deep*," Mindy said, shaking her head slowly. "*So* deep."

"We get hung up when we think our happiness is dependent on circumstances outside ourselves. I'd be happy if only this would happen, we say, or if only that hadn't happened. We have to let go of that and realize that happiness is a choice. When we can

choose to be happy *in spite* of what's going on outside us rather than *because* of it, when we can stop
letting circumstances dictate how we feel, *that* is
true empowerment."

"That's amazing. 'Happiness is a choice.' That's
so good."

I smiled humbly. It really was one of my best nug-
gets of manure, that one. I rearranged this particular
piece of…wisdom slightly after every interview, so it
sounded fresh. Hell, I knew a thousand ways to say it
by now. It was the core message of seven bestsellers.

"So did you always know you would get your eyesight back one day?"

"Not at all," I said. "In fact, I'd pretty much given
up on it. I'd had cornea transplants before, but I was
one of those rare individuals who rejected them
every time. And I rejected them violently. My doctor had to convince me that it was worth trying again
with a new procedure." That, at least, was true.

"And it worked." Mindy clapped her hands to em-
phasize the words. "What was the first thing you saw
after the bandages came off?"

"My sister's face," I said, again speaking the truth.

"Oh, that's beautiful," Mindy said in an emotional
falsetto, blinking rapidly.

"So is she."

Applause, applause.

Note to self, use that line again.

"So if we create our own experiences according

to where we put our focus, how do you think you attracted your blindness?"

Because life sometimes sucks, and I drew the short straw. Because bad shit happens, and it doesn't make any sense at all and it never will.

I nodded sagely while I pulled the appropriate well-rehearsed reply from my archives. I had them for all the tough questions. "Until we know that our thoughts and focus create our lives," I said, "we sort of create by default. Our higher selves guide us toward the life we're supposed to lead, and we either go with the flow or fight tooth and nail. I believe this was simply a part of my journey in this lifetime. I think I had agreed to it before I ever incarnated."

"Really?" she said. "You *really* think all those years of blindness happened to you for a reason?"

"Absolutely." *Because I had shitty luck.*

"And have you reached any conclusions about what that reason might have been?"

"I think I've pieced together some of it, but not all. I don't think I'll know all of it until I'm on the other side, looking back, reviewing my life and the lessons it taught me. But I do know that being blind led me to my career of writing self-help *(bullshit)* books like the ones my family used to *(push on me)* get for me when I was going through hard times. It led me to dear friends I might not have made otherwise, people in my transplant support group, the best friend I ever had in my life, Mott Killian, who's since passed over himself, and my dog, of course."

And Mason Brown. It led me to him. When he hit me with his car because I stormed into a crosswalk, blind as a bat and too mad to be careful. Helluva coincidence that he ended up donating his brother's corneas to me later that same day. Helluva coincidence.

A big smile split Mindy's face, and she lifted the book again, opened the back cover and turned it toward the camera, which caught a close-up of Myrtle sitting in the passenger seat of my precious inspiration-yellow T-Bird with the top down, wearing her goggles and yellow scarf, and "smiling" at the camera as only a bulldog could do, bottom teeth sticking up over her upper lip.

The audience laughed, then applauded again.

"Myrtle is blind, too," I said. "I might not have taken in a blind old dog if I hadn't been through what I had." Odd, that was sappy as hell, and yet it was the absolute truth. Just like the bit I'd been thinking about the way Mason and I met. I should really be using this stuff more. But it made me uncomfortable to point to true things in order to prove my false claims. Muddied the waters. I liked clear lines between real life and my fictional nonfiction.

"That's beautiful," Mindy said. "That's just beautiful. Thank you so much, Rachel. It's been a pleasure having you. I hope you'll come back."

"Thank you, Mindy. I'd love to."

She faced the camera again, holding up the book. "Grab a copy of Rachel de Luca's *Wish Yourself*

Rich, available now in hardcover and audio wherever books are sold."

Applause, applause, applause.

"And we're clear!" called the director.

I relaxed and automatically turned to see if Mason was still there.

He was. But he was looking at me with his head tipped slightly to one side, like Myrtle when I say the word *food.* Or the word *eat* or the word *hungry* or any word remotely related to a meal.

He'd just seen a Rachel de Luca he'd probably never met before. The public one. And now he was going to berate me for it throughout an entire lunch. *This should be pleasant. Not.*

Mason had never seen the side of Rachel he'd witnessed on that stage. He had read her books—the last three, anyway—and he'd skimmed the others. They were pretty much all the same—all about positive thinking and creative visualization and everything happening for a reason. He would probably have read more, because the message was so uplifting and empowering, if he hadn't known that she didn't believe it herself. Not a word of it.

It was the one thing he'd never liked about her. God knew he liked everything else about her a little *too* much. But that she was selling this spiel to the masses when she didn't believe in it felt a little too cold, too calculating. It was a side of her that he found hard to take.

But today, just now, he'd seen a hint of something else. She might *say* she didn't believe the stuff she wrote about. She might even *think* she didn't believe it. But she *wanted to*. She had practically emanated a glow on that soundstage when she was going on about her positive thinking message. He was beginning to think it might not be an act at all.

Or maybe that was just wishful thinking on his part.

She'd kept the mask in place as she'd said her goodbyes to her hostess, and the entire time she'd signed autographs for the respectable-sized group who'd gathered outside on the sidewalk, despite the fact that it was cold and starting to snow. Then the crowd fell away as they walked up the sidewalk to find a place for lunch.

"It's a great time of year to be in the city," he said.

She nodded. The Rockefeller Center Christmas tree was all lit up, and every store window was decked to the nines. "I wish I could stay, but I've gotta get home to the kids."

"Kids? Don't tell me you got another dog."

"No, Myrtle's plenty. My niece Misty is dog-sitting, though."

"At your place?"

She nodded.

"You're a brave woman, leaving a seventeen-year-old alone in your home overnight."

"Amy's staying over, too."

He grinned. "I don't think your assistant is going

to be much help, unless it's to buy the booze for the inevitable party."

"Don't judge a book by its cover," she quipped. "Amy may be all Goth-chick on the outside, but she's super responsible, and besides, she hasn't forgotten that I saved her ass a month ago."

"*We* saved her ass a month ago."

"Well, yeah. You helped."

He laughed and meant it. It had been a while since that had happened. "Why only one twin with the dog-sitting? Is your other niece a cat person?"

"My sister and Jim took Christy with them for a two-week Christmas vacation in the Bahamas. She got the time off school but had to take her assignments along and promise to bring them back finished."

"And Misty didn't go?"

"Misty had the flu. Or at least she convinced my gullible sister that's what it was. Frankly, I think it was more a case of not wanting to leave her latest boyfriend behind. The priorities of love-struck teens never fail to make me gag." She did the finger-down-the-throat thing to make her point.

"I've missed the hell outta you," he said, smiling at her gross gesture as if she were a supermodel posing in front of a wind machine. Then he added, "And your little dog, too."

"She's missed *you,* too."

But he noticed that she didn't say *she* had.

"Corner Deli?" she asked.

She'd stopped walking, and it took him a beat to realize she was suggesting that they should eat at the establishment whose wreath-and-bell-bedecked door they were currently blocking. He opened it. It jingled, and she preceded him in. They joined the line to the counter, ordered, and then she picked out a table to wait for their food. She headed for the quietest table in the crowded, noisy place. "Ahh, New York," she said. "The only place where you can order a twenty-five-dollar sandwich that will arrive with a pound of meat and two square inches of bread."

"And it'll be worth every nickel."

"Hell, *yes,* it will." She was sparkling. Her eyes, her smile, told him she was as glad to see him again as he was to see her, whether she was willing to say it out loud or not. "So how are the nephews? I'll bet this is a hard time for them."

"It's rough. Their first Christmas without their dad. It's hard on all of us."

She nodded slowly. "It's my first holiday without my brother, too. I think that's probably why Sandra wanted to get away. It's too hard."

"It's rough. Sometimes I wonder if it would be easier if they knew the truth about Eric." He looked at her as he said that. It was one of about a million things he'd been dying to talk to her about.

"No, Mason," she whispered. "No one would be better off knowing their father, husband or son was a serial killer. No one. Trust me on this."

He nodded slowly. "It's been eating at me. Keeping that secret."

"You did the right thing."

God, he'd needed to hear her say that again. He didn't know why, didn't need to know why. It was a relief, that was all.

"They must have that new baby sister by now, though, right? Marie was out to *here* last time I—"

"Stillborn," he said softly.

"Oh, my God. Oh, *my God*. I'm so sorry, Mason. I didn't know."

"I know."

"You should've called."

"What good would that have done?"

She blinked real tears from her eyes. "Poor Marie. First her husband and then her baby. I'd ask how she's doing, but…" She just shook her head.

"Yeah, she's having a hard time of it. Keeps saying she's being punished."

"For what, for heaven's sake?"

He shook his head. "She's grieving. We can't expect her to make sense."

"And the boys?"

"Josh is good. He's eleven, you know? It's Christmas. They bounce back at that age. They spend a lot of weekends at my place, including this one when I get back. I pick them up after school and take 'em to the gym to shoot hoops every Wednesday when they don't have any other commitments."

"Josh is good," she said, homing in on what he'd left out.

She was good at that. Good at reading between the lines, good at sensing the things people didn't say. He'd never seen anything like the way she could tell when someone was lying and read the emotions behind their words.

"But Jeremy, not so much?" she asked.

"He's seventeen." He said it as if that said it all, but then reminded himself that Rachel had nieces, not nephews, and it might not be quite the same. "He's not bouncing back like Josh. He's morose. Brooding. Quiet. Withdrawn. Didn't even go out for basketball this year. Would've been his first year playing varsity, too."

"Sounds like he's depressed."

"Marie thinks he's been drinking. Said she smelled it on his breath when he came in late one night."

"Shit. I'm so sorry, Mason."

"It is what it is. They'll come back around. It just takes time."

Then he lifted his head and tried to do the same to his mood. "I'm sorry. I didn't mean to dump all that on you. I should be focusing on the positive, right? That's what your books would tell me to do."

"It's hard when there's so little positive to find," she said. Then she stabbed him with those insightful eyes of hers. "What about you? How are *you* doing, Mason?"

He had to think about his answer. "Work's been busy as hell. We just had a local vet murdered, his office torched with him in it."

"I read about that. You have any suspects?"

He shrugged. "He and his wife were both having affairs, heading for divorce. The drug cabinet was demolished, no way to tell if anything was missing. Who the hell knows?"

She nodded. "But that's work. I didn't ask how work is, I asked how *you* are."

He lowered his head. "I don't know, Rache. I feel like I'm in some kind of limbo. Waiting for something really big and really bad." He met her eyes again. "Like it's not finished yet." He knew that she knew what he was talking about.

"It's got to be finished," she said, and she said it really softly. Like she was afraid to press their luck by saying it out loud.

A waitress brought their sandwiches, each accompanied by homemade chips and a six-inch pickle spear. They dug in, ate for a while. She started with the chips. He remembered a line from one of her books. *Eat dessert first in case you're going to choke to death on your broccoli.* It made him smile to see her living by those words.

When he was half finished, he rinsed his mouth with coffee and said, "So…about this case. It's a missing person. The name was familiar, and I realized it was one of Eric's organ recipients."

She went still, but only for an instant. Then she just shrugged and kept on eating. "Coincidence."

"There's no such thing as coincidence. You wrote that yourself."

"Every self-help author spews that line. No one even knows who came up with it first. It's universal. Doesn't make it true."

"I kind of think it does." But he took another bite as he contemplated, and then said, "I figured I should at least ask if you'd had any dreams. Like before."

"Before, when I was riding along inside the head of a killer, you mean?"

"Inside the head of another person who got one of my brother's organs. If you can see them when they're *committing* crimes, maybe you can see them when they're the victim of one. Right?"

She bit, chewed, swallowed, taking her time. Delaying her answer. "It was so traumatic before that I think my mind's kind of...taken over."

"In what way?"

"Every time I start to dream, I wake up. I have the same startle response you have when you dream you're falling, you know what I mean?"

He did. "So is it any time you dream at all, or only when it's one of those...psychic connection dreams?"

"How the hell would I know? The dreams never play out."

"*No* dreams ever play out?"

She averted her eyes, and her cheeks turned cherry-red. "Well, sure. *Some* do."

Was it crazy for him to hope that blush was because those dreams were about him? And that they were sexy as hell? Like the ones he'd been having about her since he'd seen her last?

"But I *can* say for sure that I haven't had *any* dreams about *any* harm being done to *any* people. Besides, you said this was a missing person, not a murder victim, right?"

"Right. It's a missing person. But…"

"But what?"

"According to the family, this isn't someone who would just up and vanish. Housewife. Soccer mom. PTA, all that. You know?" He got an idea and ran with it before his brain told him not to. "It would be like if your sister Sandra suddenly just up and vanished. You wouldn't think she did it voluntarily, right?"

"No, I wouldn't. Not like when my transient addict brother up and vanished and I assumed he'd just turn up after a while, like he always did. Until he didn't."

"I'm sorry. That was a bad— I'm sorry, Rachel." He covered her hand with his.

She nodded, then twisted her arm to look at her watch. "I have to go."

"How are you getting back?" he asked.

"Alone, Mason. I'm getting back alone." She pushed the final chip into her mouth and left half the sandwich on her plate, along with the entire pickle.

"Thanks for lunch. I hope things get better for your family soon."

He nodded. "Thanks. Merry Christmas, Rache."

"Merry Christmas, Mason."

2

I would never get tired of seeing my home. Not just because I hadn't been *able* to see it until this past August, but because it was so freaking beautiful. All steep peaks and those half-round clay shingles on the roof like broken flowerpots. It was partly rich maple wood planks and partly cobblestone, and it always reminded me of a fairy-tale cottage. Only bigger. Way bigger. It sat near the dead end of a long dirt road that bordered the Whitney Point Reservoir, which really looked more like a great big lake. The road and my wrought iron fence were the only things between my place and the shore. There were woods all around me and the giant meadow where the house sat, rising up above the rest like a jewel on top of a crown.

The driveway was gated, because, let's face it, I'm kind of a big deal. But the gates were open, as they usually were, and I drove right on through and up to the attached garage where my precious T-Bird was parked for the winter, with my niece's first car parked beside it. She'd still had school this past week, so she'd needed her car to drive back and forth. My winter ride was a Subaru XV Crosstrek, brand-new in tangerine-orange, all-wheel drive with all the extras, and tougher than nails. The thing was more sure-footed in the snow and ice of the rural southern tier of New York State than a mountain goat. I loved it. Not as much as my collectible T-Bird, but it was close. I think Myrtle liked it even better than the yellow 'Bird. Heated leather. She liked her ass warm.

Everything had been brown and barren when I'd left to hit the talk show circuit, but now there was a fluffy blanket of snow on everything. I'd never had eyesight in the winter before. Not since I was twelve, anyway. My fairy-tale cottage looked more like Santa's workshop now, and the sight of snow clinging to the branches of the towering pines had me gaping like an air-starved trout. And I'd thought fall was gorgeous.

Damn, I love where I live.

I parked outside the garage instead of taking the time to drive in. I wanted to walk in the snow and gawk at my view some more. But as soon as I was out and inhaling my first icy, pine-scented breath, the front door opened, and Myrtle came running right down the steps and along the curving stone path to my feet, where she wiggled against my legs. My gorgeous niece Misty stood in the doorway, shaking her head but grinning.

You couldn't not love a blind bulldog.

I crouched down and rubbed Myrt's ears, kissed her face. "Hey, little boodog. Did you miss me?"

"Snarf," she replied. Which meant, *only if you brought me something edible.*

Fortunately, I had. "Come on inside and I'll give you a treat."

She followed me in, trotting along all on her own. She'd become completely confident in finding her way around her home base. As long as I didn't leave things out of place, you'd never know she was blind. Away from home she was a lot more dependent, but here, she ruled.

"How was the trip?" Misty asked, moving her tall and impossibly thin frame aside to let Myrtle and me come in. Like there wasn't already room.

"It was great, but I'm glad to get home." I gave her a hug. "I brought you something, too, to thank you for taking care of Myrt."

"It was fun. We watched all your appearances. You really kicked ass, Aunt Rache."

"Yeah, I did, didn't I?" I frowned and sniffed. "What smells so good?"

"Amy's making you a welcome-home dinner. Pulled pork or something with an equally porno-graphic name."

"Ooooh." I don't know if I said that, or my stomach did. Amy worked for me, but she was not my cook or housekeeper, so this was above and beyond the call of duty. I didn't even *have* a cook or housekeeper and didn't want one. I liked my space, didn't like other people poking around in my stuff. I shucked my boots and coat, leaving them where they fell, and headed for the sofa to collapse. "God, it's good to be home."

When my short, slightly round assistant and right-hand woman finally emerged from the kitchen to tell us dinner was served, I didn't want to get up.

"Amy, if we can eat in here I'll give you a Christmas bonus."

She grinned, dark red lipstick making her teeth look whiter, thick black eyeliner making her skin look paler. She dressed like an aspiring Addams Family member. "You *always* give me a Christmas bonus."

"Then I'll give you a bigger one. Please?"

She shrugged. "It's your house."

"It is, isn't it? Then I decree we eat in front of the TV like a bunch of real rednecks."

"I'm gonna bring everything in, then," Amy said. "You clear off the coffee table."

I saluted her and cleared off the magazines, books and catalogs with a sweep of my arm. "Done."

"God help us all," Amy muttered.

"Give me your keys, Aunt Rache. I'll go get your luggage for you."

"You are definitely the good twin. I don't care what your mother says." I nodded at my coat, lying like a red puddle by the front door. "They're in the pocket."

A few minutes later we ate. My luggage was in my room, my coat and boots magically in the closet, and the gifts from the Big Apple had been delivered. I'd managed to get two signed photos from Rusted Rail, a band they both adored, who'd also been guests on one of the talk shows I'd done. I was no longer sure which one. It was a blur at this point. The girls were thrilled. We talked into the night, and then Amy went home for the first time in several days, and Misty headed up to the guest room.

I walked around the house after it was quiet again. There was no cleanup to do; Amy and Misty had done it for me, knowing I always came back from these trips exhausted. And I was.

But there was more on my mind than being wiped out. I was thinking about Mason Brown's visit and what he had said, and yes, I was feeling guilty for not telling him everything. The thing was, this phenomenon where I would start to dream, then be immediately startled wide awake, hadn't been happening all that long. I mean, I'd sort of implied to him that it had been happening ever since we nailed the Wraith and went our separate ways. But it hadn't. I hadn't had another one of those terrifying vision-dreams since, so I guess my brain had seen no point in waking me up. Until about two weeks ago, give or take. But it had happened five times since then. I would start to dream, and *bam!* I'd be sitting straight up in bed with my eyes wide open, that startle reflex waking me right up. And every one of those times I'd been sure the dream I was about to enter wasn't an ordinary one. It had felt like the other ones. Those terrible, horrible visions when I'd been seeing through the eyes of the serial killer whose heart beat in another man. And whose corneas had restored my eyesight.

Two weeks. That was how long he said the transplant recipient had been missing. A person who had received organs from the same donor. Mason's brother, Eric, the original Wraith. What if my dreams had been telling me where she was, what had happened to her? What if I could have helped her?

It's not my job. I'm not a caped crusader, I'm a self-help author.

But what if I could help? I mean, really, was it asking too much to just have a damned dream? Even a nightmare. It couldn't hurt me, after all. It wasn't real. It was a dream.

I suppose I could try to let one play out. What harm is there in that?

Images from the earlier visions started to creep in like black ink spilling over my brain, but I shoved them away. "It's just a missing person," I told Myrt. "She might be in trouble. I need to let the dream play out, because that's what any decent human being would do."

Nodding, my decision firmly made, I headed for the stairs. "Come on, Myrt. Bedtime."

She was right beside me, hadn't left my side since I'd gotten home, and she trotted up the stairs, happy as hell. She'd lost a few pounds since I'd adopted her. Our long walks were doing her a world of good, despite the fact that she acted like they were sheer torture.

I took a long hot shower while Myrtle lay on the bathmat in front of the shower doors, snoring. Then I put on my jammies—a white ribbed tank and panties—brushed my teeth and opened my medicine cabinet. There was some PM-style pain reliever, the closest thing I had to a sleep aid. I popped two of them, and then Myrtle and I went to bed.

She walked up her little set of doggy steps, and I knew she'd missed sleeping with me. I wondered where she'd been spending her nights while I'd been gone. With Misty, or in here all alone? She stretched out on top of the covers, as close to me as she could manage. I rolled onto my side and put my arm around her, and she sighed as if all was right with her world again. She was snoring within ten seconds.

And then I closed my eyes and hoped I was wrong. That there would be no vision. That there was no connection between me and the others who'd received organs from my donor. Mason's brother. The dead serial killer. None at all.

I was dreaming. I knew I was dreaming because I wasn't me, I was someone else. I was lying on my back on the ground. I could feel the icy cold earth underneath me and the snow around me. It was freezing. I couldn't move. I was awake, I was breathing, but I couldn't move, and I was terrified.

Someone was with me, crouching over me. I angled my eyes until they hurt, but I couldn't see them, really, because I couldn't move my head and I was lying flat and naked in the snow.

Naked? No, not quite. I was wearing a dress, but it lay open on either side of me, sliced up the front. I could just make it out in my peripheral vision. I could feel something tight around my waist, like panty hose. And there were shoes on my feet, a little too tight in the toes.

All I could see was the night sky, dotted with stars and—

Ohmygod, something's cutting me!

An ice-cold blade flashed in my vision and drove into my abdomen, and the pain screamed through me. And *I* tried to scream, as well, but I couldn't move. I couldn't scream. It was cutting me. Oh, God, it was cutting me. I felt the blood, warm and running over my naked skin. I couldn't breathe. I couldn't breathe!

I was going to suffocate. *Let it be fast! Faster than the cutting! Oh, God, no more.*

But there was a tearing, ripping. My lungs seemed to spasm in my chest, hungry for air, but I could not take a breath. Black spots started popping in and out of my vision. My head was going to explode. My torso was on fire with pain, and my heart was pounding like a jackhammer in my chest, or trying to.

Something was torn from my abdomen, and it rose up, into that tiny area within range of my vision. It was pink and dripping, and clutched in a gloved hand. A piece of me!

And then blackness descended. Merciful death caught me in soft hands. The pain went away from me. Or rather, I went away from the pain.

I screamed until my bedroom door was flung open and Misty stood there with a baseball bat in her hands. She wore cute flannel PJs, and her perfectly straight, perfectly platinum hair was in her face as she shrieked, "What the fuck!"

Hearing that particular word from my seventeen-year-old niece seemed to do the trick. I clamped my jaw and blinked my vision clear, pushed my hair off my own face and turned on the bedside lamp. "I'm sorry. I'm sorry, Misty, I must have scared the hell out of you."

"You okay?" She lowered the bat.

It made me proud to think she would come running to my defense if I really was being attacked in my sleep.

"What happened, Aunt Rache?"

Someone paralyzed me and cut out one of my organs while I lay there unable to move. Good God.

"Aunt Rachel?"

"Bad dream, kid. Just a bad dream."

She heaved a big enough sigh that I knew she'd been truly scared. "Jeeze, I thought someone was murdering you." She let the bat drag on the floor as she came farther into the room.

Someone was. Only not me. Another of Eric's organ recipients. Dammit, Mason was right. It isn't over.

"Aunt Rache? You sure you're okay?"

"Yeah. Fine. Look, I'm sorry, kiddo. You want to curl up here for the rest of the night?"

"Only if you promise not to wake up screaming again."

I looked at the clock. 4:00 a.m. The pills would have worn off by now. "I'm pretty sure I won't."

"If you do, I swear, I'm gonna hit *you* with this bat." She stood it up against the headboard and climbed under the covers.

Myrtle snuggled back down between us and started snoring like a chain saw.

"Hope you don't mind sharing with a bulldog," I said.

"She's been in bed with me every night since you left. I kind of missed her, to be honest."

"Yeah, she has a way of getting under your skin, doesn't she? Good night, Misty."

"Good night, Aunt Rache. Sweet dreams. And that's an order."

I turned off the bedside lamp. Of course the night-light was on. I always left the night-light on.

Saturday, December 16

Seeing Rachel again after almost a month had had an impact on Mason that he hadn't expected. He'd thought their one-night stand had been based on the drama they were going through, and the sense of intimacy between them on the secret they shared. No one else in the world knew the truth about his brother. Or that he'd concealed evidence to protect his family—his mother, his pregnant sister-in-law, his nephews. He loved those boys like his own. No one knew what he'd done but Rachel.

He knew she needed time to figure out who the newly sighted Rachel de Luca was. He'd been relieved by that when she'd said it, because he'd convinced himself that their roll between the sheets hadn't meant anything special. And he wasn't ready for anything more than that, anyway. He'd just lost his brother, betrayed his oath of service, become the only father figure in his nephews' lives. There was no room for anything else.

Even the way he kept thinking about her at odd moments, and the idiotic way he'd set his damned

DVR to record anything that had her name attached to it, had seemed like no big deal. But seeing her again...*that* had hit him like a mallet between the eyes.

And now he was starting to wonder if maybe what connected them was more than just the traumatic situation they'd gone through together, the secret that they shared. Hell, he'd seen through her masks so easily on that talk show yesterday that she'd seemed completely transparent. But she wasn't, she couldn't be, or the entire reading public would see through her, too, right?

No, it was only him. And he saw more than the mask she wore, the positive-thinking public persona. He saw through the cynic she thought she was to the *real* Rachel. And it made him want to see her even more.

A door slamming downstairs reminded him that he wasn't alone. It was the weekend, and his nephews, who usually showed up on Friday nights, had been delayed an extra twelve hours due to his trip into the city to see Rachel. They would not be put off any longer.

"Uncle Mason!" Joshua yelled. "Aren't you up yet?"

He rolled onto his side and blinked at the clock. 8:30 a.m. Kids had no respect for sleeping in. Flinging back the covers, he sat up, gave his head time to adjust to being vertical, then shouted back, "I'll be right down." He needed a shower, but in the meantime he pulled on pajama bottoms, a T-shirt and a pair of nice thick socks, because his old farmhouse had cold floors. Giving his hair a rudimentary flattening with his hands, he headed downstairs.

Jeremy was in the living room, on the sofa, already manning the Xbox controller. His expressionless eyes were glued to the TV screen, and his brown hair was even longer than it had been last weekend. He refused to get it cut.

"Hey, Jer," Mason said.

"Hey."

Nothing, not a flicker. It was par for the course with Jeremy lately. Only a little over four months since his father had shot himself in the head in Mason's apartment. Two and a half months since the teen had busted into a remote cabin where a madman was about to kill both Mason and Rachel. Jeremy had picked Mason's gun up off the floor and shot the bastard dead. Just like that. He hadn't even hesitated. The kid was depressed over the loss of his father, traumatized over having killed a man.

Mason scuffed into the kitchen where Marie had a pot of coffee brewing, and was taking mugs from the cupboard. She looked his way as he entered and smiled, but her eyes were dead, too. Like Jeremy's. Her smile was fake. Forced. Her baby girl had been stillborn a few weeks ago. Her husband had killed himself three months before that. The woman was so destroyed he thought a stiff wind would knock her over. But she was putting on a brave face for her boys' sakes, doing the best she could. It validated for him yet again that he'd done the right thing by hiding Eric's suicide note. The family was barely holding on as it was. Imagine how much worse it would be if they knew that their beloved husband and father was a serial killer.

"Sorry we got here so early," Marie said. "Josh was in the car with his backpack an hour ago. I put him off as long as I could."

"It's fine. I should have been up by now."

"It's your downtime. You know you could skip a weekend if you wanted."

"And do what, sleep till noon and stare at the walls all day? Nah. I need these guys around to keep me from going to pot."

Once again she smiled because she was supposed to. Her eyes remained stark. Dark circles under them told him she wasn't sleeping. Her pale skin and sunken cheeks told him she probably wasn't eating right, either.

How did you know when a grieving wife or son moved from ordinary mourning into a dangerous depression? Where was the line? He was going to have to find out.

The coffee was done, so he took the mugs from her and filled them. "Sit down, Marie. I'm cooking you some breakfast."

"We already ate."

"They did. You didn't. Bacon and eggs, whaddya say?"

She shook her head, but accepted the filled mug and sank into a kitchen chair, holding it between her hands as if she was cold. He spotted Joshua running past the window, red parka, knit hat with a fuzzy ball on top like a character from *South Park*. He'd taken one of the plastic toboggans from out in the barn. Mason had bought them right after the first snow. Josh was heading up the hill out back with it.

"He loves it here with you," Marie said. She'd slugged back half the coffee, though it was piping hot.

"I love having him." Her boots were still on, making puddles under her chair. He frowned. "Are you in a hurry, Marie?"

She followed his gaze and shook her head. "No, just absentminded. I'm sorry about the floor."

"I'm not worried about the floor. I'm worried about *you*."

She met his eyes, but quickly shifted hers away. "Some of my girlfriends are taking me out shopping today. They think it's time I...got over it. I just don't know how they think that's possible."

"It has to be possible," he said. "Marie, we all miss Eric, and I know you're devastated about the baby."

"Lilly. Her name was Lilly."

He knew that. It was engraved on the headstone with the little angel above the plot right next to her father's.

A dozen platitudes came in and out of his mind, things he'd read in Rachel's books. But he didn't say any of them, because he thought Marie needed to hold on to her grief a little bit longer. And that was okay. "You have a right to your pain, Marie. Don't let anyone tell you otherwise."

"Thank you for that."

"When you're ready to start to heal, though, you put your focus on those boys. They're just as precious as they were before all the losses you've suffered. They need you to come back to them."

She thinned her lips and nodded as if she was hearing him, but he didn't think she was. "I appreciate you picking up the slack in the meantime." Then she pushed away from the table and stood up. "I've got to go."

She headed out the door to her car and took off—a little too fast for the road conditions, in his opinion. He'd had a set of studded snow tires put on for her, though, so she should be all right on the road.

But she wasn't all right emotionally. He knew that.

He carried his coffee mug through the house to the back, passing Jeremy again on the way. He was as morose as his mother. Poor kid. But Mason kept going into the back room, the coldest room in the little farmhouse, which had no real purpose and would, he thought, make a great woodworking shop if he ever followed his intention to learn how to do that sort of thing. Right now it was a catch-all area for anything he didn't know what to do with. He passed the piles of junk, opened the back door and hollered out to Josh, "I'm making breakfast. You hungry?"

Joshua was at the bottom of the hill, picking himself up out of the snow and preparing to head up again for another ride. He hollered, "Come out and sled with me!"

"I need food and a shower, and then I'll sled with you."

"Awwwwl-riiiight."

"So you gonna eat?"

"How long?"

"Half hour?"

"Okay."

"That's about six more trips down the hill, Josh. Count 'em off and come on in, okay?"

Josh nodded and started back up the hill at a pace that made Mason smile. No question. The kid was going to try to get in ten. At least. Mason headed back into the living room, stopped behind the sofa and put both hands on Jeremy's shoulders to be sure he had his attention. "I need to take a shower. Ten minutes, tops. Keep an eye on your brother, okay?"

"Yeah." He didn't look away from the TV screen.

"Jeremy, that means put the controller down, get up, walk to the window and check on him at least three times while I'm gone."

"He's eleven."

"That's not an answer. Come on, Jer, help me out here."

"All *right,* I'll check on him. *Jeeze.*"

Mason closed his eyes and prayed for patience. The kid had lost his father, his baby sister and, for all intents and purposes, his mother, he reminded himself. Add to that the typical brooding of a seventeen-year-old male, and you had a recipe for frustration that couldn't be beat.

Mason headed upstairs for a shower that would compete with his record for brevity. When he came back down, hair wet, pulling on a long-sleeved green thermal shirt with a big black bear on the front, he heard voices. Female voices. He popped his head through the collar and pulled the shirt down over his belly.

Rachel was standing in the living room, eyes glued to the chest he'd just covered up and making him want to pull the shirt right back off again.

I had known from the second I woke up this morning that I had to tell Mason about the dream, because I knew damned well it *wasn't* a dream. I was pretty certain it was, instead, a murder. A real one. Maybe the murder of the woman he'd said was missing. I was shaken and trying not to show it to Misty, but she didn't miss much. Still, she was happy to go along to meet my friend Detective Brown. She was even a little excited. She knew that Mason and I had worked together to solve a string of serial killings, though she didn't know about my personal connection, that I had the damn killer's eyes in my head. And she knew Mason's nephew had saved my life by shooting the killer.

We pulled into Mason's driveway, and I saw an

unfamiliar green Jeep parked beside his classic Monte Carlo. Since he had mentioned that his nephews would be with him for the weekend, I'd stopped at Mickey D's for a gigantic breakfast order and brought it along. No use showing up empty-handed, right? When we got out of the car, and headed up onto the porch, Myrtle walking with her side touching my calf, my stomach went all queasy. Seeing Mason again was a big deal and not only because I was pretty sure I knew the fate of his missing person.

Joshua came running from somewhere out back and pounded up the porch steps, and I could have sworn he was going to hug me, but he skidded to his knees and hugged Myrtle instead. His smile was huge and aimed up at me, though. "Hey, Rachel! Where you been? It's been like *ages*."

I went soft inside at the enthusiastic welcome. "I've been busy jetting around being a famous author. I would so much rather be hanging out with you. But I brought food so you'd forgive me." I held up the bags and nodded at Misty, right behind me, who was carrying two more. "This is Misty, my niece."

"Hi, Josh," she said.

Josh said hi, getting to his feet but keeping one hand on Myrtle's head, scratching while she wriggled in delight. "If there's hash browns, you're my favorite writer," he said and, Myrtle at *his* side now, he opened the door and we all trooped inside.

"There are indeed hash browns," I promised.

"Yeah, and at least two sandwiches for each of you," Misty added.

At that moment Mason came down the stairs pulling a green shirt over his head, his chest and abs bare. My stupid stomach clenched up into a hard little knot, and I was still staring at his chest like my bulldog would stare at a steak—well, if she could see it—when his head popped into view. Misty elbowed me in the rib cage, and I dragged my focus from his chest to his face.

"Rachel." Mason seemed surprised and maybe a little flustered, but his smile was genuine. "What are you doing here?"

"I needed to talk to you about something." I tore my eyes away from him, glimpsing Jeremy, who was gaming and hadn't even said hello. "The gorgeous blonde bearing additional food is my niece Misty."

Just as I had intended, that got Jeremy's attention. He looked our way, and then he paused the game and got to his feet. "Hey, Rachel."

"Hello, Jeremy," I replied. Then I turned to Misty and said, "This is the young man who saved my life."

Misty smiled. And there had not been a teenage boy born who didn't turn to mush at that smile. It was bright and white and made her vivid blue eyes, fake tan and white-blond hair even more attractive. "So you're the one. Thanks for saving my aunt."

Jeremy shrugged and looked at his sneakers. At least he was on his feet now.

Mason clapped his hands together and said, "Well, let's eat. Fast food is best served piping hot, right?"

The kitchen table only seated four. Mason and I unloaded the bags and stacked the food in piles on paper plates. McMuffins on one, hash browns on another, French Toast Sticks on a third. The younger crew helped themselves and headed back into the living room, where Josh served as the ice-breaker, getting the conversation going while plying Myrtle with way too many treats. Pretty soon it was noisy in there, which was good, because it gave me an opportunity to say what I'd come here to say.

But Mason spoke up before I had the chance. "Look at Jeremy," he said in a stage whisper.

I glanced through into the living room, where the kids were all on the couch, wolfing junk food, playing with Myrtle and yacking, the Xbox still paused and possibly forgotten.

"I haven't heard him say more than two words at a time since October," Mason marveled.

"My niece has that effect on many of the male species."

"You should bring her around more often."

"I will."

He looked at me, our eyes locked and I stammered, "You know what I mean. If it would help Jeremy." *Damn, Rache, idiot much?*

"It would." He held my eyes a beat too long, and I looked away to pick out a breakfast sandwich.

"I, um, noticed the Jeep. Yours?"

"Yeah. I finally broke down and bought something more suited to winter driving. The Black Beast is going into the barn for a well-deserved winter nap soon."

I smiled. "I did the same."

He glanced out the kitchen window at my new Subaru and nodded. "Nice."

"Thanks. I, um, didn't get coffee, 'cause I figured—"

"Right, I've got a fresh pot right here. Marie made it when she dropped the boys off." He got up, got mugs, poured, served.

"How is she doing?"

He shook his head. "Not good. She looked like hell this morning."

"I'm sorry, Mason. Your family's a mess, and here I am horning in on you with—"

"It's good you're here. I've been racking my brain trying to figure out what to do for Marie and the boys, how to help, if it's normal grieving or if it's gone beyond that. I was just thinking I'd like to talk to you about it."

I nodded, lowered my head and took a bite of my sandwich, which was already cooling and would soon reach that inevitable stage of inedible.

"But that's not why you're here, is it?"

I lifted my brows at him, slugged a little coffee down to clear my mouth. "What do you mean?"

"I can see you've got something on your mind."

How could I have forgotten, even for a minute,

that he was every bit as good at reading people as I was? Especially me.

I lowered my voice. "I had a dream."

His eyes widened. "About the case I was telling you about? The missing soccer mom?"

"I don't know. But if it was, she's dead." I looked toward the living room, then back at him. "I was inside her head, Mason. I was there with her while she was murdered."

He looked horrified, then glanced toward the living room just like I had done. "How?"

"She was paralyzed. Drugged, I think. It was impossible for her to move. And the killer cut into her and ripped something out."

He stared at me. "And you felt it? You experienced it like before?"

I averted my eyes, nodded. I put my hands over my rib cage, poking the soft area where she—I—had been stabbed. "The knife went in here and ripped left, then right. God, the pain was just..." I'd started breathing hard and had to stop myself, rein it in.

"Dammit, Rachel." He put his hands on my shoulders. "Are you all right?"

"Yeah. I'm okay."

"I thought you said you weren't having the dreams anymore, that your brain was startling you awake every time one started?"

I nodded. "I took a sleeping pill. Figured I had to know what it was my brain didn't want to let me see. Now I know."

He shook his head slowly and started to say something, but his cell phone rang. He picked it up, spoke briefly, but mostly listened. When he put it down again he looked at me. "They found a body."

I closed my eyes. "Was it…?"

"No details, but Rosie said it wasn't pretty. I have to go."

"I'll stay with the boys." I blurted it without even thinking first, then realized I was effectively shooting our agreement not to see each other right in the foot. He noticed it, too; I could tell by the way he was looking at me, his eyes all questiony. "I've missed those two more than I thought, and Myrtle's in seventh heaven with Josh. We'll hang out. Go take care of this. I'll see you later."

"Thanks, Rachel." He put a hand on my cheek, then took it away, suddenly awkward, like he didn't know why he'd put it there to begin with. "Thanks."

He walked away, into the living room to tell the boys what was up, then up the stairs to grab his things. Then he came back down, shoving his wallet into his back pocket, his shoulder holster over his button-down shirt, gun in easy reach. And I was still sitting there with my half-eaten sandwich and my coffee, wondering how I'd gone from "We should stay apart" to "I'll spend the day in your house with your nephews, awaiting your return."

He came through the kitchen, looked me in the eye, and I knew he was thinking the same thing I was. I ought to say something. Clarify things. Right?

"I'll get back as soon as I can."

"Do what you need to. I'm not going anywhere."

He nodded, like that was enough. For now. It would have to be, because I didn't know what else to say. If I was having visions and people were dying and the two were connected, then we didn't have much choice but to be together until we got to the bottom of things.

I could have thought the freaking universe wouldn't take no for an answer. You know, if I believed in that sort of shit.

3

The body had been found in a wooded area off I-81, a few miles north of the Binghamton area. Traffic was being detoured for a mile-long stretch, so the highway was eerily quiet.

Mason skirted the detour sign and drove right up to the cop whose car was enforcing it, bubble gum light flashing. He lowered his window, slowed down and flashed his badge, and the officer waved him by.

The scene was already swarming. The state police forensics team was already there, and Rosie was waiting for him on the shoulder, hunching into his police-issue overcoat and wearing a completely non-regulation furry hat with earflaps pulled down. Yeah, it wasn't a warm day. The sun was shining, and the official temp was allegedly thirty-five, but it felt like single digits the way the wind was blowing. It was a cold wind, too. Icy.

Mason parked his new-to-him Jeep and got out, then walked onto the shoulder to stand beside his partner, the oversized and ready-to-retire, shaven-headed Roosevelt Jones. He followed Rosie's gaze down the steep slope to the bottom, where a New York state trooper supervised while two forensics guys worked. One was taking pictures, the other, measurements. The body was still there, bent and twisted unnaturally. "Looks like they just tossed her and let her roll down and stay the way she landed," he said.

Rosie nodded. "Looks like. Snow's covered up any evidence on the bank here."

"Tire tracks?"

"First responders ruined 'em." Rosie shrugged as he looked toward the ambulance and police cruiser parked a few feet ahead on the shoulder. Their tire tracks were fresh in the soft ground, right where whoever dumped the body would probably have parked.

Mason shielded his eyes as he watched the men below. "Who called it in?"

"College student. Had a flat, pulled over a few yards back to change it and saw her lying down there. I got his statement and contact info, then let him go."

"All right." Mason turned up his collar. His coat was lined denim, but he hadn't grabbed a hat and his ears were already freezing. "Ready to head down there, then?"

"I'll wait up here," Rosie said, eyeing the steep

climb warily. "Man my size gonna trip and roll right down on top of her. I don't wanna contaminate the scene."

Mason shook his head. "Creative way to get out of climbing back up, but I'll let you off the hook."

"You better."

Mason headed down, taking a route a few yards from the one the body had probably taken. The state cop on the scene was Bill Piedmont, a man Mason knew and liked. He didn't know the two forensics guys, but then, they tended to move around a lot.

"Hey, Bill. What's your take?"

"Mason." Piedmont gave him a nod from beneath his wide-brimmed gray Stetson. Trooper standard issue. "Looks like she's been here a while. Body's frozen to the ground. Probably was hidden by the snow until the wind came up and blew it clear enough so she could be spotted from the road. Ground underneath her is bare."

Mason was looking at the woman. She wore a blue dress, torn nylons, one shoe. The other was probably around somewhere. Most likely flew off her as she tumbled down the hill. She'd landed on her left side, left leg bent unnaturally beneath her, the right one folded up. Right arm extended, left one in front of her body. She had a wedding ring on her finger. Her hair was frozen to her skull. Red, he thought.

"So she was dumped before that first snowfall. What was that, a week ago?"

"Six days," Piedmont said.

"Look like she was dead before she was dumped?"

Piedmont nodded and walked around the body, giving it a wide berth so as not to disturb evidence. Not that there would be any. Mason was already certain the killer had stayed up on the road and never set foot down here. Still...

"Oh, shit." He could see the front of her now. The dress was torn from the hem up to her neck, flapping up and down in the frigid wind. She was cut all to hell and gone—gutted, it looked like. Then he looked again. Someone had cut two sides of a triangle into her skin, with its topmost point dead center just below her breasts, then peeled it back so the flap was lying folded over on her belly. He could see the edges of her rib cage and a gaping, frozen, deep red void he would rather not have seen.

It fit perfectly with what Rachel had described.

"Not another mark on her," Piedmont said. "A fucking odd way to commit a murder."

"She have any ID on her?"

"No, but we knew you had a missing woman matching her description, right down to the blue dress. So..."

Mason knelt and looked at the woman's hands. There wasn't so much as a broken nail. No bruising on her, none that was visible, anyway. "No signs of a struggle, no defensive injuries?"

"Not that I could see. You?"

Mason shook his head, then looked at the area around her. "There are a lot of weeds and brush down here. Enough to conceal her a little until someone got close enough to notice."

The guy snapping pictures stopped snapping. "I think I've got all we need. The ME's here. You can let him take her."

"Bag her hands, just in case," Mason said. She was pretty—or had been once. She'd died with her eyes open, but there was nothing in them now. No expression, not of horror, not of peace. Nothing. They were lifeless and shrunken, no longer even resembling human eyes, more like a pair of cloudy grapes long past their prime.

A team came down the hillside with a gurney and a body bag. Mason lowered his head. "I'm sorry this happened to you, Marissa. If you are Marissa, and I think you are. We're gonna get whoever did this. I promise you that."

Then he straightened and picked his way back up the steep embankment, moving at an angle to get better footing in the fresh snow. As he walked, he was tapping keys on his cell phone, keying in "location of the human pancreas" in the search bar. Then he clicked on Images, and saw that the pancreas was between the left and right sides of the rib cage and partially behind, tucked up against the liver.

That was where she'd been cut, where there was a gaping hole. Right where Rachel had dreamed of being cut, of having something torn from her body while she was still alive.

He hadn't told Rachel which of his brother's organs his missing soccer mom had received. He'd deliberately left that part out because he didn't want to influence her visions. It would be like contaminating a crime scene, leaving traces around that might later be mistaken for actual clues.

Marissa Siorse, his missing person, had been a pancreas recipient. The ME would tell him for sure, but he was pretty certain that body down there was missing its pancreas. And if she *was* Marissa, that organ had originally belonged to his dead brother.

He didn't want to think that Eric had come back from the dead to reclaim his parts from beyond the grave. But he hadn't wanted to think that his brother had found a way to continue his serial killings from beyond the grave, either, and he'd been wrong. Eric's crimes had been repeated by two of his organ recipients, men who, as far as Mason could tell, had been perfectly normal, law-abiding citizens prior to their transplants.

It's not the same. This organ recipient is the victim, not the killer.

He told himself that, but the icy dread in the pit of his stomach was colder than the December wind freezing his ears.

Joshua teased me to come out sledding with him until I finally gave in. It looked as if Jeremy and Misty were hitting it off just fine, but being teenagers, they were unwilling to bundle up and take him out themselves. I told them I thought they were both assholes—I said it lovingly, don't judge me—then dressed as warmly as possible, borrowing some gloves from Mason's closet, and took Josh out there myself. Well, me and Myrtle, that is. She was almost as eager as Josh was. Besides, I needed something to wipe the nightmare, which I knew in my gut was more than just a bad dream, out of my mind.

The air was cold, sunshine bright, snow pristine. I could see my breath in big clouds every time I exhaled. It was good. Clean. Just the prescription I needed. I hadn't seen much snow since my vision had been restored. It had only snowed once or twice so far this winter, and of course I'd been blind for the previous twenty. So I was taking it all in and loving it, like I did every new visual experience. And yeah, that made it tough to maintain my inner cynic, but I figured a few months of childlike wonder was to be expected and would pass soon enough, you know, like a bad bout of food poisoning.

Sighted people don't appreciate their eyesight nearly enough, in my opinion. Those who've always had it, I mean.

We trooped up the hill, dragging a pair of red plastic toboggans behind us, Josh talking a mile a minute about the karate lessons he wanted to sign up for and all the things on his Christmas wish list, while Myrtle trudged right beside him, paying such close attention it was as if she understood his every word. She adored the kid.

We reached the top. Josh situated his sled, then turned to Myrtle and said, "You want to ride, Myrt?"

"Josh, she won't sit still. She'll wipe you out for sure."

"I'll hold her," he said. He didn't precede it with "Duh," but he might as well have. "Come on, Myrt. Get on here with me."

"She won't like it, Josh," I said, as Myrtle responded to his voice and plodded right over to him. She sniffed the sled thoroughly, then lifted her paws and stepped on board in front of him. "She's blind. She'll be scared." If someone had said that about me, I would have punched them in the eye. I was being overprotective, and I knew it.

"I'll hold on to her. Come on, Rachel, she shouldn't miss the fun just 'cause she can't see." He leaned forward and wrapped his arms around my dog. Myrt was facing straight ahead with her teeth showing and her tongue hanging out. She knew something exciting was about to happen. I recognized that look. She was eager. Up for anything as long as her eleven-year-old buddy was involved.

"How are you going to steer?"

Josh tightened his arms around Myrtle, then reached one-handed for the rope handle threaded through the nose of the sled, which children everywhere use to fool themselves into thinking they have a modicum of control as they rocket down steep, snowy hills. Myrt whined uncertainly, and he let go of the rope and scooted forward. "You're gonna have to ride with us and steer," he told me with a smile.

"No way am I going to fit on that th—"

"There's room. C'mon, Rache, please? Try it. Just once."

I heaved a gigantic sigh and plopped my ass onto the sled. I stretched my legs, one on either side of Josh and Myrtle, planting my heels against the front of the sled, and reached around them to grab on to the steering rope that wasn't going to work, anyway. What had I gotten myself into?

Josh grinned at me over his shoulder, and I believe my heart grew three sizes that day. We all leaned forward and gave the sled a scootch or two, and the next thing I knew we were flying down the hill toward the back of Mason's house. I heard high-pitched squeals and realized they were coming from me just before we all went over sideways and tumbled into the snow.

When he sat up laughing, Josh still had my bulldog safely in his arms. Myrtle wriggled free and bounced in the snow, chest down, butt up, and wiggling in delight. She barked happily, and I knew exactly what she was saying: "Again, again, again!"

Okay, so I was wrong. Doesn't happen often, but it does *happen.*

I brushed the snow off myself and got to my feet. "I'm too old for this."

Josh stood, too. "Nobody's too old for this. C'mon, let's do it again."

"Yarf!" said Myrtle. Which meant, *damn straight,*

we're gonna do it again—and again and again until one of us is too tired to do it anymore. Three guesses who that'll be, old lady.

What? She's a very verbal dog.

Jeremy was messed up. Misty could tell. He couldn't look her in the eye for very long. Aunt Rache said when someone couldn't look you in the eye they were either hiding something, incredibly self-conscious or too distracted thinking about something else. Misty thought it was the third thing. He had a lot on his mind. She had to do most of the talking, but she was good at that.

"So where do you go to school?" she asked him.

"Holy Family. It's private."

"I go to public."

"Oh."

"Right here in the Point. Is that where you guys live?"

"A little south."

"You a junior?"

"Senior."

No encouragement to go on in his tone. Okay, whatev. She picked up a magazine from the coffee table. *National Geographic.* A good one to kill time with. Jeremy was kind of cute but a lousy conversationalist. "So what are you gonna do after graduation?" she asked after a bit.

"I don't know." He picked up his game controller, restarted his game.

Strike two, Misty thought.

"Maybe you should think about being a cop, like your uncle. I mean, you must have it in you, the way you saved their lives and all."

"I wouldn't want to have to do that again."

Eyes straight ahead on the TV screen. He must be good, to be at the level he was in the game. Her mom would say that was only proof he spent way too much time gaming. Whatever.

"What was it like? Shooting that guy, I mean?"

He froze, didn't look at her, just froze, and then the gunshot sound effects went off and the blood spatter on the screen told her someone had just offed him. Game Over.

He set the controller down and looked at her. "Not like shooting someone in the game."

She smiled encouragingly and nodded at him to go on.

He shrugged. "He was just…he *was*. And then he *wasn't*. I did that to him."

"It bothers you."

"Not really. I mean, he was gonna kill them. I didn't have a choice. I'd do the same thing again. But it's just…weird. How easy it happened." He bit his lip, looking down. "Like how easy you go from being alive to being dead. Bam. Just like that. Like nothing happened, except you're gone. You're just…erased."

She nodded. "This is creeping me out a little. Maybe a new topic?"

"Yeah, okay."

He looked disappointed. Like he'd wanted to talk about it some more. "So…are you okay? I mean, you know, with your dad, and then that guy?"

He shrugged. "I don't know. Mom made me go to therapy for a while after, but it's all bull."

"Yeah, I'll bet."

"I mean, if you pay someone to listen to you…"

"I hear you. And what do you say? You sit there trying to think up shit to take up the time, because you know it's costing like a hundred-fifty an hour, and you wind up just making shit up."

"Yeah." He tilted his head to one side, looking her in the eyes finally. "You've been to therapy, huh?"

"Uh-huh. I lost like fifteen pounds during my first soccer season and Mom was just sure I was purging. You know." She stuck her finger into her mouth and stuck her tongue out, the international symbol for gagging.

Jeremy smiled. It was very faint, just the slightest uptick at the corners of his mouth, but it was the first one she'd seen since they'd finished breakfast.

"Were you?" he asked.

"*No.* And *gross.* A halfback runs an average of eight miles in a game. I was just burning it off, that's all."

"Oh."

"You play?"

"Not this year. Basketball, usually, but…not this year."

"I wouldn't, either, if it was my dad. I'm really sorry, Jeremy."

"Thanks."

She sighed and, not sure where to go from there, got up and paced to the double sliding glass doors facing the backyard. Looking out back, she grinned so wide it hurt, pulled her cell out of her pocket and started snapping pics. "Ohmygod, Jer, look at this!"

He twisted on the couch so he could see, then got up and came over to see better as Josh and her aunt Rachel came flying down the hill on a cheap plastic sled. The crazy dog was sitting right in the front, her ears flapping in the wind and her jowls pushed back so she looked like some kind of alien. "Aunt Rachel's screaming her head off."

"Look how big Josh is smiling," Jeremy said. "He loves that dog."

"I can tell. She looks like something out of *Gremlins.*"

He sent her a quizzical look. "Gremlins?"

The trio had reached the bottom and tumbled into the snow. They were already hiking back up for more.

"It's an ancient movie my father insists on playing at least twice a year. Says it's a classic." She grinned. "I've got to get a few more pics. This is too good. I can blackmail Aunt Rache for the next six years with this."

"Is it any good?" Jer asked.

"What?" She was holding up her iPhone, waiting for the right shot.

"The movie. *Gremlins.*"

"Oh. Yeah, it's not bad. Actually, it's pretty funny. We should see if we can stream it."

"Right now?"

They were coming down the hill again. "Myrtle is so completely Mogwai." Misty snapped and snapped. Then she put the phone in her pocket and looked at Jeremy. "Maybe tonight, if we hang that long. We can order Chinese and go pick it up."

"Okay." He stuffed his hands into his pockets and looked away. "What do you want to do right now, then?"

"See that other sled?"

His head came up. He wasn't smiling, but he nodded. "You really want to do that?"

"Yeah, I really do."

"Guess we'll lose our asshole status. First, though, can I see your phone?"

"Sure." She slid it from her pocket and handed it to him. He located the pics while she looked to see what he was doing, then he sent one to his uncle's phone. She smiled. "Cool. He's gonna love that."

"I thought he was into your aunt before. But then we stopped seeing her and he didn't mention her name at all."

"I think she's into him, too. Hell, we might end up cousins."

"I hope not," he said, and then a flush of red went

right up his neck and into his face. He handed her
phone back to her, turned and headed for the coat
closet.

Mason was on his way home when he thought to
check the phone while he was sitting at a red light.
There was a text from a number he didn't recognize
that included a photo attachment, sent hours ago. He
opened it and grinned. Rachel, Josh and Myrtle on
a toboggan flying down the hill behind his house.
Rachel's eyes and mouth were wide open, and her
hat—no, wait, *his* hat—was in the air behind her,
so her hair was like a flag. Josh was smiling all the
way to his ears—laughing out loud, Mason thought.
The kid was going to be okay. And the dog... The
dog was all flapping jowls and ears and gleaming
teeth. She was wearing her goggles and her winter
scarf, and looked like she belonged in a steampunk
creature feature.

He felt something warm settle into his chest, and
it pushed away the cold darkness that been squatting
there before. He couldn't wait to get home. And he
thought what a great feeling that was.

As he stared at the photo, realizing it had come
through several hours ago, a car blew its horn behind
him and a new text message popped up, this one from
Rachel's phone. Ordered Chinese. What's ur ETA?

He went through the light, then pulled off the road
so he could reply. The other vehicle flew by him, and
he secretly hoped for a speed trap up ahead.

20 min, he texted back. Want me 2 pickup?

Sent kids. C U soon.

On my way.

He looked at the phone for a long minute. Okay, there was some interesting stuff going on in his sappy regions at the moment. Stuff that bore further mulling.

He clicked the button to make the shot his background image. It made him feel good to look at it, and Rachel's books were always saying when something feels good, pay attention to it. It was good advice, even if she didn't always practice it herself and claimed to think it was complete bull.

He looked at her face, her full mouth wide open in a shout but somehow managing to smile at the same time. She'd relived a murder last night—lived it from the perspective of the *victim.* But today she was raising hell in the snow with her dog and his nephew. Yeah, maybe she didn't *think* she practiced what she preached, but he was pretty sure he'd just been given photographic proof that she did.

He put the car back into gear, and headed onto the highway and back toward home.

I had more fun that day than I'd had since I got my eyesight back—not counting my one-nighter with Mason, which was the most fun I'd ever had. *Ever.* By the time the younger generation had been thoroughly exposed to the genius of Joe Dante through *Gremlins* and *Gremlins 2,* we had spent close to four hours in front of Mason's gigantic TV. The sixty-inch HD was his country home's one concession to modern design. Everything else looked rustic, even though he was wired for sound. He had the fastest internet connection I'd seen—essential, he said, for gaming. And his nephews loved their gaming.

We'd pigged out on Chinese, stashed the leftovers, and then re-pigged out between the two movies. We topped the evening off with warm chocolate chip cookies—the kind that came in preperforated squares you just broke apart and threw into the oven—and milk, because there was no point to warm chocolate chip cookies if you weren't going to dunk them in milk.

And then, as the credits rolled, I looked around and realized I wasn't in Mason's living room anymore. I was lying on my back on the floor staring at the ceiling of a room that wasn't familiar to me. The light fixture above my head had a ceiling fan attached—*but Mason doesn't have a ceiling fan*—ivory-colored blades shaped like palm fronds or something. It wasn't running. I tried to get a better look around me, because my current view only gave me a glimpse of the ceiling and the upper two feet of the walls. Oddly, though, I couldn't turn my head.

Oh, shit. Oh shit oh shit oh shit, it's another dream.

Something blocked out the light, and something else kicked me in the side, rolling me over so my right cheek was pressed to the floor, my right arm underneath my body.

Wake up, dammit. Wake up!

I felt something tear my blouse up the back, and I knew what was coming. The blade would be next. The cutting. I wanted to wake up. I wanted to scream. I wanted to scrunch my face up in fear, but I couldn't move at all. I felt the warmth of tears welling in my eyes and spilling over, running along my nose and onto the floor.

If you can't wake up, then look. See what's around you so you can remember.

Hardwood floor under my cheek. Mint-green paint on the walls. A brown sofa with wooden claw feet and a crocheted blanket with too many colors to count. Black, white, orange, red—

The blade sliced a path of fire across my back and lower left side, and every ounce of reason left me. Inside, my mind I was screaming. But I couldn't even open my mouth. I couldn't *breathe*. I lay there, completely helpless as the knife cut deeper, and I prayed for death to come fast.

It didn't.

4

1:00 a.m. Sunday, December 17

Mason had dozed off on the sofa. The kids had taken every other seat in the room, Jeremy in the reclining chair, Misty in the overstuffed one that matched the sofa and Josh was in a beanbag chair on the floor. Leaving him and Rachel the sofa. He didn't know if it had been intended or not, but they'd taken opposite ends, partly because the corner between the arm and the back was the most comfortable spot on any couch, but mostly because they didn't want to get too close to each other. In his case, he didn't want to slip up in front of the kids, absentmindedly start rubbing her leg or something. You could get into a movie to the point that your body sometimes acted on impulse without bothering to check in first. That was how you could crunch through an extra-large tub of popcorn in the theater, only to look down later and wonder who ate your snack.

Like that.

He didn't know what *her* reasons were, but he kind of hoped they were similar.

So he'd fallen asleep. And it looked as if they all had, except for Rachel, because she wasn't on the couch anymore. Sitting up and frowning, Mason scanned the room for her.

She was on the floor, facedown, with her head turned toward him. Her eyes were open—*wide* open—and there were tears streaming from them. Something was wrong with her. Her entire body kept going rigid, then relaxing, then rigid again. Her dog was beside her, whining and pawing at her shoulder.

Mason swore and dropped to his knees, rolling her over onto her back, moving on sheer instinct. "Rachel, what's happening? What's going on? Can you talk to me? Rachel?"

He heard the kids stirring as he shook her, trying to rouse her. "Rachel?"

She blinked, then her eyes flashed even wider as she sucked in a sudden desperate breath that must have filled her lungs to bursting. A nanosecond later she opened her mouth to scream, but he clapped a hand over it to keep her from scaring the hell out of everyone and put his face right in front of hers. "Hey, it's okay. I'm right here. It's okay."

She pulled away, scuttling out from under him. Then she sat up and reached around to her lower back, pushing up her shirt and running her palms over her skin. She was breathing fast and hard, her face damp with tears and sweat. And it was hitting him that she'd been having another dream.

"You're at my house, Rache. You're safe. You're okay."

"My back is bleeding."

"No, no it's not." On his knees, he moved closer to her, ran his own hands all over her back, up and down her skin, then brought them around and showed her. "See? There's not a scratch on you."

She closed her eyes in obvious relief. "It wasn't me."

Josh was still asleep, thank God, but Jeremy was up now. Misty, too, standing beside him. "Was it another nightmare, Aunt Rache?" she asked. She looked scared to death for her aunt.

Rachel nodded. "Yeah."

"Can I get you something? What do you want me to do?"

"I'm fine. I'm okay."

"You don't look okay," Misty said.

Jeremy crossed the room, opened a built-in floor-to-ceiling cabinet that was original to the house, reached to the top shelf and took down a bottle of Black Velvet and a tumbler. He poured and brought the glass to her.

"Thanks, kid." She slugged it back in a single gulp and set the glass down. Mason made a mental note to ask his nephew how the hell he knew where the liquor was kept. Tomorrow. It was one-something in the morning, and he needed some privacy with Rachel.

"Why don't you two take Josh up to bed? Misty, there's an empty bedroom up there you and Rachel can use for tonight. Jeremy will show you where the sheets and things are."

Misty nodded, but instead of leaving, she crouched down and put her hands on her aunt's shoulders. "Is that what you want me to do, Aunt Rache? It's probably too late to go home, anyway."

Rachel nodded. "I'm sorry about all this. I'm not the greatest company for you on this visit, am I?"

"Not really. But I'll make you take me shopping to make up for it, okay?"

Jeremy was standing nearby, and Mason had fully expected him to argue about taking his brother up to bed, because he argued about just about everything these days. But when Rachel's gorgeous blonde niece turned to him and said, "Well, what are you waiting for? You don't think *I'm* gonna carry him upstairs, do you?" he scooped his sleeping brother out of the beanbag chair, and the three of them trooped up the stairs.

Mason helped Rachel up off the floor. She kept putting her hands to her back, as if it hurt.

"There's another one, Mason," she said.

He searched her eyes. "Another...murder?"

She nodded. "What did you find out about the last one? You never said."

"Kids were around. And frankly, I didn't want to think about it."

"Think about it now," she told him, eyeing the empty glass, then the cabinet across the room.

He sighed. "Full autopsy results won't be in for a day or two, but on initial exam, the coroner said the pancreas was missing."

"The pancreas? So…what organ did that woman get from your brother?"

He lowered his head. "His pancreas."

She rubbed her back again, left of center. "I think maybe someone should check on whoever got his kidneys, Mason."

"I will." He pulled out his phone.

She put her hand over his. "Wait, I want to get this all down while it's fresh. Everything I saw."

"Shit, Rachel, you were memorizing details while someone was cutting out your kidney?"

"Just before. Get a pen and a notepad or something, will you?"

He nodded and let go of her for the first time. Hell, he hadn't even realized he'd been holding on to her until then. Her hair was tousled, plastered to her face on one side by her tears. Her eyes were red, like she'd popped a blood vessel or two. Her cheeks were tear-stained, and he could see the pulse beating in her neck.

"Stop looking at me like you think I'm going to keel over, and go get a pen and paper, Mason."

"I'm going."

He looked around the room, moving to the same cabinet Jeremy had left standing open. It had cupboards above and below, a row of three drawers in between. He pulled open one of the drawers, rummaged around for a pen, yanked out a notepad, closed the drawer and reached up to close the cabinet door, too.

He paused when she said, "Bring that BV over here with you."

He nodded. "I could use a shot myself." He grabbed another glass and the bottle. Then he set the bottle, pad and pen on the coffee table, went to the kitchen for some ice and ginger ale. A minute later he was back.

She took the makings from him, and put the pen and pad into his hands instead. Then she poured the drinks and started talking.

"I was in a house, facedown on the floor. I think it was the victim's house. There was a hardwood floor, light-colored, maybe maple. A brown sofa with claw feet. Mint-green walls. A god-awful afghan with a dozen garish colors. Looked like someone made it out of all the leftover yarn they could find. An orange throw pillow. I saw a couple of pictures on the wall, little kids, but they were old. You could tell by the haircuts and the fading. Looked like school pictures. Two kids, a girl and a boy. The boy's a little older. Carrot curls and freckles, both of them. He had a plaid shirt on. She had a yellow dress with a white collar."

He was scribbling as fast as he could. "Was there a clock on the wall that you could see?"

"No."

"How about windows, anything that would tell you whether it was day or night?"

"No uncovered windows." She bit her lip, nodded once. "There was a ceiling fan light fixture thing."

"You said you were facedown."

"I was face-up at first. I saw this ceiling fan with palm frond–shaped blades, ivory or cream. The fan was off, but the light was on. I think it was night-time, because it was darker where the light didn't touch the ceiling. Then someone kicked me over."

"Did you see them?"

She shook her head.

"Not at all?"

"No, not at all."

"Rache, if you were face-up, and they came close enough to kick you over onto your face, you would have had to have seen them."

She frowned really hard, her brows drawing to-gether. "No, something went over my face right be-fore I felt the foot in my side. I remember, something covered my eyes."

"A hand?"

"Maybe a piece of cloth. It didn't feel like a hand."

"Okay, okay. And then you felt someone kick you over?"

She nodded. "I was completely paralyzed. I couldn't move. Couldn't turn my head. Couldn't even *breathe.* I could see, but I could barely move my eyes enough to get a better look around me. But

I could feel everything." She lowered her head and hugged herself, rubbing her arms up and down. "Everything."

"I'm sorry, Rache." He put a hand on her shoulder, kneaded it softly, repeatedly, like he could massage away the horror.

"It's not your fault," she said.

"I gave you his corneas."

"You gave me my eyesight. You didn't know it was gonna come with a downside."

He lowered his head. "What else do you remember?"

"Just the cutting." She reached out, took her drink, slugged half of it. "And praying to die fast."

He swore softly, set the pen down and hugged her. He put his arms around her shoulders, and he pulled her to his chest. Her head rested against him, but her arms stayed at her sides, under his.

"Check on whoever got his kidneys," she said again, staying stiff in his arms, not returning the embrace, but not pulling away from it, either. He let go, and she sat up straight again. "You had a list before, when we were looking at your brother's recipients as potential killers. We need to check on whoever got the kidneys."

"The list was just the hospitals. Not the patients. But I think we can trace them from there. There are probably two—two kidneys, two recipients."

"It was the left one."

He nodded and wondered why he didn't doubt a

word she said. Admittedly, there was some small voice of reason way down deep inside his brain saying *Wait just a damn minute here.* Saying they couldn't be sure the victim she'd dreamed of was another of Eric's organ recipients. That the dream might have just been a nightmare and not a real event. He could say those things himself. He'd said them before, after all.

But he'd been wrong.

He went to the computer and pulled up the list he'd wheedled from a transplant-unit nurse. His brother's body parts were listed in neat rows, along with the hospitals to which they'd been sent. His kidneys were not labeled left or right. He had no idea if they should've been or not. There were two separate hospitals beside them, though. Piedmont Transplant Center in Atlanta and Strong Memorial in Rochester.

"Care to take a drive with me tomorrow?" he asked.

She didn't even ask where, just nodded her assent. "Misty won't mind me leaving her again. She and Amy were planning a Christmas shopping trip tomorrow, anyway."

"I take the boys home at noon on Sundays. So we'll go after that, all right?"

"Sure."

"Think you can sleep?"

She looked at her glass. "One more of these and I'll sleep like a baby. For a few hours, at least." She downed the remainder of her drink. "Please, God, no more fucking dreams. No more."

Sunday, December 17

"It's just a day trip," I told her for the tenth time at a quarter to one while I waited for Mason to pick me up. "I feel really bad for leaving you again so soon after the book blitz, but it's just for the day, and I'll bring you back something, okay?"

"Will you bring me back something, too?" Misty asked.

"Me, too. I want something," Amy said.

I rose from the floor, where I'd been scratching Myrtle right in front of her ears, which was her blissspot. "Yeah, yeah, I owe you both my life. If for any reason I don't make it back tonight—"

"I'll stay over," Amy said.

"Yeah, because being seventeen, I need a babysitter who's twenty-five."

"Twenty-four," Amy corrected.

Misty rolled her eyes. "I could manage just fine on my own overnight."

"I know you could." With Aaron, Lloyd or whatever her current boyfriend's name was. I just remembered the double letters at the beginning. I'd met the kid, hated him on sight. Cocky, arrogant little prick.

"I wish we were having more fun, Misty," I said in all honesty. I did feel bad. She was missing the trip of a lifetime with her family, but it was obvious she didn't mind that, and I had no doubt she'd been seeing plenty of the boyfriend while I was doing the talk show hop, with or without Amy's knowledge.

Sandra thought it was fine when I talked to her about my suspicions, said she trusted Misty. If you asked me, "trust" and "seventeen" should never be uttered in the same sentence if there was a boyfriend involved. Teenage girls loved harder than any other species. Teenage love was apocalyptic. Wild horses couldn't stop it.

"I'll get back as fast as I can and we'll do something fun. Really fun, I promise. Maybe we'll go find a Christmas tree and decorate it."

"I had a lot of fun at Mason's yesterday," Misty said. "Don't feel guilty, Aunt Rache. You always say it's a wasted emotion."

Yeah, I did say that. In print and in front of live studio audiences. That didn't make it true. Guilt was never wasted. It was going to net the kid a Swarovski crystal swan to add to her collection.

Mason pulled up in that big black boat he called a car. I closed my eyes, hitched my "just in case" bag over my shoulder, hugged Misty, then Amy, then Myrtle one last time. "Okay, I'm outta here. See you late tonight, and if there's any change, I'll call."

They said so long and I was gone. I opened the driver's door, and Mason looked up at me from behind the wheel.

"What, you want to drive?"

Damn, he's good-looking. It's like I forget just

how *good-looking when I'm away from him, and then I see him again and it knocks me on my ass.*

"I know you love your boat and all, Mace, but—"

"It's a scventy-four Monte Carlo, and it's a *classic.*"

"It's a rear-wheel-drive bchemoth, and it's an accident waiting to happen. We're heading into the snow belt. What if we hit a blizzard? Why didn't you bring the Jeep?"

He sighed. "It's a clear day, maybe my last chance to drive my baby for the season."

"Which part of the words *snow belt* did you not understand?"

"You want to take your Subaru, don't you?"

"Yes, I do. You have any objections?"

He lowered his head. "I have to tell you something I've never told you before, Rachel."

Hell, this sounds serious. I frowned, watching his face. "Go ahead. What is it?"

"I hate your driving." His head came up, and he was grinning, probably at the way my mouth was hanging open. I clamped it shut. "I don't mean to insult you, but you scare the hell out of me when you drive."

"Why?"

"Because you're always looking at everything but the road."

"I am not!"

"'Oh, pretty mountain! Oooh, what kind of bird is that? Hey, look at that cloud.'"

I bit back my automatic defensive response and took a breath. "Try being blind for twenty years and see how much looking you do your first fall, first winter—"

He held up both hands to stop me, midrant. "I *love* the way you see everything like it's the first time, Rachel. Makes me see things from a fresh perspective myself. It...enhances my every experience just being around you."

Damn. That was almost poetic. My anger cooled a degree or two.

"I just *don't* love being a passenger in a car while you're doing it. That's all. You gonna shoot me for that? You wanna use my gun? 'Cause it's right here—"

"Shut the fuck up, Mason." I dug my keys out of my pocket, hit the garage door opener button on the key ring, then dropped them into his lap. With his irritatingly perfect reflexes he caught them before they landed.

"You can drive, okay? But we're taking my car."

"That sounds fair."

"You can put your boat in the garage if you want."

"It'll be fine outside." He shut off the engine, dropped his own keys into the ashtray and got out. He had a dark green backpack on the backseat, and he grabbed that and was good to go.

So I let him drive. And yeah, I stayed mad at him for the first hour, until we drove past the wetlands preserve, partially frozen over, and I saw a red-tailed hawk dive-bomb not twenty feet from the highway, then soar up again with something furry in its talons.

"Ohmy*God,* did you see that? That hawk just nailed a freaking squirrel or something. Look, look at it go!" I was pointing and craning my neck. When I looked over at him, he managed to hold back for about three seconds and then he burst out laughing, and I did, too, in spite of myself.

"All right," I admitted, no longer angry. "I'll have to try to stop doing that."

"Don't *ever* stop doing that. That was amazing, and I never would have even noticed it if you hadn't been with me."

"Yeah?"

"Yeah." He shrugged. "Just…try not to do it when you're driving."

I rolled my eyes and returned to watching the passing scenery.

At Strong Memorial Hospital's Financial Services Center, Mason made the impossible as easy as 1, 2, 3. He got in to see a patient accounts manager, claiming to be an insurance adjuster and saying he needed to verify some information about the patient who received the kidney on August 17 of this year. Then he shuffled papers looking for the patient's name while the woman at the desk clicked her keys, bringing up the info. I waited in the hallway outside the office door, and when he sneezed, I walked up the hall a few steps, made sure no one was looking and, with a tissue covering my fingers, pulled the fire alarm.

People poured out of offices left and right, including Mason and the accounts person. I joined the throng moving forward, exclaimed, "My purse!" in case anyone was listening, and ducked into the same office he'd just left. I hurried around the desk, took a quick look at the computer and there it was. The patient's name and address. Three patients had kidney transplants that day. But only one of them received a left kidney. I scribbled the info on a notepad, jammed it into my pocket, zipped out again with my heart in my throat and caught up with the throng heading for the stairwells. By then someone in charge was telling everyone to stay calm, it was probably a false alarm. Maybe even a prank.

"Fucking kids," someone muttered.

I saw Mason talking to the woman whose office I'd just left and looking at his watch, making excuses to leave and follow up with her later. Then he entered the stairwell. I passed her in the hall as I went to join him, but there were lots of people heading down and I had to wait until we were outside. He was ahead of me, and he got into my car and started the engine. I hurried the last few steps and hopped in on the passenger side.

"You get it?" he asked.

"Henry C. Powell of Sodus Point, New York. You know where that is?"

"No, but your nav system does." He poked buttons. "Street?"

"Twenty-five Lake Street."

He punched a button, then another, and the nav system plotted a route and said it would take less than an hour to reach our destination. "We're in business. You want to grab a bite first?" It was close to four-thirty, after the two-and-a-half-hour drive out here, and the time we'd spent executing our plan. Flawlessly, I might add. Neither of us had eaten lunch.

"Yeah, but only if it's a drive-through. I'm kind of eager to check on Mr. Powell."

"Me, too."

So we grabbed some fast food and ate while he drove.

An hour later we were cruising slowly along the southern shore of Lake Ontario, which looked more like an ocean than a lake, since you couldn't see to the other side. The water was dark and moody, deep blue-black, with whitecaps like sharp teeth in the mouth of a monster. The sky matched. Of course, it would be dark in another twenty minutes, so it was already dusky under heavy clouds.

We located number 25. I'd been searching for info on Henry Powell online, via my smartphone, for much of the drive. His Facebook page relationship status was "Single," and he only had forty-seven friends, despite having posted daily up until about a week ago. He looked pale and pasty in his profile pic, and I imagined that was one of his better photos, because who uses their bad ones, right? Ruddy cheeks and pale blue eyes, blondish hair going gray, a long, horselike face.

"I don't think he won too many beauty contests."

"Does it say what he does for a living?" Mason asked.

"Retired. Doesn't say from what."

He pulled to a stop on the deserted road. I got a chill but told myself to buck up. We weren't going to know anything until we got a look inside.

"You stay here, I'll go check on things."

"Uh-uh. I need to see the inside of the house, see if it's the same as the dream."

"You described it to me. I can tell if it's—"

"I have to go with you," I said. "I don't know why. It's...personal. Like we're...related."

"That's a stretch, Rache."

"Too fucking bad, that's how it feels." I got out and slammed the door, then started up the recently shoveled walk to the front door of the little lakefront cottage. There was a white door with three diamond-shaped windowpanes, and a big picture window just to the left of it. I hit the doorbell.

"He's gonna answer the door," I said with more certainty than I felt. "He's fine. The whole thing was stress. My imagination could have spun a second murder out of the strands left over from dreaming the first one, right?"

"Right."

No one answered. The bell was probably broken.

I knocked this time. Mason moved away from the door and walked over to that big window that looked out on the lake. "Light's on. Shit."

"What?"

"That looks like the ceiling fan you saw in your dream. Palm leaves. Off-white. Window's too high, though. I can't see the floor."

I closed my eyes, knocked harder. "Henry! Henry, are you in there?"

No answer, and I closed my gloved hand around the doorknob, twisted—and it turned.

"The door's unlocked. I'm going in."

Mason swore and headed for me, but I pushed the door open and stepped inside.

Henry C. Powell was lying on the living room floor, facedown, head turned to one side, shirt torn up the back. There was a gaping hole where his left kidney should have been.

I turned to run outside, pushing past Mason. I was bent over, hands on my knees, gasping and gagging, when Mason came up behind me and put his hands on my shoulders. "Don't puke, okay? We don't want anyone knowing we were here."

I gulped air, swallowed. "Neighbors probably already saw the car."

He kept his hands on me as he looked up and down the narrow road. "Most of these places look empty. They're seasonal. It's winter."

Nodding, I managed to straighten up. "We can't just leave him there, though."

"We won't. We'll make an anonymous call to the local cops from a rest stop. They'll take care of him, notify his family. We can't get you tangled up in this again, Rachel. Last time you were too close to being a suspect."

"I know."

"If that happens, we'll be too busy trying to cover our own asses to keep on digging. And we *have to* keep on digging. No one else can do this."

"No one else would *believe* this."

He nodded.

"Mason, someone is harvesting your brother's organs."

"Maybe."

"I have his eyes."

"Yeah," he said, staring right into them. And he couldn't hide his fear.

I knew that fear. Felt it. Times ten. And I didn't like it any better than he did. He was seeing it in his mind's eye the same as I was. A horrible vision of him walking in and finding my body on a floor somewhere, with my eyes gouged out of my head.

Talk about a nightmare.

"We need to get you out of town, Rache. Somewhere safe."

"I'm not even gonna argue," I told him.

5

By the time we got back to my house it was almost midnight. Long drive, no snow, thank goodness. I missed my dog.

Mason got out and, instead of heading for his car, followed me to the front door. I turned around and tried for sarcasm to lighten the heavy mood that had settled over us on the long drive home. "What, you haven't had enough of me for one day?"

He tried it right back. "Plenty, but I'm crashing on your couch all the same."

It fell flat in both cases. For most of the ride we'd been more morosely silent than his brooding teen-age nephew. My brain was wondering why the hell his damned brother refused to die, while his was probably piecing together clues and extrapolating them into some logical explanation for two murder victims who'd both had their organs harvested—his brother's organs.

There was only one explanation in my mind. His tweaked-out sibling wanted his body parts back and had figured out a way to take them from beyond the grave. Period. And I was equally sure that meant my eyeballs were probably pretty high on his list. Mason was probably afraid that if he left me alone tonight, he would find me come sunup with two gaping holes in my head. And frankly, I was afraid of that, too.

"Earth to Rachel? Crashing on the sofa. I know I sounded all confident, but I'm still waiting for you to say that's okay with you."

"Fine, but unnecessary. I have plenty of bedrooms."

"I know, but the couch puts me between you and outside."

So would the left side of my bed.

"Suit yourself," I said, and unlocked the door and went inside. The alarm panel beside the door started flashing red, warning me that it would start screaming bloody murder if I didn't enter the code, and fast. I keyed it in while Mason looked over my shoulder. "Amy and Misty did what I told them for a change. Armed it." I'd called home after our visit with the unfortunate Mr. Powell and instructed them to lock up tonight and set the system. I looked over my shoulder at Mason. He wasn't smiling.

"Your birthday?" he asked with a nod at the keypad. "Are you shitting me?"

"How the hell do you know my birthday?"

"I think it was in one of your books. Or maybe it was in the background check I ran on you when you looked good for the Wraith killings. Or maybe I have an internet connection and a Google search bar like everybody else in the Western hemisphere."

He was worried about me. It was kind of sweet. Why did I still want to smack him?

"I wasn't aware I was in any particular danger when I set the code."

"You're a minor celebrity. You're always in danger."

"What the fuck do you mean, *minor?*"

He softened up a little. I did, too. Then he opened the panel on the control box and hit a couple of buttons until the screen read "enter code." The words flashed impatiently at me.

"I wouldn't have known how to do that in a million years," I told him.

"Pick a new code, Rache. No one's birthday, not the last four digits of your phone number or your social, and not four sequential numbers. Make them random."

"If they're random, then how the hell am I going to remember them?"

"By repetition. Same way you memorize any other number."

I scowled and entered the last four digits of my editor's home phone number. He wouldn't know that, right?

Right. As evidenced by his nod of approval. He hit another button or two and the thing read "code accepted." Then the green light went on and the moon returned to its proper orbit around the earth.

"I'm beat," I said, turning for the stairs, then stopping as my blood went cold. "I wonder why Myrt didn't come down to greet us?"

He pulled his gun. I wanted to say, "Oh, quit being so melodramatic," except I knew he wasn't. After what we'd both seen today, he had good reason to be scared. The fucking organ snatcher would be coming for me, sooner or later, and my niece, best friend and bulldog had been home alone.

I was an idiot to have left them.

Don't be stupid. I didn't know... Not for sure, anyway.

I still don't.

Yeah, I do.

He moved past me and went sneaking up the stairs like a TV cop, gun pointed up at the ceiling. I snagged my favorite baseball bat from the coat closet and hurried to catch up, walking on tiptoe with my heart in my throat, trying not to imagine my sister's gorgeous daughter with her eyes gouged out of her head because the ghost-killer didn't know the difference.

We got to the top of the stairs, and I suddenly wondered why the hell we hadn't turned on the light. There was a switch right there, so I reached for it.

Like a flash, Mason covered my hand with his,

stopping me. He had eyes in the back of his freaking head, I thought. But I left the light off and started wishing I had a better weapon than the baseball bat I'd been keeping in that downstairs closet since the last serial killer started fucking up my life.

What the hell was *that* about, anyway? How come I was attracting serial killers like a porch light attracts bugs?

'Cause you've got a killer's eyes in your head, dumbass. Technically, you're part serial killer yourself.

Mason moved silently down the hall toward my bedroom. The door was open, the night-light I never turned off emitting a soft glow from within. He moved closer, took a quick peek in, ducked back, then took a slower look.

"Grrrruff!"

Myrtle. The surge of relief that flooded me almost made my knees weak, and I couldn't wait any longer. I leaned past him and looked into my bedroom.

Misty was lying in my bed, curled up in one corner. Myrt was sprawled everywhere else, somehow making her two-foot-long body take up the entire bed. But her head was up and she was facing us in the doorway, sniffing, ears cocked and alert.

"It's okay, Myrt, it's only me."

She let out a far happier woof, then scrambled to her feet and down the little stairs I'd bought to give her easy bed access. She was at my feet in a second, so I crouched to love her up thoroughly as Mason backtracked and turned on the hall light, allowing me to verify that Misty was alive and well.

I stood up and looked at her.

There was red swelling around her closed eyes that made my heart freeze in my chest.

"Misty!" I lunged to the bed, gripping her shoulders, turning her onto her back, expecting to see blood-soaked pillows and empty eye sockets.

She blinked and scrunched up her face, shielded her squinting eyes and said, "What the hell? Oh, hey, Aunt Rache."

I frowned and searched her face more closely. Smeared makeup. Red puffy eyes. Tear tracks, not bloodstains. She'd been crying.

"What's wrong? What happened, Misty?"

She swiped her eyes, and I heard footsteps in the hall and glanced back to see Amy in her Goth girl jammies. "Her douchebag boyfriend dumped her. Hi, Mason."

"Hello, Amy. Sorry to wake you."

"He dumped you?" I was dumbfounded. What sort of eighteen-year-old boy dumped a future runway model like my niece?

"After I gave up Christmas in paradise for him," Misty muttered, and wiped at her eyes again.

"Why, for heaven's sake?"

"He wanted a blow job and she wouldn't cave," Amy said.

"Whoa." Mason was holding up a hand as if to deflect the chick-talk going on in my bedroom.

"When I'm ready for sex, it'll be a two-way street, not all for the guy. Just like you told me, Aunt Rache."

"That's my girl. I didn't like him, anyway. I promise you, we're going to have such a great time that you won't miss the Bahamas at all. Now that you don't have that lead weight holding you back, we can go somewhere fun."

She frowned at me, blinking. "We're going away?"

"Yeah. As soon as Mason and I can get the arrangements made."

"Mason and you?" She craned her neck to see him around the corner. Myrtle stood at the foot of her portable stairs, waiting to see if it would be worth the effort to climb back into bed or not. "Are you two—"

"No!" Mason and I said simultaneously.

Amy and Misty locked gazes, eyebrows arched and speaking volumes. Misty looked back at me first. "So where are we going?"

"We haven't decided yet. We'll talk more tomorrow. Get some sleep. I'll take the guest room."

"No way." Misty flung back the covers and slid out of bed. "You sleep here with the bed-hog dog. I'll take the guest room."

She shuffled out of the room, and she and Amy went back down the hall. "Night, Mason. Night, Aunt Rachel," she called back over her shoulder.

"Good night," Mason said. And then, loudly

enough for them to hear, "I'll just, uh, grab some blankets for the couch, if you'll tell me where—"

"Linen closet, third door down," I said, just as loudly.

Not that they were buying it.

Hell, I wouldn't have, either.

Mason couldn't sleep. He was glad of it, though. He wasn't there to sleep, and he certainly wasn't there to slip up the stairs to Rachel's bedroom and try to talk her into one more go-round for old times' sake.

He couldn't very well protect her if he was having sex with her. He knew from experience that his mind would be completely immersed in the task at hand.

Hell, who was he kidding? His mind was already full of her, and he wasn't even doing anything.

After an hour he got up, wandered into the kitchen and made a pot of coffee, because there was no point trying to sleep. He debated having a snack to go along with it, standing bathed in the light from the open fridge as he looked unseeingly at all the girl-food inside. Yogurt. More fresh fruit, like there wasn't enough already in the overflowing ornate basket on the counter. Fresh vegetables. Cukes and celery, green peppers, three kinds of lettuce, baby carrots, baby spinach. Where the hell were the deli meat and mayo?

"The rabbit food is for the teenage female upstairs. Check all the way in the back, third shelf, plastic container, blue lid."

He didn't jump, just straightened enough to see Rachel over the top of the open fridge door. He'd felt her there about a half a heartbeat before she'd said anything. Or maybe he'd smelled that shampoo she used that always reminded him of a summer beach. Coconut and vanilla bean or something.

She was wearing a snug-fitting T-shirt with Betty Boop on the front, and panties. And socks, he noticed, which made him realize he had just let his eyes take the scenic route all the way down to her toes.

Damn. He ducked behind the door again, digging for the promised container, pulled it out, peered through the plastic. "Is it…chicken?"

"KFC. Extra crispy. And only two days old."

"And there's enough for two." He swung the fridge door closed and took the container to the microwave, peeled back the lid, popped it in, hit a button.

"Should be some sides kicking around in there, too," she said, and when he turned it was to see her in his former position, leaning into the fridge, only way sexier, especially from behind.

He leaned on the counter and watched as her backside moved in time with her rummaging.

She stopped what she was doing. "Are you staring at my ass?"

"Nope. The panties are in the way."

"Pig." She emerged with two more containers.

"Potatoes and gravy. And I think there might be some biscuits in the bread box."

"It's a veritable feast."

"It is." She crossed the kitchen to where he stood, set the containers beside the microwave behind him and looked up into his face. "I can't reach the plates. They're..." She trailed off, pointing at the cupboard behind his head.

He clasped her waist in both hands and picked her up. She squeaked, then laughed, then opened the cupboard and took out two plates. When he lowered her again, she slid down the front of him, and he wondered why he was torturing himself like this.

"I've really missed you, Rachel."

"I know."

He rolled his eyes. Not exactly the reply he'd been hoping for. "We had good reasons for not taking things...where they seemed to be going between us."

"Yes, we did." The microwave beeped. She nudged him aside, removed the chicken and put the potatoes and gravy in to heat up next.

"You wanted to experience life as a sighted, independent adult for the first time before cluttering it up with a relationship."

"Yes, I did."

She wasn't contributing much to the conversation, he thought. "And have you done that?"

She pressed her lips together, then turned away so she could put the now-steaming chicken and the two plates on the table. She went to a drawer for utensils and yanked a couple of paper towels off a roll to serve as napkins.

"Live as a sighted adult?" she asked. "Kind of hard not to, since I am one."

"You know what I mean. Have you been…dating?"

"Have you?" she asked, turning to spear him with her eyes.

He didn't want to answer. The truth was, he had been trying, but the old Mason, the play-the-field guy he'd been before, seemed to have vanished. He couldn't find him anywhere. Every woman he took out, all he managed to do was spend the night comparing her to Rachel.

And not entirely unfavorably. Rachel was mouthier, more sarcastic, shorter-tempered, would see right through his bullshit, swore like a sailor….

And yet he always felt like he would rather be with her. Since he couldn't very well tell her that, he opted to shrug his answer, then took the potatoes and gravy out of the microwave and set them on the table.

Rachel grabbed two big spoons, plopped one into each dish of steaming leftovers and sat down, grabbing the biggest piece of chicken.

"It's only been a month, Mason."

"I know. I know."

"You had reasons, too," she reminded him. "You were nowhere near ready for anything serious, you said. You had enough on your shoulders with your brother's kids and your sister-in-law and your mother, and coping with your brother's death, you said. You needed to keep some small vestige of your private life free and easy, you said."

"I know."

"So how's that been working out for you?" She bit off a hunk of chicken, closed her eyes in approval and chewed like no one was watching.

"Fine," he said, because she'd pretty much told him she was sticking to their original agreement and he had no intention of letting on how not-fine it had been. It was hands off until they were both ready to go where this thing between them seemed likely to lead.

She blinked, and he thought maybe she'd been surprised by his reply. "Really?"

He shrugged and started eating.

It wasn't an answer. Neither of them was giving much in the way of answers tonight. And as much as he wanted to ask her if she thought they could temporarily suspend their hands-off agreement, he didn't. Mainly because he didn't think his ego could take the rejection if she said no.

He couldn't afford to have things getting all tense and awkward between them when he had to keep tabs on her, keep her safe.

"So what are we gonna do?" she asked.

He almost choked, then met her eyes, his own no doubt hopeful and eager. "Do?"

"About this phantom who's apparently going around collecting your brother's organs?" she clarified.

"I knew that." He got up and poured himself a mug of coffee. "Want some?"

"Why not? I'm not sleeping anyway."

He got down another cup and filled it. "There's a ski resort up north, in the Adirondacks. Pine Haven. New York's Aspen, they call it. Even has an indoor water park. I checked online from my cell phone earlier, and they aren't filled up this week yet."

He dared to look at her, to see what she might think of his suggestion. She was watching his face, her head tipped to one side, taking it into consideration, not ruling it out before he'd even finished suggesting it, as he'd half expected.

"It's in the middle of nowhere," he went on, encouraged. "You could take Misty along without raising any suspicions. Spend a week, stay through the holiday. No one would know where you'd gone if you kept it ultra-private. I can book it in my name, in case anyone's looking for you. You'll be safe for a while."

She blinked. "You really think we can keep our hands off each other if we spend the holiday in some winter wonderland together, Mason?"

"I...wasn't planning to go with you. I mean, I've got Mother and Marie and the boys to think about. I can't leave them for Christmas. And work is—"

"Sure. I mean, of course. I wasn't thinking."

Oh, yes, she was. And why did that make him want to grin?

She shot him a look, like she knew what he was

thinking, so he sobered up again. "I need to find this killer. That's the whole point, to get you out of his reach and give me time to track him down and lock him up where he can't hurt you or anyone else."

"Makes perfect sense." She'd stopped eating. Her face was pink. She was embarrassed.

"For the record, though, no. I don't think we could keep our hands off each other if we were tucked away in some winter wonderland together."

She smiled, her ego soothed, he thought. "Then it's a good thing you're not going."

"So you'll do it?"

"One stipulation," she said. "They have to let me bring Myrt. Otherwise, I'll take my chances with the fucking organ thief. It's my first Christmas with Myrtle, and we're not spending it apart."

"I'm way ahead of you. Pine Haven is pet-friendly. That's what made me think of it."

"I can book it myself, you know." She sipped her coffee, leaning back in her chair, her plate still half full.

"No, I don't want you online doing any of this. I don't want there to be any possible way someone could hack into your computer and see where you've been searching. It's better if I do it."

She lifted her brows, sipped her coffee. "All right."

"I'll get it done tomorrow." He looked up at the clock on the wall. "Today. You can leave before the day is out. Can you be ready?"

"I haven't even unpacked from New York yet." Then she sighed. "Yeah, I can be ready."

"Good."

Damn. He picked up the plates, scraped them into the trash, rinsed them off and headed back to the living room with his coffee like the conversation was over. He didn't even *try* to get into my pants. For fuck's sake, what did he think I came downstairs in my underwear for, anyway? Was he dense?

I heaved a pissed-off sigh as I stomped past him, up the stairs and back to bed. *Dumbass.*

He was already in the shower when I got up a very few very short hours later, and when he came out, all clean-smelling and wet, he turned down my offer of breakfast. Said he had to get to work. And yeah, he probably did, but if I was heading up to Mount Timbuktu tonight, I wasn't going to get the chance to see him again until after this thing was solved.

And after this thing was solved, my excuse to see him would be gone.

So you'll just have to make a decision, then, won't you? Decide you want to get with him or decide you don't.

Yeah, but what if I do and it doesn't work?

He borrowed my favorite travel mug and told me to be careful today. To keep the door locked, to call if anything suspicious happened, not to let any strangers anywhere near the place, not to breathe a word about our trip to anyone who wasn't coming along and to be ready to leave by 6:00 p.m.

"Leave for where?" Misty asked. She'd just come down the stairs in her bunny jammies and plush robe, and she looked like she'd been crying most of the night.

I was at the front door with Mason. He was pulling on his coat. "I'll let your aunt tell you," he said. Then to me, "See you tonight."

Did he sound eager?

Was I pathetic or what?

Then he was gone and Misty was waiting, arms crossed, foot tapping in a perfect imitation of my sister. "Well? Don't tell me you're taking off on me again, Aunt Rache, because I really need you right now."

"I know you do, kid. That's why I'm taking you on a fabulous ski vacation for the holidays."

Her jaw dropped. "Really? Where?"

"Pine…something. Up north in the mountains. It'll be great, and I would never have been able to get you to come with me if dickwad hadn't had the bad judgment to dump you."

"And that would be what? The bullshit silver lining you always say to look for, the one inside every storm cloud?" she asked, mocking one of my most famous quotations exactly the way I generally did. Did I really sound that cynical? I wondered. Wow, what must Mason think of that?

Since when do you care what anyone thinks of you, Rachel?

"Not everything I write is bullshit, Misty." *Oh, yeah? Because if that was the case, Mason would be going north with me and there wouldn't be a killer after my eyeballs.*

"But we have to be ready before the day's out, so—"

"I've got to go back to my house! I have brand-new skis I haven't even used yet. And the cutest ski-bunny outfit you ever saw, and—" She stopped there, looking at me, her head tilting to one side. "You can't ski, though."

"I know. That's why we're going. I got my sight back, so there's no reason why I can't learn to ski, right? Um, there's only one thing, Misty."

"What?"

"You can't tell anyone—and I mean *no one*—that we're going."

She frowned at me, starting to look worried. "Why?"

I rolled my eyes. "I know you don't notice it much, but, uh, I'm kind of a big deal. I can't have fans and paparazzi drooling all over me if I want to have a nice holiday vacay with my niece."

"Paparazzi. Really." The words dripped sarcasm.

"What? It could happen."

"Fine, don't tell me the real reason." But she zipped her lips anyway and headed back upstairs to get ready. We had a busy day ahead of us.

Monday, December 18

Amy headed home right after breakfast. I told her it was only a week until Christmas and she should go have fun, because I wouldn't need her again until after the holidays.

Midmorning, I dropped Misty off at her house to pack. She was still pissed that I tried to make her sit in the backseat so Myrtle could have her place of honor up front. I did give in, but only after she accused me of loving my dog more than my family.

However, *she* was the one who insisted on taking Myrt with her to keep her company while she packed. I had some fast and furious shopping to do, and neither of us wanted the poor dog sitting in the car alone waiting for me. Not that Myrt would mind. My vehicles were her homes away from home. I think she was missing riding around in the T-Bird with the top down. But it was winter. What could I do?

I was being careful. Watching my rearview mirror as I drove, keeping track of any cars that I saw more than once. But deep down, I didn't feel anything but good. I'd been gearing myself up to feeling good all night long, instead of moping that I wouldn't get to see Mason the entire time I was gone—which was the biggest downer, even though there was the strong possibility that a killer was after me, looking to gouge out my eyes. I know. Pathetic. I took a page from my own book—pun intended—and started counting everything good about this situation. First and foremost, it had brought Mason back to my door, and he was clearly still interested. He'd even admitted he'd had trouble staying away. Sort of. That was good, right?

I thought it was, even though I wasn't yet sure where I wanted this thing with him to go.

Second, this trip would give me time to think about that very thing. Where I wanted us to go. Was I ready for a real relationship? And what the hell did that mean, anyway?

Okay, to keep this trend going, my third silver lining was that I would get to do something really special for Misty. I had wanted to, had been racking my brain to think of something to make up for her missing the Bahamas and getting dumped by her useless boyfriend, so this was good.

Oh, and fourth! I was going to learn to ski.

And, of course, I'd be safe from any potential eyeball-hunting serial killers.

There really wasn't much to be bummed about after all.

I pulled into the Oakdale Mall's giant parking lot, using the same entrance I always used and parking in the same area I always parked in, no matter what store I was going to visit. It was near the spot where the taxi or Amy always used to drop me. Some habits died harder than others, and the lifelong need to do new things in the same way every time—because being blind meant I had to memorize everything just to get by—was one habit I was having a hard time breaking. I kept reminding myself that I could see. I could park anywhere I wanted and get around just fine. But no, my inner blind chick liked her routines. So I just gave in. At least I would never forget where I'd parked.

I had no doubt the mall would have everything I needed. Misty had assured me it would be faster and easier to rent my skis and all that went with them at the lodge. My main goal today, she'd insisted, was to get hot-looking ski-bunny clothes. To be precise, she'd ordered me to find "ski pants and a matching jacket that don't make you look twenty pounds heavier, and a cute as hell hat and scarf." She would have come with me to tell me what qualified as "cute as hell," but since she insisted it would take her a minimum of two hours to pack and we were short on time, I was on my own.

And it took a while. But I finally found what I needed. A pair of very thin, very lightweight black ski pants guaranteed to keep me warm at temps down to twenty below, and a black-and-white jacket that matched the one I bought for Myrtle. (Naturally I'd shopped for her first.) I headed back to the Subaru and got in, slung my bags onto the passenger seat and cranked her up. I was debating whether to get some takeout on the way to pick up Misty as I headed onto 17, whipping through traffic until I hit 81, and then taking the Whitney Point exit a half hour later. Almost home.

I decided at the last minute to grab us some subs and told my dashboard to call Misty as I took the left into the village, and sat waiting at the light.

"How'd it go?" she asked in lieu of a greeting.

"I think you'll approve. The hat is red—but you'll see it soon enough. I'm in the Point."

"Already?"

"Yeah, you almost done packing?"

"Close. Are you bringing anything to eat? Our fridge is bare."

"That's why I'm calling. You want Subway?"

"Tuna," she said. "Toasted. You know my veggies, right?"

"Lettuce, tomato, spinach and pickles?"

"Right. And some chips. Baked ones, okay?"

"Got it. I'll see you in ten. Maybe fifteen."

"Cool."

I got our subs, which took almost no time at all, and then I was back in the car and heading into traffic, past my road and on out the other end of the village, then turning onto the twisty side road that wound uphill to my sister's place.

I glanced up at my rearview mirror and saw something: a dark, hooded form rising up from my backseat, and I swear to God my blood froze and my heart tried to break out of my chest. I jerked the wheel and cringed toward the passenger side, away from the phantom, as one of its arms came around my neck. My momentum carried me though. I ripped free of the attacker's grip and felt something sharp jabbing me in the shoulder, right through my jacket, and then the car was rolling and I was being snapped left and right, up and down against my seat belt. My head hit the side window, and I didn't know anything else.

6

I woke with a sudden gasp, my eyes flying wide. I was suspended at an odd angle, up in the air, my seat belt keeping me from falling toward the passenger door. Through that window there was only the snowy ground. Through my own window, sky. I jerked my head toward the backseat, but there was no one there. The rear hatch was open, showing me a view of a rocky stream bed. But I couldn't see the entire backseat.

Was my attacker still there, crouching, waiting to spring on me?

I was shaking, and then I remembered the needle and quickly looked to my shoulder to see it still there, the tip embedded in my flesh but the plunger still extended. Carefully I grabbed it and pulled it out, sucking air through my teeth as I did, not in pain, but in fear some of the drug would seep into my flesh. I didn't want to toss the needle, but I wasn't going to pocket it, either, and risk injecting myself by accident. I aimed toward my shopping bags, which had landed against the passenger door, and dropped the needle into one of them.

I had to get help. I had to get out of this car. I had to make sure the killer wasn't still *in* the car. I didn't know what to do first.

I thought of my phone and thanked my stars I kept the thing clipped to my waistband. Still there. Thank God.

I pulled it out, found Mason's number and texted *911*. Then I hit the "send location" button and sent it.

Snapping the phone back onto my hip, I tried to make as little noise as possible as I wriggled around to get my legs and feet more or less between me and the passenger side window, which was *down* to my *up*. I wanted to land upright once I got free of the seat belt, so I could get out of the car as fast as possible, and I didn't want to make any noise and rouse the possibly unconscious killer who might or might not still be in my backseat.

I hope he's fucking dead back there.

The car was still running. What a trooper. I could get out faster if the window was open, so I risked waking my attacker by hitting the button. The driver's side window began to open, and I let go of the button to let it continue down on auto while I quickly reached for the seat belt buckle. The belt was currently supporting my full weight, so I pressed one leg to the dash, the other to the back of the passenger seat to lift myself a little, and I wrapped one arm out the window and up over the roof of the car. Then I hit the release. The buckle snapped loose and I dropped a little, but I managed to catch myself. Frantically I wriggled out of the shoulder harness, my eyes glued to the backseat, though I still couldn't tell if the killer was back there. I got my other arm out the window and pulled myself through. Once I managed to hook a foot in the steering wheel—*don't hit the horn, don't hit the horn, don't hit the horn*—it went faster. I pushed up and out, hit the horn and scared myself shitless, and finally got clear, pulling my feet out behind me like the devil was going to grab them. I ended up facedown on a steep slope, my feet on the fender of my car, which was lying on its side. I strained to see into the backseat, but the sun reflecting off the glass made it impossible. I looked around outside. Where the hell was he? Where was the killer?

I wasn't waiting around to find out. The slope to the road was steep, but I was determined. I started clawing my way up. As I went, I noticed the snow was turning awfully bloody. My head, I thought, but I didn't have time to worry about that now. I felt like someone was pursuing me, that tingle up the spine that makes you walk super-fast when you come up the basement stairs in the dark, only to the power of ten. I was scrambling like a king crab in mating season, scuttling up that slope like Spider-Man on crack. Making up metaphors like a writer having a panic attack.

And pretty soon I was dragging my sorry ass over the gravel on the shoulder of the road and onto the pavement. I saw shiny black shoes attached to legs that came running toward me, and I screamed.

"Easy, miss, easy now. You're okay." The legs crouched, and I saw the uniform. A cop. Mason had sent the cavalry. I was safe. Thank God.

By the time Mason arrived on the scene there were three cruisers and an ambulance on the side of the road. He pulled over, spotted Rachel's SUV at the bottom of a massive drop and damn near threw up.

A big hand clapped his shoulder. Rosie. "Easy, Mace. She's over in the ambulance, see?"

Mason breathed again and jogged to the back of the ambulance. A medic was cleaning the blood from a small cut on the left side of her forehead, and she was wincing in pain—until she glimpsed him. Everything in her eased when she met his eyes. Made him feel ten feet tall when he saw that.

"I need to talk to the detective," she told the medic. "Can you give us a minute?"

Mason had to force himself not to pull her off the stretcher and hug the crap out of her, because he didn't know how badly she was hurt. He settled for touching her face with one hand, her shoulder with the other.

"I'm sorry it took so long. I was doing a final check of that crime scene. Are you okay?"

"I think so. Mason, it was him. It was the organ thief."

Shock jolted him in the chest. He'd thought it was a simple car accident. "What happened?"

"He was in the backseat. He tried to jab me with a needle, and I—"

"Easy, Rache. Easy now. We need to go slow. I need to get everything. This person was in your car with you?"

She nodded, and he noticed her pupils were dilated. She was still shaken up.

"Did he get out?"

"I don't know. I couldn't see into the backseat and the hatch got ripped open, so I don't know."

"Hold on. Okay?"

He backed out of the ambulance, put his fingers to his lips and whistled. Two uniforms and Rosie gathered around him. "All right, we have a murder suspect who was inside the car before it went over. Fan out. Rosie, call it in, get a couple of roadblocks in place."

"We have a description, Mace?" Rosie asked. The other cops paused in what they were doing, awaiting his answer.

He looked in at Rachel. She shook her head. "Dressed in black and wearing a ski mask."

He nodded. "Ski mask, that's all we've got. Go." He nodded at the two uniforms. "Check the car, but be careful. The suspect is armed and dangerous. And the car's a crime scene, so don't contaminate it. Check for the suspect, then tape it off."

The two men nodded and started down the slope.

He moved back into the ambulance with Rachel. "I need to know how this person got into your car. Where were you?"

"I was at the mall. But I locked it. I was careful."

He nodded. "Did you stop anywhere else before you headed up this road?"

"Yeah. Subway. In the village."

"Did you lock the car then?"

She thought back, lowered her head, then shook it slowly. "No. No, I was in a hurry to get up to Sandra's to pick up Misty and—" Her head came up, eyes widening. "Misty! She's alone, her and Myrt, at Sandra's house."

"I already called her, the minute I saw where your text came from," he said. "Figured she should know you'd been in an accident. She was fine. I sent a uniform up to keep her posted, and I stayed on the phone with her until he arrived, just to make sure she wouldn't panic. She's safe. Worried about you, though."

She nodded. "I should call her."

"Yeah, we'll get to that. So you stopped at Subway. And then what?"

She swallowed hard, her eyes meeting his. He felt her fear. Hated it, but felt every ounce of it. And that was a lot. She didn't scare easily. She hadn't been this scared even the last time a killer had stalked her.

"I glimpsed this masked face rising up behind me in the rearview. It was a split second before he grabbed me, and that gave me time to lurch to one side. I jerked the wheel. He jabbed me with a needle, and then the car was rolling. I hit my head and blacked out."

"You keep saying he. Are you sure it was a man?"

She frowned hard at him. "It happened so fast I...I don't know. I'm assuming." She touched the cut on her forehead and winced. "How bad is it?"

"Not bad. You're gonna be okay. What about the needle? Are you feeling any side effects?"

"I don't think anything went into me. It barely broke the skin, and he never had the chance to depress the plunger. When I came around I pulled it out, and the plunger was still fully extended. I left it in the car. I managed to drop it into one of my shopping bags. I didn't stick around long, though. I was afraid he was still in the car, so I climbed out the window and got up the hill as fast as I could."

He knew that much. Had seen the bloody smears in the snow all the way down. "I don't know if I could have made that climb *without* a head injury."

"Sure you could."

Another cruiser pulled to a stop, and Misty dove out, sprinting for the ambulance. "Aunt Rache!"

Rachel gripped his arm. "I don't want her knowing what really happened. Tell the officers—"

"Aunt Rachel!" Misty climbed into the ambulance opposite Mason and hugged her aunt.

Mason gave her a nod and left the two of them arguing over whether or not Rachel was going to the hospital. He turned back. "I want you to go, Rache. Please."

"It'll take up my entire afternoon," she said.

"You know what can happen with a blow to the head. Better than it taking up your entire life, right?"

I wanted out of that curtain-draped E.R. cubicle even more than I wanted the chocolate bar Misty brought me from the machine in the waiting room. But I took the chocolate anyway. I'd been in here for over an hour and apparently was now just waiting for someone to look at my CT scan before I could get the hell out of there.

"Mason went out to check on Myrtle," Misty said as I bit into the Kit Kat bar and let it improve my mood. Slightly. It was after 2:00 p.m. The day was all but shot, and...okay, might as well admit it. I was afraid to go home. And I was afraid if I was here too long, it would be too late to hit the road out of town. And how was I going to do that, anyway, with my new car currently lying on its side at the bottom of a ravine?

I was scared, I'll admit it. And it pissed me off to be scared. "Myrt's been cooped up in Mason's car for entirely too long," I said, because it was better than giving voice to my darker thoughts.

Misty started to say something just as my curtain whipped open, and a bald guy with glasses stepped in, carrying a clipboard and looking at it, not at me. "Ms. de Luca?"

"Present."

That brought his eyeballs off the chart. "Okay, it looks like you're going to be fine. You've got a mild concussion. That means—"

"I know what that means. Bruise on the brain. Could swell or bleed. I need to limit my activity for the next forty-eight hours and come back immediately if I have any odd symptoms, like a headache that doesn't get better with Ibuprofen, dizziness, passing out, change in sleep patterns or sex drive, or—"

"Are you in the medical field, Ms. de Luca?"

"No, but my friend Siri's a freakin' genius." I held up my smartphone. "Web MD," I clarified.

He sighed and handed me the chart. "Read it, sign it and you're out of here."

"Thanks. How seriously do I need to take the 'no strenuous activity' thing? I'm about to leave on a ski trip."

"I wouldn't do any skiing for the first twenty-four hours. After that, if you feel all right, you should be fine."

Nodding, I scratched my official signature, not the one I used for autographs—every author knew those two should be as different as possible unless you used a pseudonym. Then I said, "Sorry if I was bitchy. This really messed up my day."

"I understand that. You'll be happy to know that your blood work didn't show—"

"Hold up a second, Doc." I glanced at Misty. "Would you go see what's taking Mason so long? I'm worried about Myrtle."

She looked at me, then at the doctor, then at me again, and compressed her lips. "Okay."

Once I was sure she was gone, I said, "She doesn't know about the attacker in the backseat."

"Sorry about that," he said. "My mistake. Anyway, we checked your blood for sedatives, tranquilizers and the more common poisons. It doesn't look like anything got into your system."

"But can you be sure?"

"No, not completely. We're not going to find things we don't test for. But if you're not feeling any symptoms of anything…"

I got that. "Yeah, okay." The syringe was at the police lab, no doubt. This doctor wouldn't have had the chance to see it or analyze it. He would only have been told the bare minimum he needed to know.

"Doc, is there a drug that would paralyze a person so completely that they could barely even breathe, while leaving them completely awake and lucid?"

He blinked at me like I'd turned into a brain-munching demon and took an actual step back. "Well, yes."

"Would you have found that if I'd been injected with it?"

"No. It leaves the system so quickly it barely leaves a trace. We could test for the metabolites it breaks down into. But there's no point, because you couldn't have been given that."

"Why not?"

"Because if you had, you'd be dead by now. Succinylcholine is what we use in the O.R. to keep the patient perfectly still during surgery. It paralyzes every muscle, including the lungs and, in large enough doses, the heart. It's why you always need an airway during surgery. You can't breathe on your own when your lungs are paralyzed."

"Is this—what did you call it? Sux-sin—"

"Succinylcholine."

"Yeah, that. Is it easy to obtain?"

"Almost impossible," he said. "And like I said, if he'd injected you with that, you'd be dead."

"Yeah." *But not before he'd gouged out my eyes, I bet.*

He took back his chart, peeled off a copy of what I'd signed and handed it to me. Ah, yes, my release instructions. As he exited the curtained-off area, Mason and Misty came in. I was already sitting up, long since dressed and ready to go.

"I got the all-clear, so let's blow this pop stand."

Mason asked for the paper by holding out his hand, and I gave it over. He read every word, which was more than I had done, nodded and said, "Okay.

We're going to my place for the time being, if that's okay with everyone."

"It's not," I said, sliding off the bed to my feet.

Mason shoved the paper into Misty's hands and came quick to my side, sliding an arm around my waist like I might fall down without him. Once I would have resented it, but I liked being close to him. Up against him. I liked it a lot.

Down, girl. Finish your thought, before you lose it entirely.

"I still have to pack, pick up Misty's stuff and get myself a rental car so we can go on our trip."

"We could always take my car," Misty said. "And grab my bags while we're picking it up."

"That doesn't cover the part where I still have to pack," I told her. I looked at Mason. And oddly, I knew that he knew exactly what I was thinking. *I have to pack, but I'm afraid if I go home a killer will be waiting for me.*

"I have a suggestion," Mason said.

I nodded at him to go on.

"Come to my place tonight, rest, and let me worry about getting Misty's stuff from her house and getting you a rental car. You can head up north in the morning. I'll even take you home to pack your stuff first, and then out to breakfast. What do you think?"

What did I think? I thought he was too good to be true. Fortunately I'd known him long enough by now to know that he was just what he seemed. I knew all of Mason Brown's secrets. Okay, maybe not all of them, but certainly his deepest, darkest ones. None of them revealed him as anything other than perfect. Okay, so he liked to play video games, and he'd covered up the fact that his brother was a serial killer. Was still covering it up. But he had good reasons. And really, how could he have known his insane brother would keep coming back to haunt our lives the way he seemed determined to do?

Not that it was his brother doing this. No ghost was going around injecting people with suxsy-fuck-acholine and reclaiming its lost organs. That hadn't been a ghost in the back of my car, it had been a real flesh-and-blood person. I'd felt it.

Thinking of that gave me a shiver.

I rubbed my arms until the feeling went away. "I think that's a great idea. Thanks, Mason."

"*De nada.* Let's get a move on, Myrt's getting impatient."

Mason could see that Misty was starting to wonder what the hell was going on between him and her aunt, but she hadn't asked. Yet. She probably would as soon as he left them alone at his place, which he had no choice but to do. Every Monday evening he picked the boys up from basketball practice and drove them home. It wasn't far out of his way, and he enjoyed the extra time with them. Jeremy had opted not to play this year, but he still hung out at the school gym doing homework while his brother practiced.

So he left the women at his place with Myrtle and drove to the school, pulling into the half-circle drive in front, taking his place in a long line of minivans and SUVs, and waited for the boys to come out.

Joshua emerged a few minutes later, dragging his backpack, still in his shorts and sweaty T-shirt, with a hoodie slung over his shoulder, even though it was thirty freezing degrees.

Mason cranked up the heat a little and reached across to open the door. Josh tossed his backpack into the backseat and got in.

Mason resisted the urge to tell the kid to wear his jacket so he wouldn't catch his death. He had no desire to sound like a nagging mother. If Josh got cold enough, he would put the hoodie on. All the nagging in the world wouldn't make him do it any sooner.

"You lucked out, got here before Jer and landed shotgun," he said as Josh buckled up. "What's taking him so long, anyway?"

"He didn't come. Said he'd catch a ride home with 'one of the guys who actually has a car' later on."

Mason got that the sarcasm-loaded part of the sentence had been Jeremy's, not Josh's.

A car blew its horn from behind them, and when Mason checked the mirror, a woman in a minivan sent him an apologetic shrug. He didn't like this and figured Marie was going to like it even less, but he didn't have any choice but to get going. He wasn't comfortable leaving Rachel and Misty alone, even at his place, right now.

He pulled into traffic and headed for Marie's, Josh talking a mile a minute as they went. Basketball practice, the coach, the holiday tournament being cancelled because of a flu outbreak at the hosting school, and about fifty other topics over the fifteen-minute ride.

God, that enthusiasm. He could use a dose of it right now.

He and Josh got out, and Josh ran ahead to the front door. Mason followed at a slower pace, until Joshua turned and said, "Huh. Door's open." Then he hollered, "Mom?"

Mason reacted automatically, catching Josh before he went in, pulling him back a little and pushing the door open himself. He peered inside, and saw the place in shambles. "Josh, get back in the car. Get back in the car right now and—"

But the kid shoved past him and darted into the house before Mason could finish, so he had no choice but to pull his piece and follow.

Marie was on the floor near the sofa. The coffee table was on its side, a lamp smashed on the floor near her head and the back door was standing wide open.

He lunged forward, dropping to one knee beside Marie. She was banged up to hell and gone, a huge lump, already purple, on her forehead, a bruise on one cheekbone, and more all up and down one arm and shoulder. Her eyes were closed. She was breathing, though, and had a solid, steady pulse.

He turned. "Josh, stay close to me."

Josh came to him, phone in hand, already mid-conversation with a 911 dispatcher. He put his hand over the phone. "She wants to know if the bad guy's still here," he said, and from the look in his wide eyes, he did, too.

Mason took the phone from him. "Your mom is okay, pal. I want you to pat her face a little, talk to her, try to wake her up."

"Okay." Josh began doing as he was told while Mason got to his feet again, checking the surroundings as he brought the phone to his ear. "This is Detective Mason Brown. I'm on the scene. I need backup and an ambulance. Looks like the attacker ran out the back door, but I can't leave the victim and her son to give chase."

"We have help on the way, Detective."

"Good." He set the phone down, put it on speaker, and said, "I'm going to take a look out the back door." Then, louder, "Josh, if you see anyone, yell."

"I will. Come on, Mom. Come on, wake up."

Mason went through the kitchen, which was empty, one chair knocked over but nothing else out of place. He looked through the open back door. No one out there. And the sidewalk that led around the house to the front was snow-free and dry. Not a track to be seen.

He closed the door, being careful not to touch the knob and obscure any prints, and headed back into the living room, grabbing the phone on the way. "I hear sirens now. I'm going to hang up."

Marie was sitting up, holding one hand to her head, crying softly and hugging Joshua. He went over to them. "Josh, go wait by the door and let the cops in, okay?"

"Okay."

As soon as the kid was a few feet away, Mason leaned close to Marie's face. "What happened?"

"He...just walked in the front door and started hitting me."

"He?"

She nodded. "Had to be. He was tall. Thin, but tall. And strong. He had a ski mask on. I couldn't see anything, no skin, nothing." She lifted her bruised face to stare straight into his eyes.

God in heaven, why? Why would this killer go after Marie?

"Did he say anything? Could you recognize the voice?"

She closed her eyes, shaking her head. "He was trying to jab me with a needle. I thought he was going to kill me. He must have heard you pull in and run off."

"All right, all right, it's all right now." He hugged

her, and then Josh was leading the uniforms inside. Rosie showed up on their heels.

The paramedics arrived next, and Mason backed off to let them have a look at Marie. He had the uniforms scouring the neighborhood, and everything in him was itching to go help, but he didn't dare leave Josh and Marie alone. While the medics were with Marie, he took Rosie into the kitchen, out of earshot. "It's the same guy. The organ thief."

Rosie's brows shot up. "The one that attacked Rachel earlier today?"

"Yeah."

"How do you know?"

"Dressed in black, ski mask, too similar to be coincidental. She said he had a needle."

Rosie leaned back against the kitchen counter. "Damn. Why would this guy want to bother with Marie?"

"I don't know, but if he'd come after her, he might come after the boys, too, and—" He broke off there. "Shit, the boys. I don't know where Jeremy is."

He lunged back into the living room just in time to see his teenage nephew burst through the front door, his face etched in panic, no doubt from seeing the ambulance and police cars out front. "Mom?"

"I'm okay, Jer. I'm okay," Marie said as he rushed to her. She was on the sofa now, with two paramedics attending to her.

Mason caught Jeremy's eyes. "She was attacked,

but we scared the guy off. She's okay, I promise.
I've got this."

Rosie clapped Mason on the shoulder. "You take
care of your family. I'll deal with the rest of this,
all right?"

Mason nodded, grateful, but seething inside.
"This piece of shit's gone too far, Rosie. He's gone
too far."

7

Monday, December 18

Mason called about two hours after he'd left us at his place, and to be honest, I was relieved. I didn't want to admit it, but I was scared shitless. The little farmhouse was in the middle of nowhere. Empty fields with stalky dead weeds and snow and bare earth, woods beyond them, treeless and black. A big old barn out back that could be hiding an army, for all I knew. No one knew I was there, but I was still scared. My brain wouldn't stop spinning a dozen scenarios. Suppose the killer had seen me with Mason and knew I'd be likely to hide out at his place, or followed us from the hospital and was just waiting to finish the job? Suppose it was someone we both knew?

Suppose you stop thinking about shit you don't want to attract, Rachel?

It doesn't really work that way, I thought, denying my own bestselling philosophy.

You've been thinking about Mason Brown a lot, and now he's smack in the middle of your life again.

I didn't want it like this, with another string of murders, Inner Bitch. Not like this.

Did you specify?

"Rache? You there?" Mason asked through the telephone.

"Yeah, right here," I said. I was hanging out in front of the coffeepot. Misty was on the sofa, texting with God knows who. The house was too damned creepy, and had a loose shingle or something that kept flapping against the roof every time the wind blew and scaring the hell out of me. "We were beginning to think maybe you'd ditched us." The wind howled, and I looked outside to see nothing but darkness.

"How is everything? Are you guys okay?"

"We're fine." I frowned, because his voice sounded...off. "What's up, Mason? You sound weird." *Scared. He sounds scared and nerved up. Shaken.* My knees quivered, and I pulled out a chair to sit down. Myrtle promptly collapsed on top of my feet and sighed.

"You don't miss much," he said.

"Blind people can't afford to miss much. So what's going on?" I reached for the cup I'd just filled and sipped it for something to do. The wind sent something skittering over the front porch, and I almost wet myself, then lunged to the door to look out and spotted what looked like a plastic jug tumbling off the far end. I sighed in relief and double-checked the lock.

"Marie was attacked."

Just like that and my relief went out the window. "*What?* My God, like she hasn't been through enough. Is she all right?"

"Yeah. Wouldn't even go to the E.R. She looks like she went a few rounds with a prize fighter, but I think she'll be okay."

"Son of a—"

"It was the same guy, Rache."

"What do you mean it was the same guy? That doesn't make any sense." His cop sense was off. He was too close to this.

"Since when do psychopaths have to make sense?"

He was practically quoting *me* back to *me,* I realized. I'd said something similar to him once, only a few months ago. "I know. I just… I don't get it. Are you sure?"

"I'm sure. He had a syringe."

I cussed impressively, and imagined finding this jerk and cramming his syringe right up his ass. "So now what?"

"Same plan, just more of it. Marie, the boys and I will be staying at the lodge, too. And my mother. The police are parked outside their places for the night. We'll get out of here tomorrow, maybe a little bit later than planned."

"Your *mother?*" *Did that sound as unpleasant*

as I think it did? I'd met the woman once. My first impression had been *stone-cold bitch,* but I really didn't know her well enough for that to be carved in granite.

"I can't get it out of my mind that this maniac keeps going after people connected to my brother. First, people with his organs and now his widow. If Marie qualifies just because she was married to Eric, then Mother might, too, even though Eric was adopted. I just can't risk it."

"I wouldn't ask you to." Oh, God, I did *not* want to spend Christmas with Mason's mother.

Right, but you were just wishing you could spend it with Mason. Wish and it is granted, right, Rache?

It was *just like* my inner bitch to use my own titles against me.

Besides, you like *the boys. Jeremy could be just the medicine Misty needs for her broken heart. And she might be just what he needs for his.*

Was it just me, or was my inner bitch morphing into Pollyanna?

I felt for Mason's family, I really did. His mother had lost a son only a few months ago. And Marie had lost her husband, quickly followed by her baby. Stillborn. What a nightmare. But as sorry as I felt, I barely knew them. And I wasn't exactly the warm and gregarious type.

"Rachel?"

I silenced my inner argument. "Yeah, I'm still here."

"I booked us a huge cabin. Mother refuses to stay in it, though. Says she'd rather be in the main lodge. She wouldn't take no for an answer."

"So six of us in one cabin, then? I mean, couldn't Misty and I get a room, too?"

"They're full up. And besides, the whole idea of going up there is so I can keep you safe."

"I know." But he'd been planning to send me up there all alone before this happened, and he'd presumed I would be safe then.

"I know what you're thinking," he said.

"You do *not* know what I'm thinking. You're a good cop, but you're not *that* good." I had an eerie feeling I was wrong about that.

"I decided to go to the lodge with you right after you were attacked, Rachel. I just didn't know how to broach the subject without either pissing you off or making it sound like a come-on."

I shrugged and looked away, like he could read my face through the telephone line. "It wouldn't have pissed me off. I do prefer your company to having my eyes gouged out."

"Gee, thanks."

"You're welcome." I swallowed hard. "Do you think your mother will be safe in the lodge?"

"She'll be surrounded by people at all times, and I've talked Rosie and Marlayna into coming along. They'll be in the lodge, too, for added security." He sounded guilty. "That's why all the rooms are gone. They booked the last one."

"Wow." I frowned, trying not to let my voice tremble and give away how scared I was. "You're really worried about this, aren't you?"

"I'm afraid to let anyone I care about out of my sight, Rachel. We're just going to have to make the best of it."

Wait a minute, stop the presses. Did he just say he cared about me?

"On the upside," he went on, "we get to spend Christmas in a beautiful cabin at an upscale resort in the mountains."

"Being stalked by a killer and surrounded by people I barely know." He started to talk, but I ignored him and kept going. "I know I'm being a bitch, but it's my first Christmas with my eyesight back. This isn't how I was hoping it would go down. As un-me-like as it sounds, I was hoping for a really spectacular holiday this year."

"I'm sorry. I really am. I'm just trying to make sure you get plenty more of them."

I sighed. "I know you are. And I'm grateful. Besides, it wouldn't have been so spectacular with my sis and fam out of the country anyway. I just feel like we should be trying to catch this guy, not going on vacation."

"We are going to catch this guy. We're just going to work on it together from a secure location where everyone will be safe. And Chief Subrinsky is up to speed on everything else. He's working on getting through the red tape and HIPAA laws so he can protect all the other recipients. Everything that can be done is being done."

"Okay," I said, knowing he was making way more sense than I was just now. And who was I kidding? I was looking forward to spending the holidays with Mason Brown. Family or not. *Killer* or not. Was I a basket case or what?

8

Tuesday, December 19

I steered my rented SUV, a burgundy, all-wheel-drive Ford Escape, between the giant wooden signs that read Pine on the left and Haven on the right, and actually stopped and sat there staring with my mouth hanging open. The snowy, twisty drive wound up-hill to what I could only describe as a log castle. The place had countless dormers, super steep peaks and green shutters with pine tree cutouts bracketing each and every window, including the twenty-foot-tall one front and center. Beyond that front window a massive Christmas tree twinkled with multicolored lights. Every peak and window and door was also lined in Christmas lights, white ones, all of them aglow. The driveway itself wound between pine trees, also all lit up in white.

"It's like Santa's workshop on crack," Misty said,

stroking Myrtle's head as the bulldog snored on her lap. Her legs had to be asleep by now.

The car behind me blew its horn. One little honk, but still, it pissed me off. Mason's mother was driving that car, a big flashy black Escalade. Marie was riding with her. The trunk and backseat were so full of gear that Josh and Jeremy had to ride with Mason. They were up ahead of us in Mason's recently acquired manly green Jeep. Rosie and his wife, Marlayna, who I'd met when we'd all stopped for dinner at a rustic roadside diner thirty miles ago, were bringing up the rear in Rosie's bright yellow Hummer. Marlayna seemed nice, but she was a little starstruck around me. She was my self-styled *number one fan*. Fortunately she didn't seem like the type to go all stalker on my ass.

I liked her better than I liked Mason's mother and was glad to have a female along who felt like an ally. Misty was too busy impressing Jeremy, and Marie was barely holding her pieces together. So it was Marlayna or nothing.

I got the car moving again, and resisted the urge to ooh and ahh out loud at the pristine beauty around me, glistening in the holiday lights. The place was like a Christmas card, and it was bringing my inner little kid to life. You know the one I'm talking about. The one who used to wait up for Santa Claus on Christmas Eve, struggling to stay awake to hear reindeer on the roof, and scanning the skies for a red glowing nose. I hadn't felt that way since my eleventh Christmas, which was the last one before I'd gone blind. I hadn't seen the lights since then, either. This was a first for me, and it was choking me up.

I do not get choked up over pretty lights.

Yeah, hardass? Then why are your eyes burning right now? That's right, blink it away.

Fuck you, Inner Bitch.

Hey, don't get mad at me. You wanted a spectacularly Christmassy Christmas, and it looks like that's just what you're getting. Wish and it is granted, remember?

Mason led the way, apparently following the signs, which blurred in my vision a little bit, to the parking lot around back. No covered garage. We'd have to make do. He got out of the Jeep and waited while I parked beside him, and he was smiling and rubbing his gloves together when I got out.

"Isn't this amazing?" he asked.

Good God, the man was *sparkling*.

And looking damn good doing it. Those dimples in his cheeks are ridiculous. Possibly illegal. And is that a little bit of his inner child I see in his eyes?

"It's amazing," Misty said from behind me. She set Myrtle down, and Myrtle promptly peed right where she was, unashamed. "How many Christmases has it been since you've been able to see the lights, Aunt Rachel?" Misty asked.

I shrugged and looked away, toward the giant log cabin's rear entrance: a row of glass doors that opened out onto a paved patio with a big stone fire pit in the center. Several people were milling around the fire in colorful hats and scarves. Some were toasting marshmallows. All were smiling.

Good God, I'd arrived in Happy-Joy Christmas-town.

The driver's side window of the Escalade rolled down. "Mason, why didn't you pull up to the front doors so I could have had a valet unload our luggage?"

His mother. She'd pulled into a parking spot nearby.

He looked at me, a subtle exchange to tell me she was irritating but lovable. The irritating part I got, the lovable not so much. "Mother, there was no point in the rest of us pulling up in front, since we're all staying in one of the cabins. And there's no point in them unloading the boys' luggage, since they're coming with me. I'll carry your bags inside and get you checked in, all right?"

She pouted but nodded, put her window up, shut the Caddy off and got out.

Marie got out, too. "Let's all go in," she said. "This place looks amazing."

She'd done a pretty good job covering up the bruises on her face with makeup. A cute brown hat and scarf set hid the lump on her forehead. Damn, her blond curls looked great in that set. I was a little jealous, because putting me in any winter hat and scarf, no matter how cute, just looked dumb. Her eyes were still haunted, but I thought this trip might be just what she needed to help her out of her grieving.

"I want to see the water park!" Josh shouted.

He and Jeremy had got out of the Jeep and were standing behind me, bracketing Misty. Teens must have some kind of gravitational pull on each other, I thought.

"All right, we'll check it out," Mason promised. "But listen. It's important that I know where you are at all times. And that goes for everyone. Adults included. Okay?"

The boys slid a look at their mother, then nodded at him. I could see the look Jeremy exchanged with Misty. The two of them clearly knew we hadn't told them everything. They also knew that coming up here had something to do with the attack on Marie, and I think maybe Misty also suspected I hadn't told her the truth about my "accident."

I felt guilty for being less than honest, but it was Christmas. I wasn't going to burden the kids with nightmare images of organs being cut out of living people, that was for sure. I mean, it wasn't exactly the kind of sugarplum I wanted dancing in their heads.

Mason dug through the Escalade to fish out his mother's bags, then said, "I'm locking it. Let me have the keys."

Angela shook her head. "I never take the keys out of the ignition. That's why I insisted on the external keypad, so I never have to worry about where I left the keys." She nodded at the row of numbered buttons underneath the front door handle. "Just punch in your father's birthday. Twelve-eleven."

Mason nodded and locked the oversized SUV.

Rosie and Marlayna had stopped out front and were already at the registration desk when we all trooped in. Holiday music filled the pine-scented air. I gaped like a tourist yet again, while Myrtle, insecure in a new place, pressed tight to my calf. I had a leash on her, though it wasn't really necessary. She wouldn't go far, especially if there were other dogs around.

The towering cathedral ceiling in the lobby was lined with gleaming logs that still had their natural shape, knots and all. White lights spiderwebbed above like stars on a clear night. The fieldstone fireplace was gargantuan. One entire section off to the right housed a bar, with more logs and shining shellac, and a smiling female bartender-slash-unemployed and underfed supermodel standing at the ready, nodding a happy hello to us. On the left was a gift shop, and then the front desk. I saw a sign beyond that, very rustic looking, pointing the way to Haven Spa and Salon and Pinewoods Bar, along with Northstar Dining Room, Polar Frolic Indoor Waterpark and Borealis Ski Shop. The place had everything.

Mason nudged me. I'd become hypnotized by the twinkling lights of the Christmas tree, the gleaming garland, the angel on top. I hadn't even thought I'd missed these sights. Just how much I truly had was hitting me pretty hard in my emotional epicenter and sending ripples out through my entire being.

"This must be almost overwhelming for you, Rachel," he said softly, leaning so close that his breath tickled my ear.

I sniffed and shrugged. "That sappy music they have going isn't helping any. I mean, Ebenezer Scrooge would get choked up in this joint."

"Yeah." He nodded toward the bar. "Why don't you take the kids for a hot cocoa while I get things squared away at the desk?"

I nodded. "Okay." I was not drinking hot cocoa. Hot buttered rum, maybe. Not cocoa.

The kids, Marie, Myrtle and I weaved through the customers toward the bar. We were stopped three times by bulldog lovers who wanted to pet Myrt. She didn't mind the attention at all, and I was relieved, yet again, that most people were too busy noticing the dog to recognize me. I'd put on a pair of fake reading glasses—if it worked for Clark Kent—and my hair was tucked under my hat. I mean, yes, I'd done the talk shows over and over again, and I do tend to get recognized around Whitney Point, but that's only because the locals know I'm there and have seen me out and around. In reality, who remembers the face of their favorite author? How many would *you* recognize on sight? Go on, try picturing them in your mind. You got Stephen King, and maybe Deepak Chopra, didn't you? But if you could pick Amy Tan out of a lineup of similar-looking women, with the addition of a hat and unnecessary prop glasses, I'd say you're a rare individual with a photographic memory. Eventually we found a table. A waitress was with us immediately. "Welcome to Pine Haven. Is this your first visit?"

"It is," I said.

"Where are you from?"

Oh, God, she wanted to have a conversation. "South," I said. "The kids have been dying for a cup of your famous hot cocoa the entire trip. Can I get three, please?"

"With marshmallows," Josh said.

"And for the adults?" She was still smiling. I was glad I'd managed to avoid exchanging pleasantries without hurting her feelings. She didn't look any older than Misty, after all.

"Can't I have a real drink?" Jeremy asked.

"Absolutely not, Jeremy," Marie said.

The waitress giggled. "I couldn't serve you anyway, without ID. And if you had ID that said you were twenty-one, I'd probably have to confinscate it." And yes, she said, "confinscate." And then she giggled again. *Note to self, pick a table away from this section next time.*

"I'll take a rum and Coke," I said, then looked at Marie.

She opened her mouth to speak, and Josh interrupted, in the whiniest voice I'd ever heard him use. "I just want to go to the water park! Why can't we do that now?"

"'Cause it's closed," the giggly waitress said, just like that, silencing the impending and unwinnable argument. Maybe I wouldn't have to strangle her after all. "It's open every day, noon to eight p.m. at night, and that's it. Sorry."

8 p.m. at night? The brownie points she'd gained were fading fast.

Josh sighed dramatically and put his elbows on the table, head in his hands, like she'd just told him he had six months to live.

"I'll take a hot toddy," Marie said.

"Anything else?"

"Yeah, two more cocoas." I looked at Marie and shrugged. "In case Mason and Angela want some."

"Angela won't," Marie replied. "She's too worried about her figure. Get her a martini, two olives."

"Shaken, not stirred," I threw in.

The waitress blinked like a doe in headlights, and I thought I heard crickets chirping. Josh laughed out loud, slapping a hand on the table. "Double-oh-seven!" he said. "I have that game for my Xbox."

Marie and I chatted while we waited. Was my holiday shopping done? No. I'd bought a ton of stuff for Myrtle, but no one else. I routinely bought for only a handful of people. My sister, Sandra, her perfect hubby, Jim, the twins, my assistant, Amy, and my agent, Barracuda Woman. Marie said she'd been done for a month now. It wasn't all that much fun anymore. Used to be all magic and mystery, but now the boys just basically placed their orders and she filled them.

The poor woman was so sad. I was going to find a gift for her this year for sure.

And there it is. The music, the pine scent, the twinkly lights, all empowered with the post-hypnotic suggestion to buy, buy, buy.

I rolled my eyes. Even *I* thought that was a little too bah, humbug.

"Can we at least go *look at* the water park, Mom?" Josh asked.

Marie sent a look at the waitress—Tammy, her nametag said. Of course it did. She'd just returned with our order. She was quick. Tammy nodded, set our drinks on the table and bent low to feed Myrtle a little doggy treat. "Sure, you can. It's kind of dark, because most of the lights are off, but you can see well enough."

I got a chill when she mentioned the darkness and remembered we had a killer after us. Maybe I should say something. They got up, Josh carrying his cocoa and Marie her toddy, and off they went while I debated.

"Let's go check out the tree," Misty said, and when I turned to reply I realized she was talking to Jeremy, not me. And then they were gone, as well, cocoa and all.

I downed my rum and Coke in about three swallows, picked up the martini and hot cocoa, and headed over to the registration desk with Myrt's leash looped around my wrist.

Marlayna and Rosie were on their way to the elevators, behind a guy with a rack full of luggage. Angela was with them, so I skirted the desk to catch them before the elevator doors opened.

They looked at me, Marlayna and Rosie smiling widely. "This place is incredible," Marlayna said.

"It is." I handed the martini to Angela. "Thought you might want a nightcap."

Her perfectly plucked—well, a little too thin, to be honest—brows rose in twin arches. "Thank you." It almost had a question mark at the end. I could see her rethinking her initial opinion of me, which hadn't been good, probably because I'd called her firstborn grandson an asshole during our first conversation. Don't judge me. He was acting like one.

"De nada," I said. "Are you guys on the same floor?"

"Yeah," Rosie said. "Angela's room is right next door to ours."

"Good. That's good."

He nodded. I didn't know how much his wife knew about our real reasons for being here—or Angela herself, for that matter—so I didn't say more. The elevator doors opened right then, anyway, so the awkward moment ended.

I turned to look toward the giant Christmas tree. Jeremy and Misty were still in view. Then I craned my neck to see around the corner to the right, where the water park signs were pointing, but Marie and Josh were out of sight.

Damn, this was going to be harder than I had imagined.

"We're all set," Mason said from behind me—and way closer than I'd expected. I jumped and spun so fast I slopped cocoa on my sleeve. Fortunately it had cooled off by then.

"Great. Here. Cocoa." I handed it to him, aware I'd suddenly turned into Cave-Rachel. "Um, Marie and Josh went to look at the water park, even though it's closed and there's no one down there and the lights are off."

He frowned. "I'll go get them. Where are Jer and Misty?"

"Tree," I said with a nod.

"Okay, you wrangle them, I'll get the other two. Meet you by the back doors. Don't go anywhere else, okay? The lobby's still crowded—you should be okay."

I nodded once and we split up, and it hit me how much easier it was going to be keeping track of everyone with him here to help. And how much easier my presence was going to make it on him. Alone, neither of us would have stood a chance.

Besides, what were the odds the big bad organ thief had followed us up here, or even knew where we'd gone? We'd all taken separate vehicles, left at separate times from separate locations. Mason had gone all out to ensure our safety. He'd even brought a gun and was wearing it. I'd seen it under his jacket when we'd stopped for dinner.

I went into the lobby, right up to the towering Christmas tree. *Silent Night* was wafting from the unseen speakers now, and the scent of pine, tinged with cinnamon I noticed now, was even heavier in the air. Brightly colored prop gifts with giant bows and sparkly ribbons were stacked strategically beneath the tree. Super-sized candy canes hung from its branches, and the blonde angel on top gazed down with her arms and wings open wide, apparently pouring blessings down on us all.

Yeah, sap. This place was brimming with it. And not just from all the pine trees.

When I rounded the tree, Jeremy and Misty jumped apart almost guiltily, and I wondered if they'd been holding hands just before they'd heard my approach. Or just standing close, like shoulder to shoulder or something.

Interesting.

"They always have lifeguards on duty," said a male voice, and it echoed in the giant room that housed the indoor water park. "And the kids get unlimited juice and healthy snacks while they play. All included in the park pass."

Mason tensed as he stepped into the dimly lit room, scanning the perimeter. There were three full-sized pools, two of which had water slides emptying into them, and five additional towering slides of various shapes, heights and bright colors. One was an open spiral, one an enclosed tube, one dropped straight down from a dizzying height, another two were obviously designed for younger riders. The water was turned off, none of them running, but the pools glistened and gleamed from interior lighting. Floating alarms bobbed in each pool, ready to scream if the water was disturbed during off hours.

And then he spotted Marie, Josh and a strange man standing at the far end of the park, where another set of glass doors faced a snowy wonderland outside.

"It's going to be so much fun for you, isn't it, Josh?" Marie asked.

"Yeah, if I ever get a chance to do it. Why can't we stay here in the lodge, instead of out in some stupid cabin?"

"I promise, you'll get plenty of time in the water park, Josh."

"The cabins aren't far. Which one are you in?" the man asked.

Marie looked up at him. "I don't actually know yet."

Mason cleared his throat, and Marie jumped and turned. "Oh, God, Mason, you scared the hell out of me."

"Sorry, Marie." He faced the stranger. Tall, very lean, fit the body type of Marie's attacker perfectly.

Rachel hadn't been able to guess at his size, though, since they'd both been sitting in her car.

Mason thrust out a hand. "Mason Brown. And you are?"

The man blinked, as if he was wondering about the slightly challenging tone. "Scott Douglas," he said. His grip was strong. A little too strong, like he had something to prove.

"Scott's another guest here, Mason. He was just telling us about the water park."

"Really? How long have you been here, Scott?"

"Arrived earlier today."

Interesting.

"Mason is my brother-in-law," Marie said, as if she felt a need to explain his presence. Then she hurried on. "Thanks so much for the information... Scott. It was nice meeting you."

"You, too, Marie. Um, maybe I'll see you around the lodge."

"I hope so."

She turned and headed back toward the lobby, snagging Josh's hand on the way and tugging him along beside her.

Mason caught up with her in the main hall. "Marie, we agreed to stick together." He looked behind them to be sure the attentive Scott hadn't followed.

"I was just showing Josh the water park."

"Yeah, after hours, alone, in the dark."

She snapped her head toward him, a hint of anger

in her eyes, but then she seemed to bank it. "I know. I...I forgot."

"I don't know how you can forget what happened to you yesterday, Marie."

"I know. It's—"

"And striking up conversations with strange men isn't exactly part of the game plan, either."

This time she let her anger flash at him. "I'm a big girl, Mason. And he was just being nice."

"Yeah, and did you ask yourself why?"

"Duh, Uncle Mason," Josh said.

He looked down at Josh, having forgotten he was there, and could have kicked himself. The kid just rolled his eyes and ran ahead.

Marie said, "Yeah, duh, Uncle Mason. Do you really think the only reason a good-looking single man would strike up a conversation with me is because he wants to kill me?"

"Of course I don't think that. You're a beautiful woman, Marie. I just—"

"Don't worry. I haven't forgotten your brother. I might never get over him, if that's what you're thinking about."

"It's not." Hell, his brother had been a freaking psychopath who'd left his widow and two sons because he'd been twisted and sick. He didn't deserve Marie's mourning, much less her loyalty.

"It's not," he repeated. "I actually think it would be good for you to...you know, start dating or...whatever, when you're ready."

"Right. Sure you do."

They picked up the pace to keep up with Josh, who was already rounding the corner up ahead and racing into the lobby.

"He was the right height, the right build, and he's only been here since today. We can't be too careful. Okay?"

She nodded. "I appreciate you being so protective of us, Mason. I do. I'm sorry I snapped at you, I'm just...not used to having to answer to anyone. It's been months now. And even then, Eric never... he wasn't...jealous. You know?"

"I know." His brother had had his own obsession going on. He'd been way too busy sating his sick appetite for murder to worry much about what his wife was doing.

"I'm not complaining," she added quickly. "I've always liked...my space."

"I'll try not to act too much like an overprotective big brother, then."

"I'd appreciate that."

Our "cabin" was a chalet with two stories, eight bedrooms, a huge living room with a cathedral ceiling, four bathrooms and a kitchen equipped to feed a small army. Beyond our initial unpacking, our curious exploring and the choosing up of the bedrooms, I hadn't heard or seen a soul since we'd come in.

I had taken a huge bedroom in a corner of the second floor. It had its own bathroom and a balcony—

not that I'd be likely to spend too much time out there, being that it was twenty degrees outside. But the view was beautiful. Way more snow up here than at home, and pine trees and mountains everywhere.

The bedrooms were arranged around a square balcony open down to the great room and protected by what amounted to a split rail fence. Misty had the room around the corner to the right, and Mason's was to the left. His bedroom put him right between me and Marie, who had the other corner. Joshua had the room to the left of hers, but Jeremy had taken the middle bedroom on the fourth side, across from Mason's room and with no one to his left or right. The kid liked his privacy. The other two second-floor bathrooms were strategically placed, one at each end.

I loved the place, in spite of my initial misgivings. It was absolutely perfect. I'd expected it to be rustic to the point of primitive, but it wasn't at all. Even the roomy kitchen was fully stocked. They would just tally up what we used at the end and add it to the bill.

I was unpacking my new coat and pants, and remembering the needle that I'd yanked out of my shoulder and dropped into the shopping bag with them what seemed like a lifetime ago, when Mason tapped on my door. Yes, I knew it was Mason. No, I don't know how I knew. My sightless senses had sharpened to where I could identify most people by smell, by the sound of their movements, by their energy, but usually not from beyond a closed door. "It's open," I called.

He came in with a sheaf of papers in one hand and two steaming mugs in the other. "Coffee?"

I grinned in delight and took one of the mugs from him. "Thanks. You're a mind reader."

"I owed you for the cocoa."

"Yeah, and speaking of owing…"

He held up a hand. "We've already had this discussion, Rachel."

Yes, we had. I had told him that I had plenty of money, that the bullshit I wrote had been good to me and that paying the entire shot for the whole crew would be absolutely no problem for me. But he insisted on paying his own way along with Marie's and the boys'. How he planned to do that on a cop's salary was beyond me. We were splitting the full tab for Rosie and Marlayna, though I'd had to twist his arm to get him to agree to even that much. Angela thought of herself as wealthy and was insisting on paying her own way at the lodge, which was fine with me.

"So what have you got there?" I asked, nodding at the stack of papers while taking a nice big sip of the coffee, which was perfect. More than perfect. What kind did they have in that kitchen, anyway? I was going to have to find out.

"Guest registry," he said, and I almost choked.

"You're shitting me."

"I shit you not," he said, making me grin again. "I had a private talk with the head of security while I was killing time at the front desk. You're gonna love this guy, Rache. Retired cop, so Irish he still has a brogue. Finnegan Smart."

"I love him already," I said, trying to picture the man in my mind. Was it bigoted of me to imagine him slugging a pint of Guinness and smoking a pipe? Probably.

"I showed him my ID, told him there was a very slim chance that a suspect I've been looking for is up here, and that I needed the guest list. He said he'd email it, and he was as good as his word."

"This place has a printer?"

"Yeah, there's an office downstairs."

He shuffled papers around, separating the freshly printed stack from an older one. "I also brought our lists of which organs went to which hospitals and who the recipients were, at least as many as I was able to piece together before it became unnecessary."

"We thought."

"Yeah. I figured we could compare our list to the guest list. Chief Sub's gotta wait for a warrant to get the list of recipients the regular way. We've got a head start."

"You don't waste any time, do you?"

He walked to my nightstand, set the papers down and turned. "Actually, I think I'm about to waste a little. Everyone's clamoring for a snack. Marie found brownie mixes in the kitchen and they'll be done in five. I said I'd see if I could coax you down for some brownies and coffee by the fire."

My thought bubble had Mason and me curled up

on a bearskin rug in front of the fireplace—there was no bearskin rug except in my mind, just so you know—pigging out on brownies. It sounded like heaven, until Misty, Jeremy, Josh and Marie all arrived in my bubble, crowding it until it popped. But I decided to play nice and gave him what I hoped was a convincing smile. "I thought I was catching whiffs of pure temptation while I was unpacking."

He looked past me at the bed, the shopping bags, the snow pants. "They got the analysis back on that syringe," he said.

"Don't tell me. Sucks-in-Aberdeen, right?"

"Succinylcholine."

"That's what I said."

"It's used in surgery to—"

"Paralyze the muscles. I know. And your lungs get paralyzed, too, and you suffocate if you're not on a ventilator, and it's hard to trace because it breaks down and the stuff that remains is also found in most corpses due to decomposition."

He stared at me and blinked. "How is it you're so far ahead of me on this?"

"It was my body that had a syringe full of that shit sticking into it. One push of the plunger and we'd be having this conversation over an Ouija board."

He lowered his head. "You've barely had time to process what happened, have you?"

"I don't want to process it." Then I shrugged. "Besides, I'm feeling much better now. We're up here in the middle of nowhere. No one knows where we went, and I have to believe we're safe while we work all this out."

He nodded slowly. "Yeah, I hope you're right."

"I know I am." It was a lie. I was pulling a page from my own books and thinking positively. Fake it till you make it and all that bull. Hell, you never know, it could work just this once, right?

I heard voices…singing, and I frowned, cocking my head to one side. "Is that…?"

"Carolers?" Mason asked.

"Good God, they just beat you over the head with holiday cheer up here, don't they?" And yet I moved past him into the hall, deliberately brushing against him, then hurried down the stairs to see for myself.

Yes, there were carolers. Marie had opened the door and was standing there smiling at one of them, a tall, dark-haired guy who was damn good-looking. Not as good-looking as Mason, of course. But then, who was? He was smiling back at her, too, a twinkle in his eyes.

They know each other. And that means she broke our number one rule. She told someone we were coming up here.

Maybe not. There could be another explanation. But there is something going on in the air between his eyes and hers. I don't miss shit like that.

Rosie was among the singers, his Santa-sized belly making him easy to spot, and Marlayna was tucked in the crook of his arm, smiling car to ear and singing off-key to "God Rest Ye Merry Gentlemen."

Mason and I joined the others, crowded together at the open door as the carol unfolded. A couple in the back added harmony, and the snowy night vista behind them made it picture-perfect, too. It was wonderful, and we all clapped like giddy cheerleaders when they finished.

"You have to invite us in for a drink now," Rosie said. "That's how this works."

"No, Mr. Jones, not at all," said a pale, bespectacled man I guessed was either a pastor or an accountant.

"Yes, Mr. Beckwith, yes, it does. For me, anyway." Holding Marlayna to him, Rosie pushed through the crowd and came inside. "Go on, have fun now. These are friends of mine," he added, because Mr. Beckwith looked worried.

He smiled in relief then, and waved. "Good night, Mr. Jones, Mrs. Jones."

"Merry Christmas!" called several of the group.

They trooped away singing "Jingle Bells" as Mason started to close the door. Then he stopped halfway as a car pulled up out front. Angela.

Great. Now the evening was complete.

Marlayna sniffed the air. "*Now* I know why you wanted to come in. I smell something good."

"Aw, hon, don't be like that," Rosie said. Then, to Mason, "It's brownies, isn't it?"

"Oh, no, my brownies!" Marie ran to the kitchen.

I ran to help her, hoping she'd made a jumbo-sized batch. And hoping even harder that this evening with the gang would pass quickly, so I could get back to that homework, alone in my room, with Mason.

Because...what? You want to bang him?

Yes, Inner Bitch. That's exactly what I want. Maybe.

I felt my alter ego snort in derision. *You want more than that, and you damn well know it.*

Whoa. Where had *that* notion come from?

It didn't matter, I told myself. Another one-night stand with Mason was *exactly* what I wanted. Right now. I was drunk on holiday cheer and twinkling lights and anticipated chocolaty deliciousness, and I wanted another night in his arms to go with all the other sensory delights. And if there was anything more than that in the offing, I was just going to think about that later.

Marie brought in a platter of brownies, and I saw there were at least three different varieties. Some had lighter brown swirls of what I hoped to God was peanut butter. Some had walnuts and chocolate chips, and the third batch was actually blondies, with butterscotch chips, be still, my waistline.

She set the platter on the coffee table, a giant oak slab of a thing facing the fireplace, which was burning happily, and Josh grabbed a handful before anyone else could get close.

"One," Marie said. "You take one brownie at a time, Joshua."

So he let them go. A pile of slightly mashed

brownies freshly contaminated with whatever his unwashed boy-hands had on them.

"Honestly, Marie," Angela snapped, "do you really think anyone wants to eat any of them now? Joshua, take the brownies you touched off that pile. Those will be all you get."

Mason beat him to it, taking the most mashed brownie of all and popping it whole into his mouth. Then he chewed and grinned at the same time, clearly disgusting his mother. Joshua, who'd looked wounded a second ago, burst into giggle fits.

Angela rolled her eyes. "That's good, Mason. Encourage him to be rude."

"He wasn't being rude," I said. "He was just being a kid."

Mason's mother glared at me, and I knew I wasn't scoring any brownie points. Okay, bad pun. Shoot me. The woman's personality matched her hair. White steel. And I'd been as disgusted by Josh's brownie grab as she had. I just automatically rose to Mason's defense. Which was stupid, because he certainly didn't need it.

Misty came trundling in from the kitchen with a big tray full of coffee mugs, two steaming pots and various other implements of indulgence. Cream, sugar, cocoa packets, so I presumed one pot held coffee and the other, hot water.

Jeremy jumped up from his chair to take the tray from her, and the smile she sent him was gooier than the still warm chocolate chips in the brownie I'd just picked up. Angela looked pleased and Marie looked worried. Hell, I wasn't. Misty had a good head on her shoulders.

So we sat around eating. Marie was mostly quiet. Rosie and Marlayna carried on most of the conversation. And eventually it turned to my work, as I had feared it would. It was always awkward when someone brought their adoring fandom to a family function. It clashed, you know?

Anyway, it was of course Marlayna who said, "You know, Rachel, your books really changed my life."

"Really? Well, isn't that interesting?" Angela set her cup delicately down and leaned forward. "Do tell us how, Marlayna. I never thought you were the type to go in for that sort of thing."

"What sort of thing is that, Angela?" I asked.

She smiled at me. I smiled back. *Don't even try to out passive-aggressive me, hon. I wrote the manual.*

"Oh, you know." She waved a hand from the wrist. "Airy-fairy."

Mason put his hand on my thigh. It was supposed to calm me down. It didn't. Then he went to take it away and I slapped mine over top of it to keep it there. Because while it wasn't calming, it *was* distracting in the best possible way.

Marlayna was talking again, but I'd been focused on that hand and had to quickly tune in.

"…not like that at all, Angela," she was saying. "It's…deep. She writes in truths that are so simple you just feel like you knew them all along. And I think we probably *do* on some level, we just…I don't know, forget."

"Truths, you say." Condescension dripped from Angela's tone. "Why don't you share some of these bits of genius with us, Rachel? I'm not familiar with your work. In fact, I'd never heard of you until Mason mentioned you to me."

Another slam. I was preparing to return the volley when Misty said, "Wow. Have you been living in a cave or something?"

Mason snorted coffee out his nose. Well, okay, not quite, but I thought it was close.

"I used to spend all my time worrying," Marlayna said. She either hadn't noticed the little round of slam-the-writer or had chosen to ignore it. "Every decision, every simple 'should I or shouldn't I?' was like a life-and-death choice. I'd spend hours trying to think of every possible repercussion, trying to predict other people's reactions to every decision I made. I was trying to choose between jobs when I read *Wish and It Is Granted*."

"What were the jobs?" I almost jumped, surprised the question had come from me. I realized I was leaning forward on the sofa, elbows on my legs, having forgotten all about Mason and his hand on my thigh, which was, sadly, no longer there. I was eager to hear what Marlayna was saying. *What the fuck?*

"I was a teacher at the time," she said slowly. "But I was offered a job in the administration end of things, and at the same time, I'd been playing around with website design, taking a few classes and practicing by putting up sites for friends. I was worried about money, security, retirement, work hours...everything you could think of. And then I read that book, and it was like an angel whispering in my ear, 'Just do what you really want in your heart to do, the thing that feels like the most fun. Do that, and the rest will fall into place.'"

I wrote that? That's actually not bad.

"So what did you do?" I asked, and this time I wasn't even surprised I was eager.

"I did what my heart wanted to do and started my own website design business. Within a year I was making twice what I'd made teaching, and after the second year, more than the administrative job would have paid. And I have never once regretted it."

Angela made a huffing sound, but I decided to ignore her. Then Marlayna was reaching across and covering my hand with hers. "Thank you for that, Rachel. I've been making decisions based on what my heart wants ever since, and just like you said, my heart has never steered me wrong."

"Too bad I didn't have that kind of advice seventeen years ago," Marie said softly. "I was a nurse when Eric and I first got married. But I gave it up to stay home and raise our boys. Sometimes…I really miss it."

"It's never too late, Marie," Marlayna said softly.

Everyone was looking at me—Angela skeptically, of course, but Mason was beaming like he was proud or something, and Misty had that "if they only knew" smirk on her face.

"Well, we'd best get back to the lodge and let you all get some sleep," Rosie said, maybe to break the awkward moment. "Will I see you all on the slopes tomorrow?"

"You can see me in the water park," Josh said. "That's where I want to be!"

"We'll ski in the morning, water park in the afternoon. How's that sound, pal?" Mason asked.

Joshua pouted and sank farther back into his chair. I felt for the kid. That water park was all he'd talked about since we'd arrived. Maybe I'd talk to Mason about letting him go right at noon, when it opens.

"Come on, Josh, time for you to get ready for bed," his mother said. "Me, too, for that matter. I'm exhausted." She got up and held out her hand to her youngest. "Good night, Rosie, Marlayna. Angela."

"Good night, Marie." Marlayna went to her, gave her a slight hug and whispered something that made Marie glance my way, nod and say, "Maybe I will."

Hell, Marlayna was telling her to read my books.

I just knew it. Like that was going to help after she'd lost her husband and her baby.

Angela said, "No point in you two walking back to the lodge. I have my car outside." They left, and Marie and Joshua headed upstairs, leaving Mason and me with Misty and Jeremy, who were clearly hoping we'd turn in and leave them alone.

"I'm pretty tired, too," I said. "Misty, help me with the mess, will you, so we can turn in?"

"Sure." She followed me to the kitchen, each of us carrying a pile of stuff. She wrapped the leftover brownies, while I stacked empty mugs in the dishwasher.

I said, "So listen, about you and Jeremy…"

"We only met a few days ago, Aunt Rache."

"Yeah? Well, I've been a teenager, albeit a blind one. I know the deal. You're seventeen. Are you on anything?"

"Like *drugs?*" she asked, mortified.

"Like birth control, Einstein."

She crossed her arms over her chest and turned her back on me.

"Look, I have three things to say, kid." I ticked them off on my fingers as I went on. "One. Not without a condom, not ever, no matter what. Two. Not before you're ready, no matter what, no matter who. And three. Remember that sex means something. It connects you with the other person whether you want it to or not. So understand that before you proceed."

"You sound like one of your own books, Aunt Rachel."

"That's because I'm the author. And while I've got your attention, I want you to keep in mind that Jeremy is in a really vulnerable place right now. He just lost his father, and then his newborn sister, so be careful with his feelings."

"I am *not* going to have sex with Jeremy."

"You can still be careful how you treat him."

She rolled her eyes.

"I'm done now. Use your brain. Make your aunt proud." I wiped my hands on a dish towel, tossed it onto the counter and left the kitchen in time to see the tail end of what looked like a similar conversation between Mason and Jeremy, who was rolling his eyes just like Misty had. I hoped they both listened, because we couldn't keep our eyes on them 24/7. At some point with kids you had to trust them and hope they remembered one or two of your 8000 lectures.

Mason met my eyes and nodded just slightly, telling me we were still on for that research in my room.

"I'm heading upstairs now," I said. "Good night, you guys."

"Night," they chorused.

And then I headed for my room, feeling like a hypocrite because I'd just lectured Misty on the dangers of casual sex while I was considering having some myself a little later on.

Or was I?

According to Marlayna, the crap I'd spouted in book one, crap that was really just a remix of crap I'd read myself, in braille or on audio over the twenty years I'd been told to make peace with my blindness, actually worked.

Had changed her life, she'd said.

Oh, she wasn't the first. I'd had thousands of letters and emails from readers claiming the same. I guess I'd just assumed those people had thought their lives had changed, but that they would revert in short order to whatever had been wrong in the first place. Marlayna was the first person to give me a snapshot of changes that had lasted years.

I knew the stuff by heart, the platitudes, the pseudo-science behind them. The theory that one's inner self always knew the right thing to do, and that this all-knowing, all-seeing part of us communicated to us through our emotions. When something felt great, filled us with excitement and eagerness, that was our inner self saying "Hell, yes," according to the message I preached.

My inner self was shouting a very loud *hell, yes* to a night of hot monkey sex with Mason.

Maybe, just this once, I would try a little spoonful of my own medicine. Practice what I preached. What did I have to lose?

Shit, I need to take a shower!

I hit the adjoining bathroom like my feet were on fire, cranked the taps and thanked my lucky stars that I'd packed all my inner-Barbie stuff. My sweet-smelling body wash. My extra rich conditioner. A couple of razors. I was going to do it, I thought, as I scrubbed every inch of my body. I was going to have sex with Mason tonight.

My inner idiot giggled like a sophomore.

My inner bitch was smiling like she knew something I didn't. I hate when she does that.

9

*T*ap tap tap, really softly on my bedroom door. And it was about frigging time. I'd only been waiting for close to two hours, which meant I'd had plenty of time to change my mind seventeen times and primp a little more just in case. You know, the usual stuff. Fix my hair three different ways and debate with myself over whether to wear pajama bottoms and a tank, or a T-shirt and panties. The latter would have been too obvious, so I went for the jammie bottoms and the tank. No bra. I'd just pretend I didn't realize how great my small but perky boobs looked in the white ribbed, guy-style tank top. He'd believe that, right?

Just when I decided he wouldn't, that I would come off like a sex maniac and was digging for a suitable substitution, there came that sound of someone rapping, rapping at my chamber door.

Nothing to do but buck up. I squared my shoulders, pulled my hair around to one side, which I'd decided looked sexy, and opened the door.

Mason had come bearing gifts. Leftover brownies and coffee, which he put on one of the nightstands. And the way his gaze slid over my tank top made me glad I hadn't changed. He swallowed hard, averted his eyes, and I saw the way his sexy-as-hell, stubble-coated jawline tightened. I doubted he had any idea how gorgeous he was. Or maybe he did, now that I thought about it.

He came on in when I stepped aside. He wore pajama bottoms, too, just like me. *Unlike* me, he'd chosen a loose-fitting T-shirt to cover his magnificent upper bod. I wished he hadn't. I remembered it too well. He had the best shoulders and back. Really wide and smooth, and just...*nice.*

I closed the door behind him. Too obvious?

He set the goodies on the nightstand, snatching up the file folder he'd left there earlier, then turned to face me. "Sorry it took so long."

"Did it? I wasn't paying attention."

He bit the inside of his cheek, like he wanted to grin but was fighting it. "I thought it'd be better to wait until everyone else called it a night. We can't tell them what we're really doing in here, and that means they'd jump to their own conclusions."

"Right. Makes sense." He smelled good. Damn, he'd showered, too. His hair was still damp at the ends.

My turn to avoid a full-fledged grin. I grinned on the inside, though, right to my toes.

"Where's Myrtle?" he asked, looking around my room.

"She's in with Josh because she's a dirty traitor. But I don't mind."

"He's fallen in love, for sure. So, you have chairs in here?"

"Nope, just the bed." I jumped on, scooted up until my back was against the headboard and crossed my legs in front of me. Then I patted the spot next to me.

He looked a little nervous, but he joined me on the bed. He stretched his long legs out in front of him, leaned back, positioning a few pillows behind him, and opened the file folder on his thighs.

His thighs. I remembered *them,* too. Running my hands over the soft, fine hairs on them and feeling them flex hard and let go, over and over.

"Okay, so we have—"

"We have coffee getting cold and brownies getting stale over there," I said, nodding to the nightstand on his side of the bed, because I needed to distract myself. And those brownies were pretty damn good.

He looked up from the papers and nodded. "Right." Then he passed me a mug and brought the plate of brownies over. He put it on the bed beside my legs. "There you go." Like he knew it was the brownies I'd really wanted the whole time. Hell, he probably had. We'd been together a lot, the last time his brother had come back from the dead. Figuratively speaking.

"I should at least pretend I'm not going to eat those," I said.

"Nah. I think skiing burns off more calories than you could eat if you tried."

"You haven't seen me try." I took a brownie, dipped it in my coffee and involuntarily said, "Mmm" as I bit off the soggy end.

He shifted a little, then reached for his own mug and took a sip.

"I really didn't expect we'd spend our first night here in bed together," I said.

He choked on his coffee, and I grabbed a few tissues from the box on my nightstand and handed them to him.

"Thanks."

I leaned over and grabbed my laptop off the floor where I'd left it. "So, where do we begin?"

"Let's search the net."

"Search terms?" I asked, opening the lid and signing on to the internet, pleasantly surprised by the speedy connection.

"Organ transplants, August of this year."

"Got it." I clicked keys rapidly and clicked the search button. "Hmm, over eight million hits, beginning with several from the UK."

"Yes, but now we narrow them down by hospital. We have the list from last time of every hospital where Eric's organs were sent."

I searched, but I wasn't finding what we wanted. "Most of this is official stuff. Statistics and so on. We need personal." I typed in the word *fund-raiser* with the rest of the terms, including the dates and hospitals, and sure as shit, names popped up. Actual names of actual people. Perfect. I turned the screen toward him, and he nodded.

"You're brilliant."

"Yes, I am. Thanks for noticing."

"Now we cross-check the names with the specific organs and the hospitals where they were sent, and voilà, we have our list of potential victims."

"But the patients wouldn't necessarily live in the cities where the organs were sent."

"No, that's true. The organs go to the transplant center closest to the victims. But if the fund-raiser is within a hundred-mile radius and the dates are right, we'll consider it a potential hit."

I nodded. "I'll bet not all of them had fund-raisers."

Most of them did, though. We found fifty-seven newspaper articles about fund-raisers for transplant recipients and knew we were on the right track when the results included the two victims so far. As I looked at our growing list, I nodded. "You know, Mason, I've been meaning to tell you that despite everything, I'm glad you gave me Eric's corneas. I like being able to see."

"But not what came with it."

I lowered my head. "No, being in the heads of the people who continued Eric's crimes after his death was no fun. And I've gotta tell you, being along for the ride with the recent victims was torture. But it happened. And there has to be a reason."

Tipping his head to one side, he studied my face with his gorgeous brown eyes. "Careful, Rachel. You sound like you're starting to believe in your own philosophy."

"Maybe I am, a little bit." I shrugged. "If my suffering through these…visions…can save someone's life, then maybe it's worth it."

"And maybe if we can find this person, stop him, it'll finally be over for you."

"God, I hope so."

He reached out, dragged a forefinger across my cheek. "You got some brownie on you."

When he shifted his hand away, I took it in mine and brought it back, and he flattened his palm against my cheek. I closed my eyes and rubbed against it just a little. "I really like how I feel when you touch me," I said.

"It's mutual." But he drew a deep breath and took his hand gently away. "But right now we have lives to save. Including yours."

"And Marie's," I added with a nod. "And that poor woman's been through enough for one lifetime. Maybe two."

"Yeah. She's shaky. I'm worried about the boys, too."

I nodded, and got back to our lists. We'd made our way halfway down them with no new matches when I said, "I've got a Stephanie Phelps, fund-raiser for a tendon transplant. I didn't know they did that."

He ran his finger over his list. "Nope. The only listing for Eric's tendons is Johnson City. Close to home."

I kept going on my list, reading the pertinent info aloud. "Richard Kenner has been moved to the top of the list for a lung transplant, but the surgery is expensive and insurance won't cover it all…blah blah blah, fund-raiser will be held…yada yada." I looked for follow-up pieces under his name, town and "lung transplant," and found the mother lode on Facebook. I nodded. "Richie received his new lung on August 17. The day your brother died."

"There's a good chance it's Eric's, then. Find his home address and I'll give you another brownie."

"Way ahead of you, pal." I had already started, and as it came up, I pointed at the screen, where the man's name, address and phone number appeared. "You can find anyone on the internet."

"Damn, you're good."

"As you well remember."

He closed his eyes for a moment. Good. But then he got back to business, scribbling all the information into his notebook. "That's one. We've got dozens to go," he said softly.

"I know."

"We can't let ourselves…get distracted."

Damn, damn, damn. "You're right."

"If you keep flirting with me, we're going to."

"*Flirting* with you? You're kind of full of your-self, aren't you, Mason?"

I started to swing off the bed, but he clamped a hand on my arm to keep me in place and said, "No. I'm full of *you*. You're close, and you smell good, and I'm having trouble focusing on anything except peeling that T-shirt over your head and—" His eyes were on my boobs, until he closed them and sighed. "I need you to help me stay focused. Just until we catch this guy, and then…"

"And then?" My voice sounded all whiskey and cigarettes, like Lauren Bacall.

"And then whatever you say, Rache. Whatever you say, I'm there."

I lowered my head to hide the rush of absolute pleasure that swept up into my face. I could really get in deep with this guy. My inner bitch was right about that. It wasn't just sex. I could put off the sex. But the rest of this, whatever this was, it wasn't put-offable. He was getting under my skin. Deep. I hadn't really understood that before, had I?

Not like I did right now.

"Okay, Mason. Okay." I moved his hand away, cursing the fact that it was necessary. Then I reached behind me for the little silky robe on the bedpost and draped it over me like a blanket. A thin silk blanket. "I'm a little chilly," I said.

"Yeah, I could tell." He met my eyes, and his were full of mischief.

Damn, maybe I was already into him deeper than

I'd known. I picked up a brownie and shoved it into his mouth, then dragged my focus back to my laptop. "Let's see who's next." As I searched, finding names, addresses and organs, and gaping over the personal details people shared online, I asked, "What are we going to do with this information once we have it? I mean, we're up here safe and sound. But they're out there like sitting ducks."

"I've got that covered. The chief knows we're piecing together this list. If we finish before he gets his warrant, I'm gonna fax him our list. He'll contact the local cops in each area, and have them go out and have a frank talk with the potential victims, suggest they leave town for a while and keep their whereabouts to themselves until we get this guy off the streets."

I nodded, glad no one was trying to play this close to the vest when there were lives at stake. "Does he know you have the master list of which organs went to which hospitals?"

"I didn't tell him. He didn't ask."

"But if he had, you could've been in trouble."

"Not as much trouble as those organ recipients might be."

I nodded and looked at him. Just looked. At his cheekbones, his jaw, the dark whiskers coming in that would feel like heaven on my skin. "You're really just a good person, aren't you?"

"You say that like you're surprised."

"No, I mean a really, truly good person. There aren't that many, you know."

"Oh, I don't know. I think you're a little bit of a cynic, Rache. There are more of us than you think there are."

"Not in my experience."

"No? Well, let's count, shall we? You have your sister, her husband, their girls. They're all good people, aren't they?"

"The best."

"And then there's your assistant. Amy's good people, too, right?"

"It's safe to say all the people in my life are good. They wouldn't be in my life otherwise. But out there—" I looked toward the window "—it's different. Out there everybody has an angle, everybody wants a piece of you."

"Of *you,* you mean."

"Yeah."

"And that makes them less than good?"

"Well…yeah."

He just nodded.

"Why, you think it doesn't?"

"Rachel, there's a light in you. You tend to keep it shaded in person, but it shines bright in your books. That kind of light draws people."

"And insects."

He smiled. "I think there's a part of you way down deep where this stuff you write is coming from, and I think it's real. But it's your most vulnerable side.

You protect it. You hide it behind the tough, sarcastic Rachel you pretend to be. I don't think people want to douse that light. I think they just want to bask in it a little bit. They just want to soak it up."

I was looking at him like he'd sprouted a second head, because he was talking about me as if I was some kind of saint or angel or something, and I wasn't. Far from it.

Was that how he saw me?

Was that really who he thought I was?

Because if that was the part of me he was attracted to, then he was attracted to a lie. I was not that person. I wasn't even very nice, deep down.

I lowered my head, and my throat tightened up for no damn reason.

"You don't believe me."

"I think…the person you think I am bears very little resemblance to the real me, Mason. And that bugs me, because for some screwy reason you're the only person I *want* to see the real me, not some idealized version you made up in your head, or the public persona I made up in mine."

"Your sixty million readers made her up, too?"

"I made her up for them."

"Then she came from you. I think the only one who's not seeing the real you is you."

I closed my eyes, gave my head a shake. "Can we get back to work before you give me a migraine?"

"Yeah. Who's next?"

Wednesday, December 20

When I woke, someone was pounding on my bedroom door and Mason was gone. I'd fallen asleep at some point, and I was pretty sure I'd at least been trying to snuggle—surreptitiously, of course.

I frowned, looking toward the open bathroom door. He wasn't in there. And our sheafs of papers and notes were gone. My laptop was closed and sitting out of the way on the dresser across the room. Yeah, he'd slipped out on me. The dirty rat.

The knocking came again, and I groaned, "Go away, I'm sleeping."

"Come on, Aunt Rache! Get up." It was Misty, sounding far too cheerful for this ungodly hour. "Everyone's getting ready but you."

Getting ready for *what?* was the question.

I flung my covers back and dragged my pajama-clad ass to the bedroom door, shoving my hands through my hair, which was probably standing on end as it tended to before the first comb of the day. Yeah, tangles entrapped my fingers. Ugh. Finally I opened the door, leaned on it and yawned in my niece's face.

"What's the emergency, Misty?"

"We're going to the Northstar for breakfast, and then we're skiing." She said it like one would say, "We just won the lottery!" when, in my opinion, the appropriate tone would have been more "We're going to the dentist."

"Skiing, huh?"

"Yeah, Aunt Rache. Skiing. We're at a ski resort. People come here to ski. You bought all your new ski-bunny stuff for just that purpose. Remember?"

I swallowed hard. "Far be it from me to ruin everyone's good time. You all go on, and I'll see you around lunchtime." I started to close the door.

Misty pushed back, preventing that. "I told Mason you'd try to weasel out of it, but he says you promised to do everything together for the entire trip." She grinned. "I *thought* you two had a little something-something going on."

"We do not have anything-anything going on."

She thinned her lips and tilted her head to one side.

"All right," I said, "there might be a very small thing in its formative stages, but—"

"I never even got a chance to see the clothes you bought. Did you shop where I told you?"

"Yes." I closed my eyes, but she was pushing her way into my room now, opening my closet.

"Who helped you?"

"I don't know. Some redhead."

"Char. Great, Char knows her stuff and— Ooh, is this it?"

She pulled out my brand-new ski outfit, black and white, and very much what a seasoned and competent skier would wear. It would look ridiculous tumbling down the hill with me inside it. It would probably go on strike after day one, if it had any self-respect.

She threw my ski pants and jacket on the bed. "Where's your hat and scarf?"

I just pointed. She went to the dresser, opened the top drawer and pulled them out. "Red. Perfect. Just the dash of color you need with this." She tossed them on top of the rest. "Look, the jacket has red zippers and pulls. This is super-cute, Aunt Rache. You're gonna make Mason's eyeballs pop."

"Yeah, I'm sure he'll be amazed at my grace."

"Don't be too worried. He can't ski, either."

I looked up, hope lighting a match in the darkness of my heart. "He can't?"

"He's been having the same fits you're having. All worried about looking stupid in front of you. Not that he said that out loud, of course, but I could tell. You two can laugh at each other. It'll be fun."

Four hours later I had to admit that it *had* been fun. I'd burned off enough calories to eat whatever I wanted the entire time we stayed, which was gratifying, because, in case it's not obvious by now, I like to eat. And after an hour on the bunny slope, Mason and I managed to stay upright going down some hills that were a little bit more challenging.

It was hard to keep the kids in sight, since Jeremy and Misty were experts, at least compared to us. They went whooshing past us on a regular basis. Jeremy had even been smiling once or twice, and it seemed they'd hooked up with another young couple on the slopes, because I saw the four of them together more than once.

Marie and Josh had opted to stay at the water park down at the lodge. Mason hadn't liked it, but Marie's arguments had been logical. They were safe up here. No one knew where they'd gone. They were surrounded by other guests. Angela and Rosie and Marlayna were there to back her up.

Mason had a chat with Finnegan Smart, the head of security, as an added precaution, asking him to keep an extra eye on Marie and Josh. *That* was a man I wanted to wrap up and take home, just so I could listen to his brogue day and night.

We were on yet another run, and I was literally exhausted but couldn't have wiped the smile off my face with sandpaper. I was doing it! I was *skiing,* leaning left and right, balancing with ease, speeding—for me—down a moderate slope beneath the bluest blue sky I had ever seen, with the cold air kissing my face and the smell of pine filling my lungs.

Mason came up from behind and was zooming along beside me, and I glanced his way, saw that he was grinning like a loon, too, and got stuck on him for a heartbeat too long.

Next thing I knew I was tumbling ass over applecart, as my mother used to say. He tripped over me, and then he was tumbling, too. We came to a stop eventually. I couldn't believe both my skis were still on as I sat there in the snow, pushing my fallen—but cute—hat up off my face.

Mason was pushing himself up. He rolled over

and looked at me, and his face was covered in snow. I burst out laughing before he brushed it away.

He was laughing, too.

Then he got up, got his skis underneath him and made his way over to me. He reached down, I grabbed hold of his gloved hands and he hauled me upright and brushed snow out of my hair, tucking it back under my hat where it belonged, still laughing. My eyes locked on to his, and laughter got stuck in my throat. His hands on my shoulders pulled me just a little, and his head came down. I closed my eyes, and he kissed me. It was slow, and tender, and it lasted a long time, yet not long enough. And then he straightened and said, "You okay?"

"Uh-huh."

"You want to call it a morning, head down to the lodge for some lunch?"

"Uh-huh."

"I'll get hold of the kids, then."

"Mm-hm." What had happened to my power of speech? What the hell had that kiss been about? Hadn't he just told me last night that he didn't think the timing was right? That he had to make sure we got this killer first, and that—

He pulled a walkie-talkie out of somewhere. "Where'd you get that?" I asked.

Right, your ability to speak is finally restored and that's *the question you ask?*

"It's Josh's. He loaned one to me for the morning. Jeremy has the other one."

"Smart thinking."

"Yeah, I think I'll grab another set, maybe two sets, if they have them in the ski shop. Handy as hell. But these are meant for kids. Not much range." He depressed a button. "Jer, you read me?"

He waited a few seconds, then tried again.

This time Jeremy replied. "Gotcha. What's up?"

"Ready to head down for a lunch break?"

"Yeah, we're starved. Meet you by the lifts."

Mason nodded and replaced the radio. Then he turned to me again, and his eyes got all funny. Like he was trying to think of what he should say but not coming up with anything. He started to speak twice, then stopped again.

I figured I might as well help him out. "So what did that kiss mean, Mason?"

He blinked. "I don't know. I was just being in the moment. You know, like your books always say to be." He looked down the trail, not at me. The lodge wasn't too far away. "Did you mind?"

"Hell, no."

"So then we're good."

"Yeah, I just…" *Just want to know what's next. Are you going to kiss me again? Are we dating now? Was it a one-time thing? Can we have sex tonight?*

"Just what?"

I shook my head, smiled a little and reminded myself that according to my regurgitated sermons, being in the moment meant just that, doing what felt right and enjoying it without judging it, picking it apart, analyzing it, looking ahead or looking behind. And he would surely throw all of that back at me if I said any of the things I was thinking. So instead I said, "Race you to the bottom," put a hand on his chest and pushed him. He fell on his ass in the snow, and then I pushed off with my ski poles to get a head start.

A big sign on the glass doors told us that a special holiday lunch was being served, buffet style, in the sunroom. It was a massive glass dome at the end of a long hallway, and it had a nearly 360-degree view of the mountains and pines around the lodge. And even with that, you couldn't see another home or business. Nothing but the lodge and its various structures, a few of the outlying cabins, like ours, which was a long walk or a short drive along one of the many narrow, winding roads.

The four of us hung our jackets and ski pants in the designated area and trooped inside, spotting Marie at a large table with that same man I'd noticed her looking at in the group of carolers last night.

Mason nudged me with an elbow. "That's the guy she was talking to in the water park the night we checked in."

"He was with the carolers, too. I thought it looked as if she knew him."

She saw us at the same time and waved us over.

I smiled back at her, and leaned closer to Mason. "Look at her. She looks...better."

"Jeremy doesn't."

I glanced past him at Jeremy. He looked ready to bite nails in half. Misty closed her hand on his forearm, and whispered something to him. He nodded once and seemed to relax a little as we all headed for the table.

"Josh and Angela are already in line," Marie said, nodding toward the steady flow of traffic past the buffet in the center of the room. "This is all gratis. I love this place."

The dark-haired man got to his feet. "Hello again, Mason." He offered a hand. Mason shook it, but he looked about as impressed as Jeremy did.

"I don't think we've met," I said. "I'm Rachel."

"Scott Douglas." He took my hand. Firm, but not too firm. Dry, warm. Perfectly normal hand. I was trying to compare its size to the one that had reached for me from behind that day in my car, the one that had jammed a needle into my shoulder, and decided this guy's hand seemed quite a bit bigger.

Then again, my attacker had been wearing a black glove, and black tended to make things look smaller, didn't it?

"This is my niece Misty, and Jeremy is Marie's other son."

"Hello."

"Hi," Misty said.

Jeremy tugged his hand from hers and walked away. Not a word, just walked away.

"I'm sorry, Scott," Marie said. "I'd better go talk to him."

"Why don't you let me do that, Marie?" Mason said. "It might go better."

She held his eyes for a moment, then nodded. "Scott, I think—"

"I actually have to get back," he said. Guess the guy knew when he wasn't wanted. It was a shame. I hadn't seen this much color in Marie's cheeks before today. "I'll see you later." He patted her hand where it lay on the table, but that was all.

Misty was already jogging over to get in line beside Jeremy, so I decided to sit with Marie.

"Go ahead, go get food," she said. "I can hold the table."

"I'll wait with you." She was staring at her eldest son, so I did likewise. "He's going to be okay, you know. He was actually smiling out there on the slopes today."

She sighed. "I think he likes your niece."

"I think she likes him back. You know, there's nothing like a new romance to heal a broken heart, Marie. I think Misty might be just the right medicine for Jeremy." *And this Scott character, assuming he's not an organ thief, might be just the right medicine for Marie.*

She nodded. "I just hope Jeremy's not bad medicine for Misty," she said softly. "He's been so…dark."

"He's depressed, I think. Has he seen anyone?"

"For a while, right after, but he refused to keep going. Then he came home drunk one night last week."

"Hell. Does Mason know?"

She nodded. "I don't want him to think badly of Jeremy. But…something's wrong. It's like his father's death broke something inside him. And I can't reach him anymore."

"I'm sorry, Marie. After everything you've already been through, you just don't need this."

She nodded. "Thanks for that."

"You know, maybe this time up here will help. Being around Misty, seeing everyone finding a way to go on, seeing that it's still possible to have a good time, all of that. Maybe you can both start to heal up here."

"Did you see the way he looked at me when he came in here?"

I nodded. It had been pretty hateful. "I think it was Scott. I think he's going to resent you so much as speaking to any new man, no matter how unfair it is."

"There's nothing going on with Scott," she said, color rushing into her face. "I mean, he's nice, attentive, but—"

"He's interested in you. And why wouldn't he be? You're a beautiful woman. Relax and have fun with this, Marie. You deserve a vacation. Leave all the stress and worry and grieving and death behind for a little while."

She nodded slowly, her head down, but then she brought her head up again and met my eyes. "Except death is why we came up here, isn't it? Hard to forget that. My husband is dead. My baby is dead.

Somebody wants me dead. And my son hates me. I don't know how I can even think about having a good time with all of that."

I acted without thinking first, covered her hands on the table with mine, opened my mouth and spouted a line straight out of one of my books. "The situation is what it is, Marie. You can be miserable because of it, or you can find a way to feel better in spite of it. Just reach for relief right now. Anything that makes you feel better is the right move. Okay?"

She met my eyes, tipping her head to one side. "No wonder you're so successful, if that's the sort of thing in your books. Thank you, Rachel. I'm going to try to do just that."

Huh. Go figure.

The crew returned with their plates overflowing, and to my surprise, Mason had filled one for me and Josh brought one for Marie, so we didn't have to get up and go through the line.

Waitstaff meandered through, filling coffee cups, and a woman with a face that could have won her Miss America back in her younger days stood front and center, and tapped a glass with a fork until everyone quieted down. The woman wore black leggings, furry boots and a long gold sweater with a wide cowl collar. Her hair was a mass of artfully tousled blond ringlets, and the only hints of age were the beginnings of laugh lines around her eyes. She wore no wedding band.

"Hello, friends. I'm Catherine Cole, but you can

all call me Cait. I'm the owner of Pine Haven, and I am so happy that you've all chosen to spend this special time of the year with us here."

Applause broke out. I would have had to put my fork down to join in, so I opted not to, because the food was to die for.

"This luncheon," she went on, "is my way of getting most of our guests together in one place to tell you about some of the activities we have going on this week. First, we have a Secret Santa gift exchange already underway and continuing right through to Christmas. Choose a gift, wrap it, and leave it outside any guest room or cabin door you like. There are a half-dozen lovely gift and souvenir shops in the nearby village of Blue Lake, and of course we have one here, as well."

I leaned closer to Mason, who had chosen the seat right beside me, I'd noticed with pleasure. "Great way to drive up sales."

"Cynic," he whispered back.

"We have open caroling every night from now until New Year's. Just meet up by the lobby fireplace at 7:00 p.m. to join in. There are professional photographers roaming at large, ready to take your family portraits under the tree, in front of the fireplace, on the slopes or anywhere else you like. Watch out for them, because they'll shoot you on the slopes when you're not looking, too."

Someone in the crowd moaned, and everyone laughed.

"Don't worry," Cait said. "They'll hunt you down to offer you a copy, and anything not ordered is deleted. Your privacy is safe with us. Now, beginning tonight, we'll have horse-drawn sleigh rides several times a day, but you need to reserve your spot for those. And we have even more fun planned for Christmas Eve and Christmas Day. There are flyers being delivered to every room and cabin with the full holiday schedule of events, and I hope you'll join us. Merry Christmas, folks."

Several guests shouted "Merry Christmas" back at her, while others just clapped, and she headed back to her own table, where Finnegan Smart beamed at her in what looked like more than professional pride. Huh, was there something going on there?

"Wow, what a great place," Misty said. "I'm so grateful you brought me. Thanks, Aunt Rache."

"You're welcome." I didn't exactly bask in her gratitude, since I'd brought her up here because a killer was after my eyes. But telling her that would pretty much ruin the mood, you know?

10

"What do you think about Marie and this Scott Douglas character?" Mason asked.

We were sitting on a park bench in the middle of Blue Lake, the closest village to Pine Haven, where every possible sight belonged in a Jimmy Stewart holiday movie. It hadn't been hard to find. We'd driven through it on the way north, because there was only one road from the lodge to anywhere, although there were several roads from Blue Lake to elsewhere. The lodge road was narrow, twisting, unpaved and meandered through pine forests. We'd seen a moose on the way over.

I was glad I'd given in when Misty had begged to come into the village to do some Christmas shopping for the rest of us, plus she'd thought it would be fun to play along with the lodge's Secret Santa gift exchange. After all, what was more Christmassy than

buying a present for a total stranger? she'd asked.
Jeremy had come along because he seemed perfectly
willing to go along with anything Misty wanted to
do. Since we didn't dare leave anyone connected
to Eric, via his organs or his genes, unsupervised,
Mason and I had chaperoned, and he'd insisted I
wear big sunglasses and keep my hair under my hat.
It was kind of nice that he was being so protective.
I found it odd that I felt that way. That sort of thing
would usually irritate me. The others were well-
guarded by Rosie back at the lodge, and Josh had
probably dragged them all back to the water park by
now. Besides that, Mason had his new best friend,
Finnegan Smart, keeping a close eye on them, as
well. I'd caught the two of them talking shop three
times already today, though I knew he hadn't con-
fided to the retired Irish cop—or anyone else—the
real reason we were there.

I sipped my coffee before I answered his question
about Marie's admirer. "I guess I don't have to ask
what *you* think about him."

"Why not?"

"Because you said 'that Scott Douglas character'
the way you would say 'that embezzler.'"

He met my eyes, then looked away.

"You don't like him? Is he making your cop sense
tingle or something?"

"No, he's clean. I already called and had the chief
run a background check on him."

I was halfway to another sip but stopped. "You did?"

"Of course I did. He's hanging around Marie after someone tried to beat the hell out of her. Naturally I'm going to check."

I supposed that made sense. "So he's clean, then?"

He nodded.

"And yet you're still feeling hostile toward him."

"I just think it's a little soon, that's all. I mean, don't you? My brother hasn't even been dead six months."

"And widows of serial killers should be loyal for longer than that?"

He narrowed his eyes at me a little. I'd hit a nerve. Okay. "She doesn't know what he was," he said.

"She might not have known what he did, but I don't think you live with someone for eighteen years and don't know who they are, deep down, Mason. And besides, she knows he took his own life. He chose to leave her, alone with two boys and a baby on the way. How is that supposed to inspire her endless devotion?"

He clutched his coffee cup a little tighter. "It's too soon. The boys aren't ready."

"The boys aren't dating him."

His head came up fast. "You think they're *dating?* Did Marie tell you that?"

I set my cup down. "You know, the way you're acting, I'm wondering if you kissed the wrong woman on the slopes today. Are you in love with your sister-in-law, Mason?"

"Don't be ridiculous."

I watched his face, then closed my eyes and *felt* him. He'd withdrawn from me, leaned back a little, when I asked the question, and pulled back his energy, as well. The idea repelled him. Thank God.

I opened my eyes again. "Well, you're acting like a jealous boyfriend."

His lips tightened. "She was married to my *brother*."

"I know. But he's beyond caring. And she's the one in pain. She's lost so much lately, Mason. How can you deny her a harmless flirtation with a nice, good-looking stranger if it makes her feel better?"

His gaze shifted past me, looked horrified, and I knew in that instant that the kids had come out of the shop and were standing behind me. "Oh, shit." I turned.

Jeremy was standing there, his face expressionless. "I don't think he's a stranger," was all he said.

"Jer, I'm sorry." I turned around. "I…I'm sorry. I know this is hard for you. I didn't mean—"

"What do you mean, he's not a stranger?" Mason put a hand on my shoulder to make the interruption less irritating. It worked.

Jeremy shrugged. "I'm pretty sure he's the same guy I saw her talking to outside the grocery store one day. I don't think him being here is an accident at all. And I hate her for it."

"Jer, don't say that," Misty said.

He lowered his head and headed for the car, then got in and slammed the door without another word.

"I guess the shopping trip's over," Misty said.

"I'm sorry, Misty. I didn't mean to ruin the day for you two."

"You didn't. I've been telling him the same thing you just said. It's just bugging him, that's all. It was his dad, you know?"

"Yeah, I know."

She lifted her bag. There were four more sitting on the sidewalk near our bench. We'd had a busy day. "I got some really cute things for Secret Santa, though. I can't wait to scope out the guests and decide who gets what."

"I think you're just supposed to pick a random door."

"It's mostly kids' stuff. I need to figure out who has kids." She looked toward the car. "I'll bring Jeremy around, don't worry."

"You're good for him, Misty," Mason said. "I'm glad you're with us."

Her smile almost reached her ears. "Thanks, Mason." Then she turned and jogged to the car to join Jeremy.

Mason heaved a giant sigh that made his big chest expand bigger, which made me want to lay my hands on it. Sans shirt. "So is that what I'm acting like?"

"Not to the same degree."

He nodded. "I'll try to rein it in."

"I know you will."

"More importantly, I need to figure out if she did know him before they met here. That could mean we didn't come up here as anonymously as we think we did."

"I was thinking the same thing. I thought it when he was with the carolers. Should have told you then."

"Why didn't you?" he asked, looking at me with a curious crook of his brows.

"Doubted myself. Figured I must have had my antennae kinked or something."

"Never do that, Rache. Your antennae are the best I've ever seen."

Aside from Jeremy's morose attitude and stony silence all the way back to the lodge—which was only fifteen miles away, though the dirt road made it feel like forty—the day had been a good one. I was starting to feel safe at Pine Haven. Yes, I was a little bit worried about Marie's new...friend. Not overly worried that he might be a threat to *me* specifically, though. I hadn't sensed anything hostile about him. I was more worried that he might have told someone where he was going or who he was going to meet there, which might put us all in danger.

I thought the chances of that were pretty slim, though. If they'd been seeing each other and trying to keep it to themselves, they would have as much reason to be discreet as anyone else.

I wondered if I was being overly optimistic. After all, I hadn't sensed anything dangerous about the *last* serial killer I'd known, either, and he'd nearly killed Mason and me both. Still, I didn't think Scott Douglas was out to hurt anyone. I supposed the atmosphere up here, snow and pine trees and twinkling lights and Christmas magic everywhere you looked, might be skewing my blind-chick sense a little. I was starting to buy into all the happy holiday energy around this joint.

You know, until we got back to the cabin.

We'd stopped at the lodge to pick up Marie and Josh. Josh threw a fit, because he'd discovered an entire arcade just off the water park area and didn't want to leave.

I promised him twenty bucks' worth of quarters the next day if he'd just shut the fuck up and get in the car, and yes, that was exactly the way I put it. He laughed but complied. Angela was mortified but happy, I think, for a break from her demanding, exhausting grandson.

So we arrived back at the cabin with my rented Ford crammed full of passengers, shopping bags on every lap just to make room, and as we unloaded and headed for the door, I stopped, because there was a gorgeous wreath hanging there that hadn't been there before. It was just after dark, and the wreath was real pine, entwined with holly vines, berries and all, and accented with red and white poinsettia blossoms, also real. It had to have come from a florist.

Dangling from it by a red ribbon was a tiny package, wrapped in red foil paper with a minuscule green bow on top.

"What the hell?" I looked at Mason.

"Secret Santa!" Misty shouted. "Has to be!" She shouldered past me to tug the package free, then turned it over and gave an exaggerated pout. "It's for you," she said, and handed it to me.

Sure enough, the tiny package bore a tiny tag that had my name on it in microscopic letters. *Rachel de Luca.*

"I thought the Secret Santa thing was supposed to be anonymous?" I said, looking at each of them. "Random, right? Did one of you…?"

Every one of my cabinmates denied being responsible. Then Misty and Jeremy headed inside with Joshua tagging along behind, talking a mile a minute. He'd purchased a cheese-filled bone-shaped delicacy for Myrtle to make up for us leaving her alone for a few hours. Kid had no idea she actually preferred sleeping all day.

Mason took my elbow and steered me in, too, even though I was already trying to unwrap the tiny box. Way too much tape. Clearly someone who knew me personally must have left this, and that meant someone in this cabin, whether they would admit it or not. I wasn't even registered under my real name. No one else knew I was here. I heeled off my boots and shed my coat, shifting the gift from one hand to the other as I did, and then headed straight to the nearest chair, which was in front of the fireplace. The fire had gone out, and that was sad, but I didn't let it distract me from my mission.

Finally I got the wrapping off, revealing a small white box like you'd get from a jeweler. I took off the lid and looked inside.

A folded scrap of paper lay on top, so I took that out first and opened it. It was a clipping from a magazine, and I recognized the line. "Rachel de Luca is the archangel of new-age spirituality."

It made me smile. It had been part of a stellar review of one of my books, *Create Your Life,* which had been the one that launched my career into the stratosphere.

Feeling warm inside, I moved some cotton padding to reveal a tiny angel brooch. The little angel was gold-colored, heavy enough to be real though it clearly wasn't, and she had sparkly bits of lead crystal in her halo. But there was something wrong. Something about her eyes, which were empty sockets, not even gold, just dark.

I picked her up for a closer look and saw two tiny blue stones in the box beneath her. I lifted my head, searching for Mason. He was right there, really close. My hands started to shake.

He read me in that uncanny way of his. "What is it? What's wrong?"

I held up the angel and whispered, "Her eyes have been gouged out."

Mason felt the bottom drop out of his stomach as he saw Rachel's terror.

Misty leaned over from behind her. "Gouged out? Grim much? They must have *fallen* out. It's okay, though. I grabbed some glue today so I could fix my favorite bracelet. You can fix her right up!" She ran to get the glue.

No one else seemed overly interested. But then, no one else was aware of the implications. Marie was in the kitchen, putting away the extra groceries they'd picked up in the village. The boys were on the sofa with their handheld gaming devices, earbuds in place.

"Do *you* think her eyes fell out, Mason?" Rachel whispered.

"I think that would be a hell of a coincidence."

"I don't believe in coincidence."

"Put it back in the box. Let me take it."

She didn't seem to hear him. "He's here, Mason. The killer followed us here. Somehow he knows. He's coming for my eyes."

The angel fell from her hands back into the box, and Mason reached down to take it from her lap, along with the lid, the clipping and the wrapping paper. He was careful not to touch anything more than he had to.

"Lock the doors," he said for her ears only. "Do it as casually as you can while I take care of this, all right?"

She nodded, got up to wander casually over to the front door and turn the dead bolt, then picked up her dropped coat and hat, and put them away in the closet. He knew she was checking to make sure it held only coats. No organ thieves. Mason looked around at the others. No one was paying her any mind, so he took the evidence up to his room before anyone could ask questions. He deposited it in the top drawer of his nightstand, which would do until he could grab a zipper bag from the kitchen without drawing undue attention.

And then he took the time to search the entire second floor, every bedroom—including under the beds. Every closet. Every bathroom. Everything.

He didn't find a killer hiding anywhere, nor any evidence there had ever been one around. He did find a bottle of Jim Beam in Jeremy's closet, tucked in the back behind a carefully placed gym bag.

He took the bottle, shaking his head slowly, then walked it to the bathroom, tossed the cap into the wastebasket and poured the whiskey down the sink. Then he jotted a note, rolled it up and tucked it into the bottle. He did not need another complication right now.

He was scared, and he had a lot to handle in very

short order. He had to get hold of Scott Douglas and have a frank conversation with him about how long he'd been seeing Marie, and who he'd told that he would be coming up here to meet her. He had to get a stronger read on the guy, see whether he could possibly be a cold-blooded murderer, and whether he was in the medical field and had ready access to succinylcholine. He had to get the angel brooch to a forensics lab to check it for trace evidence—fingerprints, fibers, a stray piece of DNA—and get a handwriting analysis on the gift card. He had to figure out where one of those pins could be bought and who had bought this one. He had to fill Rosie in on everything. And now he had to deal with a seventeen-year-old sneaking booze.

And he had to do it all while keeping Rachel and his family safe, and not letting on that there might be a killer after them. Marie and the kids had been through too much to handle news like that until and unless it was absolutely necessary.

It was a tall order. He didn't know if he was up to it, or if keeping the family in the dark was still the best option. For tonight, though, it would have to be.

He checked every window on the second floor, made sure there was no attic in the place and then did a thorough search of the ground floor, trying not to be obvious.

He knew he'd failed when Misty, sharp as a tack, asked what on earth he was looking for.

He couldn't help the quick look that passed between him and Rachel, but he looked away fast and thought faster. "My cell phone charger. Damned if I know where I left it."

"Well, I doubt you left it in the coat closet."

Rachel forced a laugh, though it sounded more like she had something caught in her throat. "You never know with this guy, Misty. He's so absent-minded sometimes that I'm afraid I'll find his car keys in the fridge." It was a blatant lie, and they both knew it.

Misty frowned from one of them to the other. The girl was too perceptive to be fooled so easily. "That must make being a big-shot detective a real challenge." She sighed, shrugged, turned away. "I'm gonna see if Marie needs any help with the lasagna she's making for dinner. That woman can cook like no one I know."

"Ask her if there's enough for company," Mason said. "I want to invite Rosie and Marlayna over to-night. And, um...and Scott Douglas."

Misty's eyes widened, and she sent a look at Jeremy.

He caught on and tugged his earbuds out. "What?"

"Mason, I don't think that's such a good idea," Rachel said.

"Don't think what's a good idea?" Jeremy asked. "Why's everyone looking at me?"

Josh pulled out his earbuds, too. "What's going on?"

"Your uncle wants to invite that Scott guy for din-ner," Misty said.

Jeremy's jaw dropped, and his brows drew close. "No fucking way."

Rachel glared at him. "Watch your mouth, kid."

"You should talk!"

Mason glanced toward the kitchen, where pots and pans were banging and a vent fan was running, and lowered his voice. "Look, I'm as uncomfortable with this guy as anyone else. But don't you think the best way for me to figure out where he's coming from and what his motives are would be to hang around him a little bit?"

"I think the best idea would be to tell him to take a hike and never come back," Jeremy said.

"We could tell him that," Mason replied. "But do you really think he'd do it?"

"Then I'll *make him* do it."

Rachel rolled her eyes. "Jeremy, stop. Your mom has lost so much. I know you think you're being loyal to your father, but you have to remember that he chose to leave her. She didn't choose to be alone. He took that choice away from her. From all of you."

"I'm not listening to this." Jeremy got up off the sofa and started for the stairs, but Rachel jumped up and got in his face.

"You need to hear this, Jer. I'm really sorry it's harsh, but you're not being fair to your mother, and your father's beyond caring."

"Listen to her, Jer," Mason said quickly. "She knows this stuff. She wrote a whole book on it.

Whatever was broken in your dad when he was here, it's better now."

Rachel met his eyes and gave the most subtle shake of her head that she could possibly give. *Don't go there.* But it was too late. Jeremy was looking at her now, and his expression dared her to try her best platitudes on him.

"My father was an asshole. He's probably in hell."

Mason's throat swelled shut when Jeremy said that. His eyes burned. His brother was a serial killer. Of course he was in hell.

But Rachel didn't even flinch. She put her full focus on Jeremy. "Why do you think your father would be in hell, Jeremy?"

Jeremy averted his eyes, and for the first time Mason wondered if the boy knew more than any of them realized.

He looked at Rachel again, pleading with her with his eyes. And she conceded with a nod. "I don't believe in hell, you know. You don't have a body when you die. You don't feel pain. There's no torture, just bliss."

Marie came as far as the doorway that separated the kitchen from the living room and stopped, but Rachel didn't see her. She was focused on Jeremy.

"Your father's okay, Jer. He's better than he ever was. Whatever flaws he had when he was alive, they're gone now. Death erases all that. Heals it. He would want you to be happy, and he would want your mom to be happy, too."

"He was a selfish asshole incapable of loving anyone but himself."

"Jeremy!" Marie's face had gone white.

"It's true!" Jeremy yelled. "He was always out doing his own thing, coming home in the middle of the night, never with any kind of explanation. Like you've been doing lately, Mom. Seeing that freaking Douglas guy, right?"

"Jeremy, don't do this, please."

He had tears in his eyes now. "You want to invite him to dinner, Uncle Mason? Fine, invite him. I'll leave. I'll go bunk with Marty and Chelle at the lodge." He pushed past Rachel and up the stairs to his room.

"Who the hell are Marty and Chelle?" Mason asked.

Misty spoke up. "Just some friends we made out on the slopes today."

He shot Rachel a look. She jumped in. "What do you know about them, Misty?"

Misty frowned at her. "Marty is twenty-three, a physical therapist. He and Chelle are engaged. She works in a day-care center. They're from Erie. I didn't get their last names or social security numbers."

Rachel sighed. Mason wondered if a PT guy would have access to a drug used in surgery. Maybe.

"God, what's wrong with you two lately?" Misty demanded.

Mason didn't answer. He was worried about Jeremy and half wished he hadn't dumped out the kid's booze. He could probably use a swig about now.

"What set him off this time?" Marie asked.

"I did," Mason said. "I'm sorry, Marie. I suggested inviting Scott for dinner tonight, along with Rosie and Marlayna."

Her hand fluttered to her chest. "You did?"

"Yeah. But it's too soon. I didn't think it would send him off the deep end like that."

She shook her head rapidly, then crossed the room and wrapped Mason in a hug. "Thank you for that, Mason. Thank you."

He nodded, hugged her back, then let her go and turned to Joshua, who was sitting on the sofa, right where he'd been. His eyes were red and wet. "Are you okay, Josh?"

The boy blinked. "I…I didn't think Dad was a… selfish asshole. He was just Dad." He inhaled a little brokenly. "I miss him."

"I know you do. I know." Mason went to Josh and sat down, putting an arm around him and hugging him close. He sent a look at Rachel, a look that begged for her help. She held his gaze and shook her head clearly this time, a definitive no.

"Rachel, please," he said aloud. "I know you have things to say on this. I read *The Truth About Death*. Tell Josh what you wrote there."

She closed her eyes, and he felt her anger. He understood it, too. She said she didn't believe the things she wrote about so beautifully. She claimed to think it was all bull, although he didn't think she did. Not really. How could anyone write so eloquently and so convincingly about something they didn't really believe? It was beyond him. She was a puzzle.

"Please?" he asked again.

Sighing heavily, Rachel went to the sofa and sat on the boy's other side. "Okay. So, Josh, this is just my theory, okay? I don't think people go away when they die. They come out of their bodies like a butterfly coming out of a cocoon."

"It's not like that, though." Josh's voice was raspy. "A butterfly is still here. You can see it, touch its wings."

"I know, but just hear me out on this, okay? See, we're used to being able to experience each other with our five senses. Seeing, hearing, smelling, tasting, touching, right?"

Josh sniffed hard and lifted his head. "Right. Except for tasting."

She laughed a little. Marie came closer, her expression rapt. "But we have way more senses than just those five. I learned that from being blind for so long."

"Like what?" Josh asked softly.

"Well, like when you dream. You see things in your dreams, right? But your eyes are closed. I saw things in my dreams even when I was blind. Really clear things. Bright colors, light and shadow, people the way I imagined they looked. You can hear things in your dreams, too, but you're not hearing with your ears, are you?"

He frowned. "I never thought of that." He frowned hard. "How does that work, anyway?"

"When we're sleeping, we forget all about what we think is possible and what we think is *im*possible. So those beliefs don't get in the way like they do when we're awake. All our limits are gone in our dreams. We can talk to famous people, we can fly around the world, we can do anything. I think that's the way we have to learn how to experience the people we love after they die. With our other senses, the ones we don't know we have and hardly ever use."

"In our dreams?" Josh asked. "We just tell ourself to dream about them and then we do?"

"Yeah, if we're persistent and patient. But you can do it when you're awake, too. I think we do it all the time and just don't recognize it for what it is. Like, do you ever see something and suddenly it hits you what your dad would have thought of it? Sometimes you can even imagine what he would say or do, or how he would look if he was there?"

Joshua's tears were drying fast. He nodded hard. "I was just thinking that on the water slides today, how if he was here, he would wait for me at the bottom, or maybe he'd go down it with me and how loud he would laugh. I heard it in my head."

"That's *exactly* what I mean. That wasn't pretend. That wasn't make-believe. He was really there, laughing and watching you on the slides. You were experiencing your dad through your other senses, the ones we don't even know we have. We lump all those senses together and call them the imagination, but they're not imaginary. They're real."

His eyes widened slightly, and the most serene look came over his face. He turned to look at his mother, who was standing behind the sofa with her hands on his shoulders. "You think she's right?"

Marie nodded. "I talk to your father all the time. And I try to imagine what he'd say back to me. I really *hope* she's right. I really hope one of these days I hear him answer me."

"Choose to believe it, Josh," Rachel said. "Choose to believe it, and then it's as real as you want it to be."

Josh smiled a little. "Thanks, Rache. You're…" He shook his head, then looked at Mason. "She's so awesome. I hope you guys never break up." Then he bounded off the sofa and ran upstairs, maybe to try to pass what he'd just heard along to Jeremy. When they all turned to follow his progress, Mason saw Jeremy duck quickly out of sight. He'd been near the top of the stairs, listening.

Marie met Rachel's eyes. "Thank you for that. I think it actually helped him."

Rachel only nodded. Her eyes were tearing up.

Marie said, "Mason, don't worry about inviting Scott tonight. The kids need time. But if you want to have Marlayna and Rosie, there will be plenty of lasagna." Then she walked slowly back into the kitchen, leaving Mason and Rachel on the sofa, with the space Joshua had occupied still between them. He looked at her.

And she looked back, but her look was angry. "How could you make me do that?"

"Comfort a grieving child?"

"*Lie* to a grieving child. Mason, you know it's all bullshit as well as I do."

"No, Rachel. I don't. How can you even doubt it, after what we've been through? The way Eric's organs..." He lowered his voice, leaned closer. "The way they somehow transferred his evil to the recipients. The way you can see through their eyes. You *know* there's more to life than what we can see and touch. You *have to* know it. You couldn't write about it the way you do if you didn't believe it on some level."

She shook her head. "You know what I think this is?"

"What?" He immediately realized he probably shouldn't have asked.

"I think you're starting to fall for me, and that I'm not really the kind of woman you want, so you're trying to convince yourself that I'm something else. But I'm not, Mason. I regurgitate the garbage bestsellers have been spouting for years, put my own spin on it and laugh all the way to the bank. Period."

She was absolutely right about one thing, he thought, staring at her. He *was* starting to fall for her. But the rest was all crap. He knew the woman better than she knew herself. He'd seen the true believer in her, even if she insisted on keeping that part of herself buried. And he wondered why.

But he thought he'd pushed her enough for the moment. There was a lot going on, and she was stressed, on edge. He shouldn't push her too hard right now.

"I need to call Rosie."

"Yeah. I'm going to spend some time online. See if I can find out where the angel pin came from." She got up and headed up the stairs. "Have Rosie check to see if they carry them in the gift shop on his way out, will you?"

"Yeah." He wasn't sure, but he thought maybe he'd made a mistake with her just now. Maybe a big one. He hoped he could keep her alive long enough to fix it.

11

Marie's lasagna was lacking something. Attention, I thought, my grim mood getting grimmer. I didn't blame the woman. She had a lot on her mind, with her new boyfriend so close yet out of reach, and her teenage PITA son Jeremy pouting in his room.

Could be worse. She could be aware that her attacker is somewhere at this damned lodge, waiting for his moment. If she did know about it, though, it would probably comfort her to know he'll come for me first. After all, she *didn't get a creepy fucking Secret Santa present, did she?*

Misty insisted on taking a plate of lasagna up to the shithead. I thought he should go hungry until he could quit being a jerk, but what did I know? Yes, that was hard and cold. Yes, he'd recently lost his father. But people die. My parents did, when I wasn't much older than Jeremy was now. Their first vacation without a kid—a cruise they'd always wanted. I'd flown the coop and was in my third year of college, Tommy was off finding himself in California, and Sandra was safely married with six-year-old twins. Mom and Dad thought it was the end of the world when she got pregnant during her freshman year, but it all turned out just fine. She was happy. Jim was perfect. The girls were thriving.

Everything was right with the world, and then they took a cruise, and then they were dead. People just die. It happens. Life sucks sometimes. What Jeremy wasn't getting was that you don't have to turn into an asshole over it.

Although I suppose some would argue that was what I did. I guess.

Misty took Jeremy's meal upstairs and her own with it, and I wished I could get rid of Marie and her younger, more pleasant son so Mason and I could hash out the case with Rosie. Probably Marlayna would have to go, too.

She was a nice woman, and funny as hell now that she was starting to get over being all starstruck around me. She was tall, solid, in an athletic way. Bigger than me in every dimension, but still lean and toned, and I'd bet my last nickel you couldn't guess her age and come anywhere close. I liked her.

"Well, you did the cooking, Marie," Marlayna said when the conversation hit a lull. "You have to let me handle cleanup."

"I'll help," Marie said.

Josh bolted from the table the minute his mother got up to start clearing, heading upstairs and granting me my wish.

Wish and it is granted.

Shut up.

It was just Mason, Rosie and me now. And though I looked like a jerk for not helping the other women out, I vowed I would make up for it later. I leaned over the table the minute we were alone and whispered to Rosie, "Did you check the gift shop?"

"Yeah. They got a pile of 'em in a basket on the checkout counter. I bought one for comparison." He pulled it out of his pocket. It was in a tiny two-inch square zipper bag.

I nodded. "It's the same." Only this one's blue cut-glass eyes were still sparkling in their sockets where they belonged. "No box?"

"Nope, they're loose. I had the clerk check, but she didn't have a record of selling any in the past few days. Still, it'd be easy enough to swipe one."

I shot a look at Mason. A scared look.

"It doesn't necessarily mean he's here," he said.

"No? Then why steal it? Why not just buy it, unless he didn't want anyone to know he'd bought it?"

Mason's lips thinned. "How much are they, Rosie?"

"Three-ninety-nine."

Mason sighed and got up. "Rosie, I need to get the pin, the box, entire thing, to headquarters fast. Any ideas?"

"We could probably get a courier up here first thing in the morning. Seal everything up and have him drive it back."

"Think we could get one out here tonight?"

"You pay him enough, you can get one whenever you want," Rosie said.

"How's five hundred sound?" I asked.

Rosie looked at me. "That's a lot of money, Rachel."

"I value my life, Rosie. Not to mention my eyeballs."

He nodded. "I'll take care of it."

"Talk to Finnegan, Rosie. Maybe one of his security guys would like to earn an extra five Benjamins for a six-hour drive."

Rosie nodded. "You guys gonna be safe out here tonight?"

"I'll make sure of it," Mason said. "Keep an eye on my mother. She could be a target, too."

"Will do. Anything else?"

"Nothing more you can do tonight. It's already late," Mason said.

He was tense. I could see it in him all of a sudden. His neck was more corded than usual, the muscles tight, and his back was rigid. His jaw, too.

"Hey." I put a hand on his shoulder. "We're gonna be all right, Mason. We survived the Wraith, we'll survive this organ thief, too."

He met my eyes and nodded as if he agreed, but it was pretty clear to me, because I read people so easily, that he was lying. He wasn't the least bit convinced that we were going to be all right.

Marlayna and Marie returned from the kitchen, and I quickly stood and started gathering up the remaining dishes.

Mason said, "I'll go get that package I need you to send for me, Rosie," and headed upstairs.

And that was it. That was all we could do at the moment, so there I was four hours later, in the clean kitchen, staring into the open fridge because I hadn't had the appetite to eat my dinner, and feeling like a sitting duck. I had the kind of chills you get up your spine when someone's standing behind you, or hiding just out of sight and watching you. I'd had them ever since I'd looked at that stupid angel pin.

"Hey."

Mason. His voice smoothed the chill away from my spine like a hot-oil massage. I closed the fridge. "Everyone gone to bed?"

"Yeah. I've been waiting to get a minute alone with you."

I turned and leaned back against the refrigerator. "Mason, in case you're not aware of it, you can have as many minutes alone with me as you want. Just say the word."

He smiled but it didn't reach his eyes. "I thought you were mad at me."

"Yeah, but I still want to have sex with you."

He smiled a little bigger, and his cheeks got red.

"I'm sorry about before. I honestly don't want to change you. I like you pretty well just the way you are, in case you didn't know that."

I shrugged. "I know I'm abrasive sometimes. I'm mouthy. I'm cynical. I swear like a Marine. I know."

"I know it, too." He put his hands on the fridge on either side of my head. "I'm still here."

Heat flooded my face, and a smile pulled so hard it hurt, until I had to give in to it. Maybe he didn't have delusions about the real me after all.

"So?" he asked softly, leaning in a little closer. He brushed a kiss across my mouth.

"So...my room or yours?"

Mine, as it turned out. It had been more than two months since I'd had this man in my bed, and once I got his clothes off and my own down to bra and panties, I just relaxed there on the mattress, looking at him. He was lying on his back, I was on my side, trailing my fingers over his abs. "You've been working out all this time, haven't you?" *Washboard* was an understatement.

"I wanted to be suitably impressive if I ever managed to get you in the sack again."

"All this for me?"

"Uh-huh."

My fingertips wandered up to his chest, out to his shoulder, then trailed down to his biceps. "Damn, Mason, you are *ripped*."

"Thank you. You're not so bad yourself." He reached for me, pulled me over on top of him and nuzzled my neck. He had just enough raspy whiskers to make it delicious, and I shivered right to my toes.

He unhooked my bra while I was distracted and feasted on my boobs while I straddled him, and I finally managed to pull away enough to kick free of my panties. I was breathless and eager.

He was, too. I stretched out on top of him, just rubbing my body against his and closing my eyes so I could fully appreciate the sensations. Being sighted was a distraction I didn't need just then. Yeah, he was beautiful to look at. But he *felt* even better. He smelled even better, too. And that unidentifiable thing every human being gave off—the thing I could always read to tell their mood, their nature, their intent, their honesty—was beaming a vibe so strong it was louder than an air raid siren and brighter than a beacon. He was as into me as I was into him.

That description only scratched the surface, but it was as deep as my mind cared to delve just then. Sensual pleasure was my goal tonight, not emotional undercurrents.

I didn't want to go there, down into the depths of what this was. I didn't want to probe and analyze and pick it apart. I just wanted to relish it. Yeah, just like a line from one of my bullshit books. I guessed the bit about living in the moment wasn't such garbage after all. That was three or four of my crapola platitudes I'd decided were actually valid over the course of this holiday getaway slash serial-killer dodge. Go figure.

He wrapped his arms around my waist and held tight as he rolled us both over, and we were making out all the way, like teenagers after prom.

And then there was a loud bang from downstairs, like the front door slamming, and Mason shot out of the bed like he'd been electrocuted.

He had his pants on before I'd even reached for my robe. No shirt, gun drawn. Shit, where had he been hiding that?

"Stay here. Lock your bedroom door."

"Lock it my ass, I'm going with you." I threw on my robe and sashed it tight. I skipped my slippers. Slippers were...well, slippery. If I had to run, or kick someone's face in, I damn well wanted the benefit of bare feet.

We crept down the stairs, him in front, gun leading, me behind, one hand on his back, because touching him made me feel better somehow. The house was dark, but there was still some light coming from the fireplace, which was burning low.

I heard soft sounds, breathing. No. Crying.

Mason got to the bottom, reached around the corner and turned on the light.

Marie jumped to her feet from the sofa, startled, her face wet with tears, her hair wet with melting snow. Some flakes still showed, and I looked out the window to see that it was coming down pretty hard in the gleam of the outside light. She swiped at her cheeks with an angry palm. "Mason, you scared the hell out of me."

He lowered the gun, breathing again. "I heard the door slam. What happened, Marie? Are you all right?"

She sniffed, shook her head. He tucked the gun into the back of his jeans, which must have been really cold on his bare skin. Marie sank back onto the sofa again. She was still wearing her long coat, buttoned all the way from neck to ankles, and her gloves, too. But she'd taken off her boots and was sitting in her sock feet. "I went out," she said.

"Scott Douglas?" Mason asked.

She nodded, sniffed again. "I was supposed to meet him. We were going to have a nightcap together. I bundled up and walked all the way to the lodge, but…he didn't show."

"He stood you up?" Mason sounded like he was actually sympathetic.

I felt a surge of anger. "That bastard. I oughtta kick him in the balls when I see him again." Because the poor woman needed a break for once, and also because, by standing her up, Scott had fucked up my little rendezvous as well as his own.

Marie shook her head at me, and I was reminded that she was still in the heartbreak phase. Nowhere near the anger and vengeance phase, which was really the fun part of any breakup, in my humble opinion. Still, the heartbreak phase didn't call for threats of violence. It called for soothing. So I reined in my anger and asked myself what my sister would do in this situation. And then it came to me. "I'll make tea. And check the freezer for Häagen-Dazs."

I went to the kitchen, trying to listen as best I could but missing part of the conversation while I ran water and put the kettle on a burner. I hurried to grab cups and teabags. While the water heated, I checked for ice cream, but there wasn't any, so I found a few leftover brownies and put them on a plate instead. Then I headed back in, tea and brownies in hand, to get the scoop.

Mason was all the way up to, "Is it true, what Jeremy said? That you were seeing him before you came up here?"

Sniffling hard, Marie nodded. "I thought I was being so discreet." I handed her a cup of tea. She set it down without sipping. "I met him a few weeks ago."

"How?"

She lifted her head and looked right into Mason's eyes. "I'm sorry I lied, Mason. I was afraid you'd suspect him of being the one who attacked me if I told you the truth. I even made him use a fake name. Scott's his brother's name. He's actually Alan Douglas."

I frowned, because *that* name was giving me a little itch. I'd heard it somewhere before.

"Why would you feel the need to do that, Marie?" Mason frowned. "Has this guy got something to hide? Something in his past you didn't want us finding out?"

"Nothing like you're thinking." She lowered her head. "I was afraid you'd think it was weird if you knew. He's—he's got Eric's liver."

I damn near dropped the plate of brownies and settled for landing it noisily on the coffee table. "You're shitting me."

"That's how I met him," Marie went on. "A request came through the Transplant Network. He wanted to meet his donor's family. I...I said yes."

Mason looked at me. I stared back at him. Drawing a deep breath, he said, "And he didn't show up to meet you tonight?"

She shook her head.

"Did you try calling him?" he asked. And I knew what he was thinking. That Marie's new boyfriend was either lying in his hotel room minus a liver, looking to become the next internet urban legend—just add ice—or he was out stalking other organ recipients. Like me, for example. No, we hadn't considered that a recipient might also be the organ thief. Yes, we were both considering it now. I could read Mason like a book.

I came around the table, tea and brownies forgotten, and sat on the couch next to Mason. He was facing Marie, so his back was toward me, but I needed to touch some part of him just then, and his big broad shoulders would do just fine.

"I called his cell," Marie said. "He didn't pick up. I left a voice mail, waited at the bar for over an hour, even tried using the house phone to ring his room, but—"

Mason swore under his breath and looked at me over his shoulder.

"We've got to tell her," I said.

"Tell me what?" Marie stopped crying. She looked both curious and worried now, her eyebrows twisted up like question marks as her eyes darted back and forth between Mason and me in tiny jittery movements.

Mason swallowed hard and put both his hands on Marie's shoulders. I noticed how thin she seemed, underneath the coat she was still wearing. "Okay, Marie, don't panic, but two of Eric's organ recipients have been murdered."

"What?" She shot to her feet so fast his hands fell away. "When? Why didn't you tell me about this?"

"I'm telling you now." He stood up, too. "Rachel's car accident was no accident. Someone was in the backseat. I think it might have been the same person who attacked you later that day."

"What makes you think that?" she asked.

"The description. The clothing. The needle you said he had."

She finally looked at me. "I don't…"

I stayed seated, but I could tell she still wasn't getting the connection. Mason was going too easy, not wanting to give her the gory details, but I had no such compunction. Frankly, I thought we should have told her from the start. "The killer is taking the organs," I told her. "So far one kidney recipient and the woman who got the pancreas are both dead, and the organs are missing."

"Oh, my God." She wobbled, then hit the floor before Mason could react. Her knees bent, her butt touched down and she just sat there, blinking, stunned.

"Then I received that Secret Santa gift," I told her. "An angel, with no eyes."

Marie looked up at me, her eyes wide with fear, but at least now she understood. "Because you have Eric's corneas."

I nodded. She knew because Mason had told her a while back. But the boys didn't know I'd received their father's eyes, and we'd all agreed it was best not to tell them until they were older, if ever.

"The…the killer followed us here?" Marie swung her gaze from Mason to me and back again. "He's here? Oh, my God, what if he got to Alan?"

Shaking her head slowly, as if she was in some kind of a daze, she said, "We have to find him."

* * *

Mason asked Rachel to walk Marie to her room and check on the kids while she was up there. Marie was already halfway up the stairs, hadn't even taken off her coat, she was so upset. Rachel grabbed the untouched tea and went up behind her.

He had calls to make. Rosie picked up on the third ring. "Dude, I am in bed with my woman," he said.

"I know. Something's up."

"Was, anyway, till you interrupted." Rosie laughed soft and deep, and Mason could picture his face. He suspected his partner would have preferred being awakened from a sound sleep.

He'd had the same sort of interruption himself earlier tonight and regretted it to his toes. And yet look what had happened while he'd allowed himself to be distracted. Marie had managed to slip out without him even knowing. It could just as easily have been the organ thief.

The idea sent a chill down his spine. "It turns out Marie lied to us about that Scott Douglas guy. His real name's Alan, and she's been seeing him for a few weeks. He's the guy who got Eric's liver, and he seems to be missing."

"Hell. Shit just got real up in here, didn't it?"

"Looks like. I need you to check on him. Get a key to his room, get in there. But be careful, 'cause if he's not dead, he's a suspect."

"According to what logic, pal?"

234 *Maggie Shayne*

Mason said, "He's the right build for Marie's attacker, according to her description. And he has a connection to the other victims, as well as to Marie."

"It's thin," Rosie said.

"It's all we got. Check on him."

"Will do."

"Did you get that package out?" Mason asked.

"Not yet. Turns out they have a FedEx pickup here every morning at nine. I'll get it out tomorrow."

"Perfect."

"Anything else, Mason?"

"Yeah. Check on my mother, if you can do it without waking her up and scaring the hell out of her."

"Now just how the hell am I supposed to do that?"

"I don't know. Use your imagination. I'd come do it myself, but I don't dare leave everyone here alone."

"Mason?" Rachel called.

"Gotta go," he said quickly into the phone. "Get back to me, okay?"

He hung up and headed into the living room. Rachel was trotting down the stairs with a paper bag in her hand, and it was clear by the way she held it what was inside. A bottle.

She held it up. "I found this on the floor in Jeremy's room. He's passed out cold, and he reeks."

Mason took the bag from her and pulled a small vodka bottle from it. The thing was more than half empty, and his stomach clenched into a hard knot. "Where the hell did he get this?" He looked inside the bag. A small white receipt lay damp in the bottom, and he fished it out.

"Winter Thaw?" he read.

"Wasn't that the name of the liquor store in Blue Lake?" Rachel asked. "It was right next to that souvenir shop the kids were in for so long. I remember thinking it was a cute name."

"So he sneaked over there without us noticing?"

Rachel came closer, standing beside him in a way that had her entire side pressed to his, and looked down at the damp receipt. "Look at the time stamp, Mason. The ink's running, but it looks like—"

"Eleven forty-seven p.m. December 20. That was only two hours ago." Mason shot a killing look up the stairs. When he got his hands on his nephew...

"We're doing a hell of a job watching everyone around here, aren't we?" Rachel shoved both hands through her hair, flustered. No. Scared.

He looked at her. She looked right back, not hiding her fear, even though she had to know what he was going to say. "It's because we let ourselves get distracted."

She didn't even argue. "Yeah. It could just as easily have been..."

"I know. I was thinking the same thing."

"We can't afford to let that happen again. Can we?"

She sounded almost hopeful, as if he would say, *Don't be silly. It'll be fine.* But the truth was, he agreed with her. Before he had a chance to answer, his cell phone chirped. He glanced at the screen, then answered. "Yeah, Rosie?"

"Your mother's fine. I made Marlayna wake her to borrow some pain reliever. She's probably mad as hell at her, but—"

"And what about Douglas?"

Rosie sighed. "He's not in his room. His coat, gloves, hat and scarf are all missing. And so's his cell phone."

"Hell," Mason whispered.

12

Thursday, December 21

The six of us were all crammed into Mason's Jeep for the trip from our cabin to the lodge. Josh had to sit in the cargo bay in the back, but it was only a few hundred yards. It was a quarter past dawn—only a slight exaggeration—and snowing like I had never seen it snow in my life, and *that* was not an exaggeration at all. Okay, I know that's not saying much, since I'd been blind for the past twenty years, but still...

Finnegan Smart had asked us to meet him in the cutely named but deadly serious Security Shack, where he was organizing his team to go out and search the slopes for Marie's missing boyfriend. Mason had called him last night, and Smart had searched the lodge and nearby grounds, but this snow made it useless to do more until sunup. We had to see to it that the rest of the gang were safe and sound before we could join him and his men in this morning's wider search.

It was storming too badly for anyone to want to ski, but lodge owner Cait met us in the lobby and promised she had tons of holiday fun planned for the day. Songs around the lobby's twenty-foot tree, a wreath-making class, gourmet hot cocoa brewing taught by the head chef and something called a Santa Swim in the water park.

Yeah. Frankly, I'd *rather* be out searching for a missing guest.

Rosie was on the job to keep track of the family, so I wasn't overly concerned about leaving them to join in the search. In fact the lodge, with its holiday cheer and happy guests, was feeling more and more like the safest place to be.

I was nervous this morning. I hadn't dreamed of a brutal murder, thank goodness, so I hoped that meant Douglas might still be alive. It would have helped if Mason hadn't been scared, too, but he was. Still strong, confident and determined, but worried. I knew it when he handed me a gun before we left for the lodge. He knew I could use it and feared I might need it. No words were necessary. That shook me more than anything else, I think.

Once Marie and the kids were settled in at the lodge, Cait donned a white parka with a fur-lined hood and walked us out the front door to the small log cabin a few hundred feet away. It had a rustic wooden Security Shack sign hanging over its red front door. She didn't knock, just pushed it open, stomped the snow off her boots and went inside. We followed.

Finnegan had been talking to five members of his security team, but he met her eyes and stopped speaking. Tufts of fading red hair were sticking out from under his blue knit hat. His flannel shirt, worn over a thermal undershirt, was tucked into ski pants, and his crew of four men and a woman were standing around wearing various levels of outerwear. Clearly they were getting ready to begin the search.

"We can't have guests going missing like this," Cait said, accepting a mug of coffee from Finnegan. "If Mr. Douglas never came in from the slopes, we should've caught that last night." She unzipped her parka but didn't take it off. "What's the plan, Finn?"

"A straight-up search of every slope and patch of woodland in between," he said. "We'll find him, Cait. There's no need to worry."

"This storm is giving me plenty of need to worry," she said, turning to gaze toward the window. Then she snapped her sharp eyes our way, fixing them on Mason. "Finn tells me you had reason to believe some kind of suspect might be hiding out at the lodge?"

He shot the other man a look, then shook his head. "It was a hunch. It didn't pan out."

"Is that why you've been keeping such tight tabs on your kids?" she asked.

Mason hadn't been ready for that, and I saw him

struggling for a reply so I jumped in to save him. "Hey, if you knew those kids, you'd watch them like a hawk, too. Trust me, you don't want Joshua climbing your Christmas tree."

She held my eyes for what seemed like a long time, then looked away. I think she had an inkling we were not being completely up-front with her, and I wasn't entirely sure it was the right call. But for now, there was no time to get into things. She went behind the desk and sat down in what I presumed was Finn's chair. There was a radio system on a counter, kitty-corner to the desk, and she slid the chair over to it and began turning dials. "I'll get Weather Service updates and keep you posted. You keep me up to speed on your progress. Go."

So we went. Finnegan handed us each a walkie-talkie as we headed out the door.

We took snowmobiles. There were rows of them lined up outside the security shack, many with keys in the ignition. I didn't know if the guests were allowed to use them or just tended to be well behaved enough to be trusted, but it would have been awfully easy to take off with one.

Then again, where would you go? We were in the middle of nowhere. Mason had obviously driven one before. I had not. My first winter with eyes, after all. So I got a quick lesson, and then followed him, away from the lodge and onto an uphill trail.

Man, it was coming down. I was wearing my ski mask under my helmet, and my brand-new thermal cold-weather coat and ski pants, and I was still freezing. After an hour my hands were frozen and my left thumb was aching from holding the accelerator down for so long.

We rode up and down the all-but-abandoned slopes. Oh, there were a few diehards out there trying to get a run or two in between blinding gusts of wind-driven snow, but they were having very little luck. I saw one guy topple, and I was sure the wind was to blame. I wondered why Cait hadn't closed the slopes yet, then figured she knew best. They probably got storms worse than this on a regular basis this far north.

There wasn't going to be any sort of trail to follow, that was for sure. Not with four fresh inches of snow overnight and more coming down every minute.

After two hours of searching, Finnegan radioed everyone to convene near the top of one of the highest peaks, where a small log cabin sat off to one side of the ski slope. I hadn't been up this high before. One by one, the powerful machines pulled up side by side and their motors went quiet. Everyone pulled off their helmets and headed inside.

Mason came over to me just after I climbed off my snowmobile, and was peeling off my ski mask and shaking out my hair. "How are you holding up?"

"Good." I held up my mittened hand. "My thumb is tired of that throttle, though. It's a stretch for someone with small hands. Other than that and freezing my ass off, I'm good."

"Good." He took my arm, like that was something he would normally do. It wasn't, but I liked it.

You are being such *a girl, Rachel.*

So what, Inner Bitch? I can be a girl once in a great while.

Since when?

Since I said so.

I bent my knees to loosen them up, then twisted at the waist, stretching the kinks out, while Mason smiled like he was watching a kitten bat a ball of yarn around. I stuck my tongue out at him for that and caught a half-dozen snowflakes by accident. That's how hard it was coming down.

We headed toward the cabin with the others. "I'm getting texts from Rosie every fifteen minutes," he said as we walked. "Everyone's fine. Apparently the water park is getting a workout today."

"The Santa Swim," I said. "If we find Scott or Alan Douglas, aka the man of way too many first names, all safe and sound somewhere, remind me to thank him for sparing us the Santa Swim."

"I hope that's exactly what we get to do."

We stopped at the cabin door, and I turned to look back behind us, through the falling snow. "There must be a beautiful view, up this high, when you can see it."

"Yeah. This is a lousy time for a snowstorm."

He opened the door for me, and we went inside. The cabin was stark, just a shelter, really. Several thermos bottles lined a flat counter along one wall.

There were scattered chairs and some tables, a couple of freestanding cabinets, a stack of emergency first-aid kits, a fireplace with wood and kindling stacked high, and matches on the mantel. It was, I realized, a place to go in case of trouble. And it had a huge map tacked to one log wall with a red X beside the words *You are here.*

The others were gathered near that map now, everyone holding a cup full of something steamy. I grabbed a pair of cups from the stack on the counter and poured from a random thermos, having no idea who had brought what. Coffee, black, emerged. It would do. As I handed a cup to Mason, Finnegan moved closer to the map and cleared his throat.

"Since there's no sign of Mr. Douglas on the trails, we have to assume he wandered off them. So now *we've* got to go off-trail, as well." He drew a line with his finger along the edge of the ski slope we'd just ascended. "Mason, I'll have you and Rachel tackle the woods along either side of this trail, since we're already here, and I don't want to risk you guys getting lost, too. This storm isn't letting up as quickly as I'd hoped. The rest of us will split into teams and search the other woodlots. Pick your way through, up one side, down the other, going a little deeper into the woods with each pass. Go slow'n'easy. The woods aren't intended for snowmobile use, and this snow could be hiding all kinds of hazards. We're going to make several passes through the woods on each side. The final pass ends at the Security Shack. Stay in contact by walkie-talkie." He looked at Mason. "Can you handle that?"

"Yeah, we can."

"Good. Everybody finish your drinks, partner up and pick a woodlot." He moved away from the map, and the other five on his team crowded around it, talking low, fingers touching the woodlots that separated the many slopes.

Mason met Finnegan by the counter. I stayed put, edging only close enough to hear the conversation.

"Do you think it's time to call in outside help?" Mason asked the older man.

Finnegan was refilling his cup and sipping without even giving the steaming coffee time to cool down. "We'll finish up this search. If we don't find him by then, we'll call the state police."

Tell him, I thought. *Tell him about the murders.*

"That sounds about right," Mason said.

What the fuck did he mean, it sounded right? There was a killer up here, for crying out loud.

Mason sipped his coffee, then lowered the cup again. "Are you at all concerned about this storm?"

"Truth to tell, I was. But Cait's been keeping us up to speed on it. The Weather Service says it's just skirting us as it moves north. Should be sunny and clear again by mid-afternoon."

Nodding slowly, Mason took his sweet time. I tried not to be obvious about my eavesdropping, moving nearer a window but still within earshot, pretending to gaze out at the curtain of snowfall that made it impossible to see more than ten feet in any direction.

"Finnegan, would you handle this any differently if you had reason to believe Douglas might have been the victim of foul play?"

The man's pale red eyebrows rose over light blue eyes. "That's an interesting question, Mason Brown. *Do* I have reason to believe that?"

Mason just looked at him, not saying yes or no.

Finnegan sighed. "This suspect you said you thought might be up here—it's a more serious thing than you led me to believe, isn't it, Mason?"

Again Mason stayed silent. As a cop, Finnegan would understand *need to know.*

"Well, if there's foul play afoot, we'll be having a mob of panic-stricken guests and a lot of ruined holidays. People'll be looking to leave in droves, and right now, I'd say that might not be possible, at least for the rest of the day. It'll take the town boys that long to clear the roads once the snow lets up. And panicked people who are also stuck where they are can be a very bad thing."

"I agree."

Finnegan nodded. "So let's give this search our best shot, hmm? God willing we'll find Mr. Douglas safe and sound and shivering under a pine tree. If not, then we'll call in the troops and you can tell us what you have to tell us."

Mason nodded. "Okay, that's what we'll do."

Finnegan looked troubled as Mason made his way

back to me. He took a long pull from his cup, then walked over to the map again, into the huddle of his team. "Slight change of plans. At the bottom of your first pass, stop at the Shack and arm yourselves."

"Wait, what?" one guy asked. "Weapons?"

"Handguns oughtta be plenty. Load 'em up. Might be there's more going on here than meets the eye. Be wary. Stay together. And if you see anyone on the slopes, tell 'em we've closed 'em down due to foul weather and send 'em back to the lodge."

As everyone muttered among themselves, he pulled out a walkie-talkie, contacted someone at the lodge and said, "Shut down the lifts. I'm clos-ing the slopes 'til further notice due to the weather. Tell Cait it won't be for long." He hooked the walkie to his belt, nodded at me. "She have a sidearm?" he asked Mason.

"Yeah."

"You know to use it, missy?"

I smiled a little. "Point it at the bad guy and squeeze?"

"Sassy one, ain't she?"

"You don't know the half," Mason said. He drained his coffee, tossed the cup into a nearby trash can, which was a wooden whiskey barrel with the top cut out and a bag lining the inside, and pulled his gloves out of his pocket. "Let's go."

We drove the snowmobiles down through the woods on one side of the slope. It was rough going, because the visibility stank on ice, and the trees alongside the ski trails were thick. We had to pick our way, and I was no expert with a snowmobile. When we got to the bottom, we crossed to the other side and headed up again. Everything took a lot longer than it seemed like it should, but by the time we were on our final pass down, I was confident that if Alan was anywhere nearby we would have found him, despite the snow. It wasn't as deep in the woods. Those pines made for a thick canopy.

I was also convinced that the Irish cop and the Weather Service were dead wrong about this storm. If anything, it was getting worse.

By the time we'd finished our area and met at the Security Shack once more, we'd completely missed lunchtime and it was pushing on toward dinner. It felt even later. The storm was so intense that it was dark far earlier than it should have been.

I shut off the machine and brushed the snow off my clothes. I swore I could still feel the motor's vibration right to my bones.

The other sleds were already lined up in front of the shack. There was a big, fluffy, snowy wreath on the Shack's red door that hadn't been there before. It gave me a chill at first, making me think of the wreath that had magically appeared on our cabin door with that nastygram angel attached. But Mason knew the minute I went stiff, and apparently knew why. He put a hand on my shoulder and then pointed at the lodge a few yards away, where brightly gleaming outdoor lights cut through the snow to reveal that every door bore a matching wreath. It was fine.

I sent him a silent thanks with my eyes, and he nodded a you're welcome.

We went inside.

Finnegan had arrived before us and was alone at his desk, looking worried. I didn't see anyone else.

"Where's the team?" Mason asked.

"I sent 'em to get some dinner. There's no way they can get home in this, so they're gonna have to bunk here tonight. We have a barracks for that, though." He sighed in exhaustion. "I take it you didn't find anything."

"No." Mason sighed, too, setting his walkie-talkie on the desk. I set mine next to it. "I think it's time we call the police," he said.

"I already have, my friend. Unfortunately, I waited a wee bit too long." As Mason frowned, Finnegan nodded at the computer monitor on his desk.

We both moved around so we could see the weather site's radar screen tracking the monster-sized storm. He poked a finger at its westernmost edge and said, "This is us. The wind changed, folks. There's a major blizzard heading right for us. What we've had today was just the leading edge."

"Holy shit," I muttered.

"State police will be out first thing in the morning. They're advising us to call off the search until then, for fear we'll lose someone else. Not that we could do much in the dark anyway. We're in for seventy-mile-an-hour gusts, starting within the next couple of hours. It's gonna be a helluva night."

I closed my eyes. "If he's out there, he'll be dead by morning."

Mason looked at me, and I read his thoughts clearly. *If he's the killer, then let him freeze. And if he's not, then he's probably already dead.*

The Security Shack door opened and Cait walked in.

"You want to tell me why you shut down the lifts in the middle of the afternoon?"

"The storm—"

"Is bad. Terrible. Far worse than predicted. But it wasn't when you made the call. We've left them open through far worse than what was happening at that point."

Finn looked at Mason. So did Cait.

"Spit it out, then," she said. "What's going on with this missing guest? And why is there a detective involved?"

Finnegan gestured to Mason as if to give him the floor. Mason took a deep breath, looked at me. I nodded. It had to come out. It was serving nobody to keep this thing secret, not now.

So he told them a version of the truth, just the bare basics. That the man he'd been tracking was a killer. That he'd taken precautions not to tell anyone where he was going for his vacation, because that was his habit due to the nature of his job, and that now he was afraid the killer might have found out and followed him here. Nothing else. By the time he finished, Cait had sunk down into a chair as if her bones had melted.

"It seems odd to me," Cait said, "that the killer might be chasing the cop instead of the other way around." She shifted her intelligent green eyes from Mason to Finn and back again. "Are you sure there's not more to this?"

"Nothing I'm at liberty to divulge. I'm sorry, Ms. Cole."

She gave him a steely-eyed stare. "This lodge is my life, Detective Brown. If it wasn't for the weather, I'd throw you out. "

"I wouldn't blame you," I said. "I'd do the same."

That seemed to take the edge off her fury just a bit. She said, "You'll want to leave your Jeep in the parking lot for the night. You'll never make it back to the cabin in this storm. Take a pair of snowmobiles back with you in case you need them." Then she left the shack to tend to her guests, while I hoped like hell we didn't end up ruining her business.

Finnegan fired up a large vehicle that ran on tracks like a tank, which he called the Abominable, to transport the rest of the family back to our cabin, and Mason and I took snowmobiles, as Cait had instructed. Rosie and Finn himself both rode along in the Abominable with Marie, Jeremy, Josh and Misty, to keep them safe.

Mason and I rode on either side of the road, just

like we had before, headlights on, searching through the falling snow for signs of Alan Douglas. But just like before, we didn't find anything. Truthfully, in the full darkness and snowfall, I didn't think we would have seen him unless we ran over him. Rosie said good-night at the front door, started to turn to go, then turned back again, pulling a familiar zipper bag from his coat pocket and handing it to Mason. "You may as well hold on to this, pal. FedEx never made it this morning, due to the storm."

The eyeless angel, in her little white box, lay inside that bag. Just seeing it there gave me a chill.

Mason pocketed it with a worried look my way. Then Rosie got back aboard the Abominable and it started back to the lodge.

Sighing, I walked up the front steps to open the door, switched on the lights and was promptly bashed in the shins by the hard head of a little blind bulldog. I yelped. She backed up and hit me again.

"All right, all right. I know, you've been neglected all day. Let me get your leash—"

But there was no keeping her. She weaved and dodged and bounced between incoming feet and down the steps while I swore, yanked the leash from the hook on the wall and went charging back outside after her.

"Rachel!" Mason shouted.

"She's gotta go bad to be this speedy in a strange place! I don't have a choice here!" I slammed the door behind me.

"I know you must be about bursting, Myrt. But dammit, wait up!"

She was bounding around the cabin at a dead run, her short legs throwing snow behind her and her broad chest acting like a plow. You would have thought she could see where she was going, for God's sake. I darted after her, leash in hand, wishing I had a flashlight. "I said I was sorry. It was an emergency." I'd made it to the back of the house, but Myrt wasn't there. Her trail led into the woods behind the cabin. The very *dark* woods behind the cabin.

I didn't miss a beat going after her, even though my brain was finally blasting warnings into my ears. *It's dark, you're alone, there's a killer on the loose who wants to gouge out your eyes and you're a dumb shit if you take another step, Rachel de Luca.*

I stopped walking for one brief second. Because there was less snow in the woods her trail was no longer obvious. It was also darker than a dungeon, and I could barely see my hand in front of my face.

And then my heart, normally the strong, silent type, urged me on. *She's your dog, she trusts you implicitly and she's fucking* blind, *you coldhearted bitch. Move your ass and find her before something awful happens. Besides, you have a gun stuffed in your coat pocket if you need it. And Mason will come chasing us down the minute he makes sure everyone in the house is safe and sound.*

I started moving my ass, whisper-shouting, "Myrtle! Where the fuck are you, you little shithead?" I knew it was stupid, because if you're going to whisper, it shouldn't be at the loudest volume you can manage. I doubted any serial killer would have a lick of trouble hearing me in the deep, silent pines. "Myrtle!"

"Snarf!" said Myrtle.

She sounded far away, but the pines probably muffled sound, right? "Myrt!" I didn't bother whispering this time. "Myrtle, come on, girl!" As I moved in the direction I thought her bark had come from, I had a brainstorm, yanked my cell phone from the depths of my pants pocket and opened the flashlight app, sighing in relief at the pathetic steam of light it emitted and aiming it ahead of me. It wasn't the app's fault it didn't do a whole hell of a lot of good. It was made for finding your keys on the floor of your car, not maneuvering through a pine forest in a blizzard on the darkest night since the moment before the Big Bang.

"Myrtle?"

I heard a series of barks that were so deep and menacing that I thought she'd started up a range war with some other dog. But as I followed my cell phone beam closer, I knew that was her bark. I'd just never heard it that way before.

Something was wrong. I stuffed the leash into my pocket and pulled out the gun.

I heard Mason calling my name, and he sounded so far away that I got a cold chill up my spine. I couldn't have walked that far. I told myself it was the snow and the pines making him sound so distant.

But then I pushed through some interlocking pine tree boughs and saw my dog crouched as low as she could crouch and barking up a storm at a lump in the snow.

"Oh, shit."

I aimed the light at the lump that wasn't a lump at all. It was a body. It was Alan Douglas's body, lying beneath the sheltering arms of the pines. The snow around it was stained dark with his blood, and I knew without checking that it was probably missing a liver.

I tucked the cell phone back into my pocket, but kept the gun in one hand as I ran to Myrtle and wrapped both arms around her, picking her up as she wriggled and fought me. She was agitated. She couldn't see, but she could smell. Death. Blood. Human liver. I'm sure she smelled every bit of it, and probably the stench of the killer, as well.

Is he still out here?

I backed away from the body and the blood, and, turning, started moving as fast as humanly possible back through the pines toward the cabin. I didn't know how I would make use of the damn gun while carrying the dog. I wasn't even 100 percent sure I was actually going toward the cabin.

"Rachel?"

"Mason! Out here! Hurry!" My breath was making steam clouds in front of my face, and I could only see them because they were a lighter shade than the darkness. Then I heard him, his footsteps strong and fast, his body brushing against the needled limbs, releasing their scent even more strongly. Finally I saw a light bobbing closer. "Over here," I said.

And then he was right there.

"You okay? What happened? What were you thinking, coming out here alone?"

"Myrt ran off," I said. "I followed her before I thought better of it. And then what was I gonna do, abandon her?"

He sighed, and rubbed the little dog's face. "She okay?"

"She's in much better shape than Marie's new boyfriend is."

He looked at me. His flashlight was pointed away, but it threw enough light that I could see his face, and the expression it wore was saying, *Don't tell me what you're about to tell me.*

"You found him, didn't you?"

"No," I said. "Myrtle did."

I remembered—somewhat belatedly, I know—that I had a leash in my coat pocket. So I put Myrtle down and snapped it on. Then she and I led Mason back to the spot where Myrt had found the body. I stood back while he went closer, flashlight in hand. I tried not to follow the beam of light as he aimed it at the dead man. But I followed it anyway. I saw the way the new snow had fallen over the pool of blood, so the deep black-cherry color glistened and sparkled. I saw the layer of snow coating the pale face and gaping mouth and wide-open eyes, sort of shrunken now. I saw that his clothes were mostly snow-covered, but where they weren't, they were so bloody you couldn't tell what color they were. They'd been cut open up the front, coat, shirt and all. There was a big dark gash under his rib cage, where his liver had probably been once. Other parts were spilling through the chasm someone had left in the poor man.

"He's been here a while," Mason said. "Probably killed last night. Lay here all day while we were out searching everywhere else." He aimed the beam at the area around the body, making ever-widening sweeps. He found a glove a few feet away. And something else, something that caught the light and gleamed. It was partially covered in snow, but I thought it was a pocket knife. And near it, a syringe in the snow.

"Son of a bitch, he was alive, just like the others," I said softly. "This sick bastard."

Mason nodded, crouching near the syringe. "Why didn't you have a vision this time?" he asked me.

"I've been wondering about that since he went missing. I think it's because I didn't sleep. This time I'm only getting them as dreams. And I never slept last night. You and I were... And then Marie came in and—"

He rose to his feet and came toward me, and I frowned, because the pocket knife that had been in the snow was no longer there.

"What arc you doing, Mason?"

He got to where I was, took my arm and headed back the way we'd come, Myrt hustling along beside us, eager to be done with this disturbing walk. "Taking you back to the cabin. It's not safe out here."

"That's not what I mean and you know it."

"No?" He kept walking.

"Mason." I jerked free of his grip and planted my feet. "What did you just pick up out of the snow?"

"I don't know what you're talking about," he said, but he wouldn't meet my eyes.

"The hell you don't. I saw it. What is it, Mason?" I reached for his coat pocket, and he jerked away hard, then stood staring at me.

"You're gonna *lie* to me now? You're gonna start keeping secrets *now,* Mason? When it's *my* fucking eyes he's after? What do you have in your pocket? Tell me right now, or I swear to God I'm going back to that cabin, packing my shit and heading home, storm or no storm."

He closed his eyes, then opened them again. "Okay. Okay." He reached into his pocket and pulled out a jackknife with a handle that was apparently made of real antler, what kind I couldn't have said. There wcrc initials engraved into the bone. I frowned, reached for my phone, and aimed the flash-light app at it. J.B.

J.B.

And then it hit me and my eyes must have gone as big as the humongous snowflakes falling between us.

"Fuck, Mason, is this *Jeremy's?* Tell me this isn't Jeremy's knife."

He lowered his head. "Eric bought it for him last Christmas. I helped him pick it out."

"But...but..." I shook my head. "No, this doesn't make any sense. It can't be Jeremy."

He swallowed hard, pocketed the knife and re-sumed walking.

"Mason, what are you going to do?" I said, hur-rying to keep up. "Are you going to cover this up?"

"I don't know yet. I need time. I need to pro-cess—"

"Process, my ass. You're a fucking cop. Are you going to make a habit out of hiding evidence to pro-tect your family and the hell with the rest of the world?"

He spun around so fast I actually ducked, like I thought he'd deck me. Or maybe I thought *I'd* have decked me, if I'd been him. I don't know. But I do know that when I ducked, he looked like he wanted to throw up. He shook his head, reached for me, cupped my face in his palm. "I won't cover it up. I just need to figure out what it means. Just give me a little time, Rachel. We'll watch him every minute, we'll make sure he's not out of our sight until we get to the bottom of this. Just give me some time."

I went soft inside. "Hell, it's not like I wanted you to turn him in. I just… There has to be another answer, an explanation." I said it as if I believed it. But inside, I was feeling pretty sick at the idea of how much time Jeremy had been spending with my niece. Often alone. And how it would feel to find her bloody body dead in the fucking snow. And how I would manage to look my sister in the eye and tell her that I'd taken her daughter up into the mountains with a serial killer and let him murder her.

But then again, it wasn't Misty who had Jeremy's father's eyes in her head. It was me. And I was having a helluva time working up a healthy fear of a seventeen-year-old, no matter how morose and troubled.

We were almost back. I could see the cabin's lights gleaming in the distance. "I think you're right," I said. "I think we need some time to process this."

"I'll contact Finnegan as soon as we're inside. Have him get the police up here. I imagine they'll move faster knowing it's a homicide, not a missing person. And I need to let Rosie know what's going on."

I nodded. "I'm so tired, Mason. But I'm scared shitless to let myself sleep."

"We'll sleep in shifts. I'll watch him while you catch a nap, then you can return the favor."

"Are you gonna talk to Jeremy?"

He looked up briefly, and I could tell he didn't know the answer to that. We got back to the cabin, Myrt huffing and puffing as if she was about to pass out at any moment. As we went in the front door, everyone looked at us expectantly, and it was only as Misty's eyes widened that I realized I was still holding the gun.

I handed it to Mason like it was burning me, stomped the snow off my boots and crouched down to remove Myrtle's leash.

"There's no easy way to say this," Mason said softly. "We found Alan Douglas. He's...dead."

Marie clapped a hand to her mouth, but the yelp came out anyway, like a dog getting hit by a car. Brief, pain-wracked. Tears filled her eyes. Misty went to stand beside her, put a hand on her shoulder. Josh gasped, his innocent eyes widening. Jeremy went wide-eyed with shock, then turned to his mother. "I'm sorry, Mom."

"The hell you are," she whispered. "I hope you're happy now, Jeremy." Then she turned and fled up the stairs. I heard her bedroom door slam.

Jeremy looked at the floor. He was dead silent. No tears in his eyes, but I felt the sting of the slap his mother had just delivered.

"What happened to him?" Joshua asked. "Did he fall skiing or something?"

"That can't be it," Misty said. She moved closer

to Jeremy, sliding her hand into his. I saw his close around it, and I wondered just how close the two of them had become. "He's near here, isn't he? You found him just now, didn't you?" I nodded at her. "He must have had a heart attack or something on his way to visit your mom," she told Jeremy. "You saw the way he was eating the other day. He had steak *and* chicken."

So had I, but I wasn't going to point that out.

"What happened to him, Uncle Mason?" Jeremy asked again.

Mason stared at his nephew, and I saw his eyes brimming. "I don't know, Jer. But I promise you, I'm going to find out."

If the words had the suggestion of a threat, it seemed to be lost on the kid.

I closed my eyes and tried to *feel* Jeremy, the way I so often could with people.

I was still crouching, petting my dog calm again, scratching the spot right in front of her ears and keeping my face downturned, eyes closed. "Your mom didn't mean what she said, Jer," I told him, because I needed him to talk. I needed to hear every warble in his voice, every pause, every syllable. "She's just upset."

"She meant it." I could feel him shrug. "I don't care. She's right, anyway. I'm glad he's out of the way. No matter how much of an asshole my father was, it was wrong for her to be seeing somebody this soon." He shook his head. "She shouldn't have done that."

I got a chill right down my spine, because my extra senses told me the kid meant every word of it.

13

Thursday, December 21

Mason had made the calls. Rosie, Cait and Finnegan had shown up an hour later in the Abominable, which was pulling its twin behind it. I had been wondering why it took them so long to arrive, but when Mason opened the front door to go outside and join them, I knew why. The storm had worsened.

He was gone a long time. Long enough for the kids and me to have baked, cooled and decorated four dozen Christmas cookies. Joshua kept looking outside with his wide, frightened eyes. You couldn't see anything from the kitchen windows, but I imagined the thought of a dead body nearby was scaring the hell out of him. The only thing that distracted him was Myrtle. She was mainly lying as close to our work area as possible in hopes of falling crumbs. But every time Josh walked away from the counter to look out that window, she would haul herself to her feet, plod over and bang him in the leg with her head. If he ignored the first assault, she would start hitting him with a forepaw and whining softly. It was pretty clear to me by then that my dog thought of Joshua as *her* boy.

We'd just finished frosting the last batch of cookies when flashlights came by the cabin's windows. I caught enough shapes through the veils of snow and night to deduce that they were carrying the body back to the Abominables. And then they moved toward the front of the house and out of sight from the kitchen windows again. Mason would be in soon.

I met Misty's eyes and was impressed and glad when she read mine and nodded very slightly. Taking Josh by the arm, she said, "I don't want any part of cleaning up the mess. How 'bout you, Josh?"

She was growing up pretty damn nicely.

He slid his eyes my way and shrugged.

"Oh, really?" I asked, hands going to my hips. "I suppose you think *I* should clean up this mess?"

"Yup," Misty said. "Because A, we did most of the frosting. B, this entire mess was your idea to begin with. And C, we have a Mario Galaxy tournament that we need to finish before bedtime. It's up to me to carry the banner for the female gender, and frankly, I'm not doing so hot."

I tilted my head to one side, pretending to consider, then nodded. "All right, I give. The reputation of womankind is more important than a messy kitchen. I'll do cleanup. You go play video games.

But take a bunch of these cookies with you or I'm going to get fat just from being around them."

"You already licked so much frosting your tongue is stained green," Misty said, laughing. Josh giggled, too. Yes, she was good, my niece.

Jeremy was silent, staring through the living room toward the front door, waiting for Mason to come in. His mother still hadn't come down from her room, and I didn't blame her. She must be feeling like a tragedy magnet about now.

Misty piled cookies on a plate, handed it to Josh, then pulled three glasses out of the cupboard and started filling them with milk.

Jeremy glanced at her, then shook his head. "None for me. I'll be up in a while. I want to talk to my uncle first."

Misty darted a look at me, as if to ask if that was okay and I shrugged, having no idea. "Okay, Jer," she said at length. "But don't be too long, okay?"

He nodded, but if his expression was anything to go by, he didn't intend to head upstairs any time soon.

Misty picked up the two glasses she'd filled. "C'mon, Josh. You can show me some of your skills while we wait for your big bro."

Josh followed her, and Myrtle followed him. I thought he was happy for the distraction. Myrt was just happy that the scent of Josh and the smell of cookies were moving in the same direction. There were bound to be crumbs. And I was mondo impressed with my niece for taking charge like she had, getting the kid out of range of the discussion when she must be as curious as anyone else about what had happened to poor Scott-slash-Alan Douglas.

The entire kitchen was covered in glittering red-and-green sugar and my fingers were stained with food coloring. I started on the mess and said, "Jeremy, if you're gonna stick around, you might as well help."

He looked my way, then nodded and started putting the rows and rows of artfully—well, if we'd been a group of six-year-olds—decorated cookies into the giant teddy-bear-shaped cookie jar. I ran a sink full of sudsy hot water and started washing the cookie sheets and empty frosting bowls, coloring my dishwater, while he cleaned the glittering, frosting-splotched countertop where we'd done our work.

Mason came in just as we were finishing up, looked from me to Jeremy and back again.

I decided to give him the straight scoop, digest style. "Misty took Joshua upstairs to play video games. Myrt's with them. Marie's still in her room. And Jeremy wants to know what's going on."

Mason looked at Jeremy, who nodded and said, "I know something is. This is all connected, isn't it? That attack on Mom, you bringing us all up here on the spur of the moment. You have to tell me, Uncle Mason. What's happening?"

Mason sighed heavy and deep. He looked exhausted, almost defeated, as he sank onto a stool near the countertop.

I poured him a cup of strong coffee, fixing it just the way he liked it best, light, no sugar. He said, "The state police can't get out here tonight. The storm." He shook his head. "The timing couldn't be worse. But there's nothing we can do about the weather but wait it out. They told us to take pictures and then move the body under cover, figuring that will preserve more evidence than leaving it out in the woods, with the animals and everything."

I bit my lip and turned my head away. "I didn't need to know that part, Mason."

"Sorry." But he went on. "Finnegan brought big lights and a camera. We took shots from every angle. It's snowing so hard, I don't know what else we'll get out there, but we roped off the area anyway."

Jeremy was looking from one of us to the other. "It wasn't a heart attack, like Misty thinks, was it." It wasn't really a question.

Mason's eyes met mine. I wished more than anything that I could help him, but I was damned if I knew how.

He looked back at Jeremy again. "Alan Douglas was murdered."

Jeremy had been standing in front of a stool. He sank onto it with those words. "Who did it?"

"We don't know."

Blinking hard, looking at nothing but clearly

searching his mind, the kid asked, "Is it the same person who attacked Mom?"

"We don't know."

"But you have an idea."

"I'm a cop, Jer. Until I have proof of something, I don't know anything. That's how I operate. I follow the evidence to see where it leads. It's true, I did bring your mother and you boys up here to get her away from whoever attacked her. But I don't know if this murder has anything to do with that attack or not."

"And what about Grandmother and Rachel and Misty? You brought them, too, so they must have something to do with it, right?"

"I was attacked, too, Jeremy," I said. "Same day as your mom. We thought if we went somewhere out of the way, we could have a safe, fun holiday while trying to figure out who did this."

Nodding slowly, Jeremy slid off the stool, standing up and towering over his uncle, who was still sitting, and me, though I was standing. The kid was six-two in sock feet. "And no one knows who's doing all this, or why? That's it? That's everything?"

Mason seemed to consider for a long, long moment. Then he said, "No. Actually, it's not." Then he went back into the living room, all the way to the front door, where he'd left his coat hanging. He reached into the pocket and pulled out a handkerchief-wrapped bundle.

"Mason," I said, "I don't know if this is the time to—"

"I don't have a choice," Mason said, cutting me off as he rejoined us in the kitchen. "Grab me a zipper bag, Rache."

I rummaged through the cupboards and found one, then held it open for him. He put the bundle inside, holding one edge of the cloth and letting the weight of the jackknife unroll it. I focused on Jeremy, watching him carefully as the knife fell to the bottom of the bag.

First the teenager frowned, tilting his head and leaning closer, and then he jerked backward as if a snake was snapping at him. "That's...that's my jackknife."

"I know."

He looked from the bag to his uncle and back again. "But...but where was it—where did you—"

"I found it in the woods near the body, Jer."

The kid was shaking his head. "No. No way. That doesn't make any sense. I didn't even *bring* my knife up here. This is crazy, man."

"I know it's crazy. I know, but I'm a cop, and I have to follow up on every clue, even the ones that lead to places I don't want to go. So I have to ask you..." He lowered his head, gave it a shake, then put both hands on Jeremy's shoulders and looked him right in the eyes again. "I'm sorry, kiddo. I wish I didn't have to, but I don't have a choice. I need to know where you went last night."

"Uncle Mason…" He couldn't say more. He was backing up, away from Mason's hands, shaking his head, mouth agape. "You think…you think I—"

"No, Jeremy, I don't think you did anything. You need to be very clear on that. I do not believe for one minute you had anything to do with this. I know you couldn't do something like that."

I heard the doubt in Mason's voice, though, and I knew what he was really thinking. He, a detective, had missed all the clues when his own brother had turned out to be a serial killer. Could it be happening again? Had the urge to kill been somehow genetically handed down to Jeremy? Had Mason missed the signs all over again?

I hoped Jeremy didn't hear the doubt beneath Mason's words, because I thought it would destroy him if he did.

"Neither one of us believes that, Jeremy," I said when the silence drew out too long. "But others might, because somehow your knife ended up out there. That means Mason has to know everything so he can protect you. Do you understand? He's not trying to prove you did anything here. But he might have to prove that you didn't."

Mason met my eyes briefly, and his were filled with gratitude. Then he was focused on Jeremy again. "We know you bought some booze and drank yourself into oblivion last night. You must've been gone quite a while to get all the way to the liquor store in the village and back again by—"

"I didn't go anywhere." His voice was dead. He'd withdrawn completely.

"The sales receipt was in the bag."

"I know." Jeremy spoke in a lifeless monotone. "Misty and I met a couple on the slopes yesterday. Marty and Chelle. I mentioned them before. Marty said he and his girlfriend were going into the village to party last night, so I gave him fifty bucks to pick me up a bottle. Told him if he'd bring it to my window when he got back, he could keep whatever was left over."

"It was a twelve-dollar bottle," I said.

"It was worth fifty to me."

Mason was looking at the floor. "I need to know the guy's last name, Jer."

The spark came back to Jeremy's eyes, but it was an angry one. "Why? So you can arrest him for providing alcohol to a minor?"

"So I can ensure you don't end up arrested for murder." He stared hard right into his nephew's eyes, and I hoped Jeremy could see as clearly as I did that his uncle was dead serious. "I need to protect you, Jeremy."

Jeremy dropped the attitude. He looked scared. *Good,* I thought. *He should be.*

"I promise, I won't file charges because he bought you the booze. I just need him to back up your story that you were here."

There was a sigh, an eye roll, no answer.

"Okay, that's my limit." I put my hands on Jeremy's shoulders, even though I had to reach up to do it, and turned him to face me. "Your uncle concealed evidence to protect your ass. He picked that knife up out of the snow so no one else would see it. If anyone but me knew that, he'd be the one facing charges. And you'd better believe his career would be over. He risked his job and his freedom for you. The least you can do is participate in your own defense, you stubborn little fuck. Give him the name."

Jeremy blinked, then looked at his uncle. "You did all that for me?"

Mason said nothing.

I shook him a little. "The name, Jeremy."

"I don't want to get the guy in trouble. He did me a favor."

I dropped my hands and turned away, frustrated. "Why are kids so damn *dumb?*"

"He did not do you any favors, Jer," Mason said softly. "You have a problem with alcohol, but we'll discuss that later, because right now you have a bigger problem."

"Give your uncle this guy's name, Jeremy, or so help me, I'll grab you by the balls and twist until you do."

They both gaped at me.

I threw my hands in the air. "*What?* We need the name. If there was ever a time for enhanced interrogation techniques..."

"All right, all right. It was Marty Spencer."

Mason was giving me a look that said I might have crossed some kind of line, but I ignored it.

"Can I go now?" Jeremy asked. Then with an angry look at me, he added, "If the *interrogation* is over?"

"Yeah," Mason said. "But listen up, I don't want to catch you with another drop of booze for the remainder of this trip. There's a killer on the loose, Jeremy. One who's trying to point the finger at you. I need everyone on their toes. You need to stay sharp for your own sake. All right?"

"Yeah, yeah." He was already walking out of the kitchen.

"And don't say anything about this to Joshua," I said to his retreating back. "He's already terrified."

No response.

Mason's insides felt as if they were being eaten away by battery acid. The cookies and milk Rachel was pushing on him sat untouched on the end table. He was pacing, thinking, his mind racing in a thousand directions. She was sitting in a rocking chair with her laptop open, clicking keys at what sounded like light speed while the fire crackled and popped in front of them.

He stopped pacing long enough to wonder what had her typing like she was running on rocket fuel. He looked at her. Her eyes were intent on the screen, and she was barely blinking. She had this faraway look, and her lips moved every now and then. The look on her face was just…rapt. Man, she was focused. He almost hated to butt in, but he needed her right now. He needed her sharp mind, and maybe one of her no-nonsense smacks upside the head to snap him out of the downward spiral that had him in its grip.

"What are you writing?"

Her fingers stilled the minute he spoke. She blinked twice, and then she seemed to…surface. As if she'd been out of her body for a while there and was just now reentering.

"Everything," she said.

"Everything?"

"About the murders, what we know, what we don't, what the possibilities are."

"You're *writing* about it?" He was more than a little bit horrified, and she must have seen it, because she made a disgusted face at him.

"Not for public consumption. Jeeze, Mason, what do you think I am, anyway? This isn't for anyone but us. It's just… It's hard to explain. It's my process. It's how I think."

"By writing."

She nodded. "Something happens when I write. Not in the first few lines, but soon after. Something…takes over. Everything flows. I *get* stuff."

"You get stuff?"

"Yeah."

"Like the stuff you write about? All that positive-thinking stuff?"

She nodded again, her eyes dipping back to the screen. "Yeah, most of the time. Not now, though. This is different." He sensed he was going to lose her to her thoughts if he didn't hold on.

"So then it's *not* all bullshit, like you keep saying it is. If you're *getting* it from…somewhere, it's more like it's channeled."

Her head came up fast and sharp. "Oh, come on, Mason. *Channeled?* Did you *really* just go there?"

"Well, what would you call it?"

She just looked at him for a second, then turned to the screen again. Yeah, he was losing her.

"So what did you come up with? Anything brilliant?"

She nodded fast, scrolling now. "Yeah, maybe."

He moved around behind her to look over her shoulder as she scrolled up toward the beginning of the torrent of words. Some lines consisted of nothing but random words and a lot of abbreviations, nothing that made a lot of sense to him. She was writing in some kind of shorthand only she could read, he guessed.

She found what she was looking for and stopped. "Okay, so if the guy who attacked Marie was the same guy who killed Alan Douglas, then that means he was inside Marie's house, right?"

"Obviously."

"So that means he had the opportunity to take Jeremy's knife."

Mason just stood there in front of the fireplace

with his ass getting hot, gaping at her while a ten-thousand-pound boulder lifted half its weight from his shoulders. She had just shown him that there was another way, an obvious way, that knife could have managed to end up at the crime scene. A way he'd missed entirely because he'd been so horrified that the evidence pointed to his nephew. Thank God.

No. Thank Rachel.

He couldn't help the sigh of relief that rushed out of him.

"Good, right?" she asked.

"More than good. More than good, Rachel. It hadn't even occurred to me."

"There are other possibilities, too. Joshua could have brought Jeremy's jackknife up here. You know how little brothers are, always into their big brothers' things. Josh has been all over this resort. He could've had the knife in his pocket and dropped it anywhere. Or the killer could have found it that day he left the angel pin at the door. Maybe it was here in the cabin, and he got inside and took it."

He was nodding, willing any of those possibilities to be true. "But why? Why would he want to do that?"

"To frame Jeremy for his crimes," she said quickly. "It makes a lot of sense, when you think about it. Jeremy's mother is seeing the killer's intended victim and Jeremy's pissed about it. He makes the perfect scapegoat. Not to mention that implicating your nephew throws us off track and *you* into a state where you can't even think straight. Giving the killer the chance to get away or continue his mission or…who the hell knows why? I mean, someone who kills people and cuts out their organs isn't exactly operating from any sort of logic we can relate to, right?"

"Right." He nodded slowly, moving to the sofa and sitting down because he was feeling almost weak with relief, not to mention exhaustion.

"Wait, I have more…." She got up, moving to the sofa to sit close beside him, bringing the laptop with her. He didn't imagine she had any idea how much he needed to feel her just then, touching him. It didn't even matter where, so long as she was just touching him. "Right, here we go. How on earth would Jeremy get hold of succinylcholine? Hmm?"

He shook his head. "I never suspected him of the other crimes."

"Come on, Mason, if he did this one, he did them all. The guy's liver was cut out. So just think for a minute, think like the cop you are. Is there any way Jeremy could have gotten his hands on that drug? Any hospital break-ins or—"

"The vet murder."

"What?"

"Remember I told you about the vet who was murdered and the office burned down? We thought it was drug-related. It was impossible to tell if any drugs were missing, because of the fire damage. But it stands to reason that a vet who did surgery on animals would need the same kind of drugs as a doctor who does surgery on humans."

"Succinylcholine. So they don't move. And that gives you another way to protect Jeremy. Just verify where he was when that crime was done and he's ruled out in at least one crime where he might have gotten the drug. Just like he'll be covered for a chunk of tonight when we talk to this Marty person who bought him the booze."

He looked at her. She was animated, blue eyes damn near sparkling, cheeks flushed. "You're amazing. Do you know how amazing you are?"

"Of course I do." She lowered her eyes a little, though. "You are, too, Mason. And for what it's worth, I think you did the right thing taking that jackknife from the scene."

He felt his shoulders sag a little. "Tampering with evidence is against everything I have ever believed about what kind of a cop I am."

"And what kind of *man* you are. I know."

"I made the wrong call with my brother."

"He shot himself right in front of you. It's not like you were even thinking straight in that moment, Mason." She was looking at him intently. "And then, right on the heels of that, you read his suicide note confessing to thirteen murders. He's dead. His boys are just kids. His wife is pregnant. Your mother is fragile. You were protecting *them* by hiding that note. And it wasn't like he could go on killing."

"But he did. Somehow, he did."

"No. Some of the people who got his organs did. And I don't even pretend to have a clue how that happened. But it's not anything you could've predicted. Nostradamus couldn't have foreseen that, Mason." She set her laptop on the coffee table, turned toward him and grabbed him by the arms. "But we stopped that, too. You almost got killed making it right, but you did. You found the bodies of his victims. You gave the families closure. You saved my ass in the process. Everything worked out."

He wanted to believe it.

"God, the guilt is still eating you alive, isn't it?" she asked softly. "Mason, you have to let it go."

"I don't know *how* to let it go."

She drew a breath, a really deep one, then nodded firmly. "Okay, all right, it is what it is. So you don't know how to let it go. Then you have to set it aside, just for now. Because this is a whole separate thing."

His jaw tight, he whispered, "Is it? Are you sure about that, Rachel?"

"I am. Look, we've got some crazy fuck trying to reclaim all your brother's parts and kill everyone connected to him for God only knows what insane reason. It's not a recipient. We've ruled out most of them already. We have to find out who's doing this and put a stop to it, and we can't do that if you're too busy taking a ride on the guilt train. You need to focus, Mason. If you want to crucify yourself with guilt, then you can do it later. After we fix this. You got me?"

His eyes snapped to hers. This was the smack upside the head he'd been hoping for. "I've got you. And you're right."

"Damn straight I am. So can you do it? Let go of everything that happened over the summer and just focus on the here and now?"

"Yeah. I can. I will."

She smiled at him. "Good. Now eat a damn cookie and let's figure out who could be doing this."

He reached for a cookie. "No. Let's figure out *why.* I think that'll tell us who."

"Okay, let's work on why. But I'll tell you right now, I do not for one minute believe it's your nephew."

Friday, December 22

Strong coffee kept us going until sometime after 4:00 a.m., which was the last time I looked at the clock. After that I must have dozed off. I woke at 7:30, and I was alone on the sofa with a big fat pillow under my head and a heavy blanket tucked around me. On the table in front of the couch the cookie plate was bare except for a few crumbs, and the glass of milk was empty.

I sat up and stretched my arms over my head. It was still pretty dark outside. I knew the sun must be up, even though these were the longest nights of the year. Only three days until Christmas. Some holiday this was turning out to be.

I got up and shuffled into the kitchen to put on a pot of fresh coffee, noticing things as I did. Mason had lined up rows of wineglasses on the floor in front of the back door. Clever. I would have heard anyone who tried to get in. Once the coffee was brewing and I headed back into the living room I saw the same thing in front of the front door.

He'd gone upstairs at some point, but he had made sure I would be safe down here while he was gone. I tiptoed up to check on everyone else. Misty's bed was empty. That gave me a scare on more levels than I cared to analyze at that moment. But I found her soon enough, and Myrtle, too. Both of them had curled up on Josh's bed. Poor little guy must have been too scared to sleep. They were all still snoozing, so I backed out quietly and continued on my way.

Mason was in Jeremy's room. He'd tossed a pillow and a blanket on the floor and was lying there, awake, watching his nephew sleep.

That kid wouldn't be sneaking booze again. Not on Mason's watch.

Mason met my eyes and put a finger to his lips, and I nodded and backed out into the hallway, then waited.

He joined me a few seconds later.

"Did you get any sleep?" I whispered.

"Yeah, a couple of hours. I'm good now. Could use a shower, though."

"Take a quick one and I'll make breakfast."

He looked back worriedly toward the bedroom.

"It'll be okay. He's a teenage boy—he's not going to wake up for at least an hour. You can shower inside ten minutes. Right?"

He nodded.

I said, "Thanks for the blanket and pillow. And the wineglasses in front of the doors. Nice touch."

"I doubt anyone would bother us right now, anyway. Have you looked outside?"

I frowned. "No. Why?" We were outside my bedroom by then, and he nodded at the open door. So I went in and took a look out my bedroom window. The sky was gray and dull, and the wind was blowing snow sideways. I couldn't even see the trees out back. "Holy crap, this is worse than last night."

"Way worse. We've got a meeting with Finnegan, Cait and Rosie this morning. They're coming to us."

"Then I'd better make a quadruple batch of whatever it is I'm making for breakfast. What time?"

"They didn't say. What are you making?"

"I have no idea. Something easy. Waffles and sausage?"

"Sounds great," he said. "But…that's easy?"

"Waffles are one of the few meals I do well. And I saw a waffle iron in the kitchen and a mix in the cupboard. I'll need the shower when you're done, so be quick, okay?"

He nodded, but didn't turn toward the bathroom. He just stood there, looking at me until I wondered if I still had food coloring staining my teeth from the cookie frosting marathon of the night before. *"What?"*

He shrugged. "Just...thanks. For putting all that togcther last night. For giving me hope."

"Oh. Yeah, you know." I shrugged. "It's kind of what I do."

"And you do it well. Really well, Rachel. You're a modern-day guru in complete denial."

"Yeah, right. Send me fifty bucks and I'll see to it you reincarnate as a prince." I winked. "Go soak your head, Mason. It's full of cobwebs."

I walked away. And I totally ignored the rush of blood to my face and pleasure to my belly that his un-deserved praise gave me. I ought to be irritated that he was still insisting on seeing me for who he wanted me to be instead of who I was. But at least this time it was because of something I'd actually done. So I decided to accept the compliment gracefully and let it go at that. And to make waffles. Stacks and stacks of waffles. And sausage. And a lot more coffee.

14

Friday, December 22

Finnegan Smart, Rosie and Cait Cole were sitting around the kitchen island by the time Mason got out of the shower, dressed and followed the scents of breakfast sausage and fresh coffee downstairs. When he walked in, Rachel was filling coffee cups and setting stacks of blueberry waffles in front of the guests. Her hair was in a messy ponytail, and there was flour on her cheek. She was wearing a little snowflake-patterned apron.

An *apron.*

She met him in the doorway, ostensibly to shove a hot mug into his hands, and whispered, "You didn't tell me they'd be here in minutes."

"I didn't know." He eyed her attire. "You look like a regular Suzy Homemaker."

"I had to cover up the fact that I'm not wearing a bra."

He choked on his first sip, drawing the gazes of everyone in the room.

"Mornin', Mace," Rosie said.

Mason nodded at him, noted the tight and drawn expression and frowned. "Marlayna didn't come with you?"

"She's...pretty pissed I didn't tell her why we were really coming up here."

"I don't blame her," Cait snapped. "I'm pissed, too."

"Now, Caity—"

"Don't 'now, Caity' me, Finnegan Smart. These people brought a murderer to Pine Haven at the height of the holiday season. This could ruin me."

"Watch what you say, Ms. Cole," Rachel said. "There are kids in the house who don't need to know all the details about this right now." She leaned through the doorway to check for accidental cavesdroppers, but Mason was pretty sure they were all still in bed.

Cait paced to the window, coffee mug clutched in her hands, staring outside and apparently not inclined to apologize. No doubt from her point of view they had far more to apologize for than she did.

"I'm sorry," Mason said, stepping up. "I hope you know we had no idea this person would manage to trace us up here. We booked under my mother's name, and we didn't tell anyone we were coming."

"Someone found out. Murderers are clever that

way, aren't they?" She didn't face him as she spoke, but her anger was clear all the same.

Sighing, Mason gave up. "What's the situation, Finnegan? I assume you've talked to the authorities?"

The older man dragged his eyes from Cait's rigid spine. "Not since last night. The phone lines and internet are down, and something's interfering with the radio at the moment. Walkie-talkies are still good, of course, but they only have a ten-mile range. I sent a team out this morning by snowmobile to assess our predicament, and it's a doozie, I'll tell you. The only road out is completely blocked. The only cell tower in the entire area has an eighty-foot pine lying across it. For all I know, that could be the same problem the radio tower is having, though my team didn't go far enough to find out for sure. It could just be cloud cover."

Mason swore and looked at Rachel. She'd gone white.

"Are you saying we're trapped here?" she whispered.

"For the time being, yes, but—"

"No. No way," she said. "We can get out with that giant machine. The Abominable. Or the snowmobiles, what about those?"

"And go where?" Finnegan asked. "The village is just as snowed-in as we are, and their power went out last night, to boot. We're all on the same grid. When we're down, they're down. At least we've got the emergency generators."

Mason frowned. "I didn't realize we'd lost power."

"You're not supposed to," Cait said. "We have a state-of-the-art backup system. The whole lodge is wired, as are all the cabins. It kicks in automatically." She sounded proud and heartbroken at the same time. "You wouldn't have noticed more than a brief flicker of the lights."

"I assure you, Ms. de Luca," Finnegan said, "if the radio towers are intact we'll have radio contact with emergency services again the minute the storm begins to ease."

"And how soon will that be?" she asked.

He shook his head. "It's a whopper of a storm. Last time I could get the radar map up, it looked as if it could take 'til the wee hours of tomorrow morning. The police'll be out to check on us just as soon as they can safely get through, though. They know about the killing, after all."

Rosie was the only one eating, but he stopped long enough to say, "You all ought to pack up and move into the lodge. We stick together, we'll all be safer."

"We can't do that," Rachel said softly. She looked at Mason.

He read her loud and clear. If there was any chance, even a minute one, that Jeremy had become violent, they could not bring him into a lodge full of potential targets. No, it wasn't likely that any of the guests were recipients of his father's organs. But violence didn't have to make sense, or even be consistent. They had to keep him here, where they could watch him carefully.

Everyone else was staring at her now, though, expecting an explanation.

Finnegan said, "Frankly, Detective, I could use all the help I can get protecting the guests."

"I know. The thing is, Rachel is a target. Taking her to the lodge might mean we bring the killer with us."

"On the off chance he's not already there, you mean?" Cait asked. She was looking at him now, narrow-eyed. "Which begs the question—if he's not at the lodge, then where the hell do you think he *is,* Detective?"

Rachel stood a little straighter, and she moved to put herself between him and the angry resort owner. "He could be anywhere, Ms. Cole. Serial killers are pretty good at staying under the radar, or they wouldn't be on the loose long enough to get to *be* serial killers."

"With any luck he was staying somewhere else," Mason said, "and is stuck there now."

"With a whole other roster of potential victims," Rosie muttered.

Mason shot his friend a quelling look. "Stop borrowing trouble, Rosie. There's nothing we can do about that right now."

"So what exactly *can* we do right now?"

Mason lowered his eyes. His best friend was upset; it was probably killing him being away from his wife while a killer might be on the loose. But he couldn't help that. He wished to hell he hadn't asked Rosie along and put him in this situation. He nodded at Finnegan. "Did you find that guest I asked about?"

"Young Marty and his fiancée checked out early yesterday morning, before the storm moved in," Finnegan said.

"Marty who? What's this about?" Cait asked, finally turning from the window. "Is he a suspect?"

Mason held up a hand. "No. I thought he might have seen something, that's all." So Jeremy's alibi was out of reach, at least temporarily.

Shit.

"We'll have to call him as soon as the phones are back," Rachel said. "I assume you keep contact numbers in your records."

Cait nodded. She paced to the island and set her empty mug down on it none too gently. "How the hell do I protect my guests from a serial killer while we're all snowbound? Tell me that."

"Well, we can't tell 'em, that's sure," Finnegan said. "They'd panic, and that would make things worse."

Mason nodded. "I agree on that. Cait, this guy is going after a very specific group of victims. I am extremely doubtful any of your guests fit his profile."

She looked him squarely in the eye. "One did."

"He's the only one."

"Are you going to tell me what this profile is?

What the victims have in common—besides being connected to you, that is?"

"No," he said. "I'm not."

She glared at him. Finnegan broke her stare by grabbing her mug from in front of her and holding it up as if to ask whether she would like a refill. She shook her head no.

"I believe the wise course of action," Finnegan said, "is to behave as if everything is fine. We'll institute some security measures, lay everything off to the storm. We instruct guests to go about the lodge in groups of two or more, in case the generators go out and they're trapped in an elevator or a pitch-black corridor. We insist no one ventures outside until further notice, because whiteouts up here can have a man lost a hundred feet from his front door."

Cait heaved a sigh. "Those are good ideas, Finn. But are they enough?"

"My entire security team and two shifts of the staff, minus one or two, are snowbound here like the rest of us. We put 'em all to work, let 'em know we need their eyes and ears open, to report anything unusual. Say there might be a fugitive from the law hiding out here, and tell them no more than that. Swear 'em to silence on it, as well."

Mason nodded. This guy was good. "Meanwhile," he added, "we can start interviewing some of the guests."

"That's over four hundred people," Cait said.

"We rule out anyone who was here more than a day before we arrived and anyone who checked out before Douglas went missing."

Grudgingly, the woman nodded, her short blond curls moving with the motion. "That should rule out a few of them, at least."

"My instincts will rule out a lot more," Rachel said.

Mason shot her a look. She couldn't be at the lodge interviewing guests, and neither could he. He had to keep her here, safe, where he could protect her, not to mention Marie and the boys. And he had to keep a constant eye on Jeremy.

She looked back at him, seemed to read him and nodded. Wordless communication. They were getting better and better at it. He noticed it, wondered at it, then forced his focus back to the job. "We should take another look at the scene now that it's daylight. Though with the snow, I doubt there'll be much to see." He got up from the table, leaving an empty plate behind him. Cait hadn't touched hers. Rosie got up rather reluctantly, eyeing the stack of waffles still left behind.

Marie came into the kitchen then. She looked far better than she had last night. She must have managed to get a few hours' sleep, Mason thought with a surge of relief. She'd needed it.

"What's going on?" she asked.

"I'll fill you in, Marie," Rachel said.

Mason nodded his thanks to her, grabbed a waffle off the stack, rolled it around a sausage and led the way back through the house, eating on the way to his coat and boots.

I didn't get the chance to fill Marie in on much, because two minutes after Mason, Rosie, Cait and Finnegan were out the door, the kids came dragging in, with Myrtle in tow.

Marie picked at her food for a while. Jeremy and Josh ate like a pair of horses. Big ones. Budweiser Clydesdales. But Misty seemed to be forcing herself. I could tell from the look on her face that Jeremy had told her about the murder, about him being a suspect and maybe about Marty bringing him the booze. She kept looking at me like she wanted to talk about it, then looking at Josh and biting her lip. Like me, she wanted to keep Josh as much in the dark as possible.

And he seemed okay, amazingly. He wolfed down a half dozen syrup-soaked waffles while Myrtle lay under his chair, scarfing every dropped crumb with uncanny accuracy. Josh held an entire sausage link down, thinking no one noticed, and she snagged it without even sniffing first. Fussy, she wasn't.

After she swallowed and Josh stopped laughing at her, I said, "She needs to go outside. And as much as I love her, you need to ease off on giving her junk food, Josh. It's not good for her."

At the word *outside,* Myrtle's ears perked up and she looked in my direction.

"I'll take her!" Josh volunteered.

"I don't think—"

"It's okay," Marie said. "I'll go with them. I need to stretch my legs anyway, get some air."

I put a hand on her shoulder and nodded. "Okay. You'd both better bundle up, though. Put Myrt's sweater on her, too, would you, Josh? It's still storming like crazy out there." I met Marie's eyes as Josh scrambled to get the sweater and leash. "Don't go far from the cabin, okay?"

She covered my hand with her own. "Thanks for caring."

"I do, you know," I said. And then I wanted to gag at my uncharacteristic bout of female bonding. *We should just break into a round of "Kumbaya" already.*

Marie went to the closet to begin donning her layers. Josh and Myrtle were already there. The bulldog would follow Joshua off the edge of the planet. The minute the front door closed behind them, Jeremy said, "Did Uncle Mason talk to Marty yet?"

I drew a breath. "Not exactly."

He frowned at me. Misty put her hand on his shoulder and said, "What do you mean, not exactly?"

"Marty and his fiancée checked out yesterday morning before the full brunt of the storm hit."

"So call him." Jeremy pulled out his cell. "I have his number right here."

"It isn't going to matter, Jer. The tower is out. The power's down, too. This entire place is running on backup generators."

Misty got up from the table and went to the back door, parting the curtains to look outside. "I didn't realize the storm was so bad."

"They've even closed the slopes. Everyone has to stick to indoor activities until further notice."

Misty turned from the window and met my eyes. "We should just leave, Aunt Rache. If there's a killer here somewhere, we should just—"

"The road is completely blocked."

"Oh, my God," she whispered. "This is like something out of a slasher flick."

She looked at Jeremy. He got up from the table and put his arms around her.

"Whoa, no PDAs, all right? You're too fucking young."

"Get over it, Aunt Rache," Misty said, gripping his wrists to keep his arms right where they were. "We have a connection."

"Yeah, it's called hormonal overdrive."

"Don't assume I'm driven by the same shit you are," she snapped.

My jaw dropped. I clamped it shut. "God, I hate when you sound like me."

She rolled her eyes and turned to look back outside. "Josh and Myrt are heading back."

"What about Marie?" I asked, going to the window to look over her shoulder.

"I saw her heading into the woods. I think she went out to find Mason."

"And left Josh out there alone?" Jeremy turned

and went into the living room, grabbing a coat and opening the front door before he even put it on. Conscientious about protecting his kid brother. That didn't really seem in character for a crazed teenage serial killer, did it?

"You don't really think Jeremy had anything to do with Mr. Douglas's death, do you, Aunt Rache?"

I turned to my lovesick niece. "I wouldn't tell you so even if I did, so the question is moot. And it doesn't matter what I think, anyway."

"It does, though."

"Why?" I asked.

"What you think matters to Jeremy. And to me. And what Mason thinks matters more to him than whether the sun rises tomorrow morning. Just so you know."

I nodded slowly. "Okay, what we think matters to Jeremy. But it's not going to matter to a criminal investigation. We need to *prove* he's innocent before the police get out here and start digging around."

She nodded slowly. "He's been drinking, Aunt Rache. A lot. I'm trying to help him with it."

"If you want to help him, you need to convince him that he has to stop, Misty. He has to stop entirely. Not one sip, not one beer, not a glass of wine, nothing. Ever. No exceptions."

She pressed her lips tight. "Seems kind of harsh."

"Look at this way. If he can do it without much effort, he doesn't have a problem. He can drink again, within reason, when he's legal. On the other hand, if he can't stop easily..."

"Then it's a real problem." She nodded as if that made sense to her.

Then the door opened, and Jeremy, Josh, Myrtle and a huge blast of wind-driven snow came in.

The spot where Scott Douglas had been disemboweled had only a couple of inches of snow, and it was sheltered from the brutal wind today, too. Mason could still see the blood, veiled only a little by the white powder. He was moving around the crime scene on hands and knees, brushing snow away as he went in an ever-widening circle. Rosie and Cait were circling the woods a little farther out, and Finn was searching for signs of how the killer had come and gone.

And then Mason spotted something in the snow.

A cell phone.

He picked it up carefully, using his gloved thumb and forefinger and turning its face toward him as Finnegan came closer.

"What've you got?" the other man asked.

"Phone." Mason pushed the power button. "Dead. Wet, too. If we can dry it out and charge it up, figure out whose phone it is, we might have our man."

"Unless it's the victim's phone," Finn suggested. "We didn't find one in his room."

"No, and not on his body, either," Mason said. "Still, we can hope."

Finn held out an open plastic bag. "Best let me get the thing under lock and key. I'll take it back to the Security Shack until we can hand it off to the police tomorrow."

"You really think they'll be able to get to us that soon?" someone asked.

They both turned. Marie was standing a few yards away. Mason dropped the phone into the bag and moved toward her. "You shouldn't have come out here alone, Marie. It's not safe."

"I just… I wanted to see where Alan…" She lowered her head, closed her eyes.

Mason sighed and put his arms around her, hugging her hard. "You've been through so much. I'm sorry, Marie. And I'm sorry I was a jerk about him at first, too."

She let her head rest on his shoulder. "I know you are." Then she straightened. "It's not like we were in love or anything, I just… I really liked him. He was a nice guy, you know? A genuinely nice guy."

"Take your sister-in-law on back to the cabin, Mason," Rosie said, as he and Cait returned to join them. "We're about done here anyway. And I have got to get back to Marlayna or she's gonna skin me."

Mason nodded, but he shot a look at Finnegan for confirmation.

"I don't know there's any more we can do here," Finn said. "Time for us all to get back and try to keep everyone safe and calm until the roads are cleared and the police can get here."

"All right," Mason said. "Drop that phone into a bowl of rice for a while. Maybe we can dry it out and find a charger to fit it."

"No doubt about that. We have in the neighborhood of a hundred and seventeen phone chargers in our lost and found. We let guests borrow one when they've forgotten theirs at home."

"Don't let any guests borrow them today, at least not until we find one that fits," Mason suggested.

Finnegan nodded and stuffed the bagged phone into his pocket as Cait walked over to join him. Mason tucked Marie under one arm, and they all started back through the pine forest to the cabin.

But when they got there, Marie abruptly stopped. Mason looked down at her with a question in his eyes, but she just waited while Finnegan, Cait and Rosie got into the Abominable. Finn turned the lumbering beast around, and they started back toward the lodge.

Finally, Marie said, "I don't know what's happening, Mason. It's like I'm cursed. Everyone I care about dies."

"No. Not everyone."

"Eric," she said softly. "Our baby. And then poor Alan." Her eyes were dry, but red, as if she'd cried for so long there were no tears left. She looked empty, hollow. Defeated. "And now Jeremy…" She trailed off, shaking her head.

"What about Jeremy?" he asked. This was important, he sensed it right to his toes.

She shook her head and turned toward the front door, but he caught her arm and turned her around. "Finish the thought, Marie. It's important. What about Jeremy?"

Marie lowered her head, sighed heavily. "Eric used to go someplace where I couldn't reach him. Someplace...inside himself. Did you ever see that happen?"

Holding her gaze, he nodded. He'd seen it. He just hadn't realized what it meant. "The silences, the brooding. Staying in his room for hours at a time without a word, just staring at nothing. No TV, no music, nothing, just...nothing," he said. "He's always done it, even as a kid."

"So you know," she said softly. "I never understood, I just... I resented that I couldn't reach him there. He seemed so far from me during those times."

"Mom took him to a psychiatrist once. But Eric said he was fine, and the doctor didn't find any reason to disagree. He could fake it really well, Marie."

"I wonder what he was hiding in that dark place inside him," she mused.

That he was a serial killer, Mason thought. But he would never tell Marie that. He'd put his career on the line to protect her and the boys from that ugly truth. "It doesn't matter," he said. "He's at peace now."

"But Jeremy isn't. And now he's doing the same thing. Going to that dark place where no one can find him. And it scares me, Mason. It scares me to death, because I don't want to lose *him,* too."

Her words sent a chill right to Mason's bones. "We're not gonna lose him," he said. "I plan to hold on to Jeremy for all I'm worth. I won't let go. We'll pull him through this, I promise you. No matter what it takes."

And he meant it. If Jeremy was infected with whatever evil had poisoned his father, if it was genetic, then Mason would get him into treatment, onto medication, whatever it took.

If.

And it was a very big *if.* The biggest. Because he knew he couldn't trust his instincts where his nephew was concerned.

But he *could* trust Rachel's. They were good, better than his cop sense—which had been called uncanny—at its best. Rachel didn't believe Jeremy could have killed Alan Douglas, much less anyone else. He was holding on to that trust, holding on for dear life. And just like he'd told Marie, he wasn't about to let go.

15

It wasn't that bad a day, considering there was a murderer somewhere nearby waiting for a chance to steal my eyes. Aside from that, it was actually pretty good, mainly because there was nothing we could do but wait for the police to arrive and the plows to clear the roads.

We'd all done a fair amount of shopping before the storm hit, and Misty had stocked up on gift wrap and bows on our trip into the village. So we worked on wrapping our gifts, all of us together, hunching over our work spaces, so the others couldn't see their surprises. Mason actually took an hour-long nap after that. Misty and Marie and I talked about whether we'd still be here—here at the lodge, not here among the living—on Christmas Day, and what we'd do if we were. Make dinner here or venture out to the lodge to celebrate with the other guests. The thought of being so exposed sent a shiver up my spine, but I pretended it was a logical discussion to be having, even with a serial killer after us.

Then again, he was really only after me—and Marie, though I still had no idea why he had gone after her. I mean, I didn't doubt it. She'd been attacked, had the bruises to prove it, but still... My extra senses were reading that signal as indecipherable. It made no sense.

Josh was having a fit most of the time, because he wanted to be at the lodge with his grandmother and the water park and arcade—not necessarily in that order. But he forgot not to have fun every now and then.

At some point we'd given in to the kids' begging and put a pumpkin pie into the oven to bake. The supplies that had been waiting when we'd first arrived had included all the ingredients from filling to pre-made pie crusts, thank you God and Caity Cole, and lots of other holiday things like canned cranberry sauce and boxes of stuffing mix. I bet there was a turkey in the freezer, and at the thought I got a little warm glow in the pit of my belly.

I smacked it upside the head and got my focus back. Killer, remember?

It was that damn Christmas thing in the air, infecting me like it seemed to infect everyone else I knew at this time of year. It was only three days away. With the smell of the fireplace and the pie in the oven, I was damn near whimsical. Almost ready to think some holiday magic was going to happen to fix all this before I wound up paralyzed under a pine tree with a scalpel-wielding killer and my eyes wide open.

I closed them quickly, gripped the edge of the counter and bowed my head. I didn't mean to, it just happened. That image had hit me hard.

"Hey, what smells so good down here?"

Mason. I hadn't realized he'd come back downstairs and automatically looked at the clock. "You only slept for an hour."

"From the looks of you, it was an hour too long. What happened?"

I shook my head and stood up straight, crossing my arms. "Nothing. I was just walking down dark alleys in my head. Places I've got no business going."

He came right to me, like it was an everyday thing, squeezed my shoulders and leaned his face close to mine. I was ultra-conscious of Misty and Marie standing a few feet away, watching us, and then I felt his breath on my mouth and didn't care if the Pope was standing there.

"I'm not going to let anything happen to you, Rachel. I promise you, I'll be the first and last thing standing between you and this maniac, and he'll have to kill me to get by."

It dawned on me that this wasn't a romantic embrace at all. It was a solemn vow, and he was standing so close to make sure I got it.

And I did, I got it, and then I was completely dumbfounded. Because he meant it.

I moved my face even closer to his, and I said to him, "I will never let you die for me, Mason Brown. Don't you even think about doing something that stupid. You think I want that on my shoulders for the rest of my life? No fucking way."

He blinked like he was stunned.

I felt bad, so I added, "That was probably the most amazing offer I've ever had, though. Thanks for that."

"I meant it."

"I know you did." His eyes were searching mine for I didn't even know what. Everything inside me was jiggling like St. Nick's bowlful-of-jelly belly, and there was this urgent feeling in my soul. I wanted him like a vampire wants a pint of A-neg straight from the donor. Right there. In front of the whole fam-damily.

The oven timer pinged, and Marie cleared her throat. I blinked myself back to reality and stepped away. Misty scampered for the living room, bending close to my ear and whispering, "That was like the most romantic thing I've ever *seen!*" as she passed. Marie took the pie out of the oven, set it on the counter and followed Misty.

I stood there, shaking. "Well, you certainly distracted me from my morbid thoughts."

"You distracted me, too."

I nodded. "We can't be distracted right now,

though." It was what he would say, I knew, and after the other night, I had to agree with him. But I wanted him anyway. In ways I was too afraid to think about.

"No, we can't." He went to the counter and leaned down to smell the pie. I watched his chest expand and ached for him. "This smells so good."

"We can have some as soon as it cools off a little."

"With hot cocoa," he said. "By the fire. This is really starting to feel Christmassy, in spite of everything, isn't it?"

I couldn't seem to generate a snarky comeback to save my ass and instead found myself nodding with a faraway look in my eyes. "I was just thinking that. This damn holiday gets into the darkest spaces, doesn't it? It's like..."

"Magic." He drew a deep breath, let it out slowly. "So, for what it's worth, I don't think it's the extreme situation this time, Rachel."

That startled me. Because he wasn't talking about the holiday anymore, he was talking about us. And I was interpreting his words to mean that he thought there might be something more between us. Something real. Even thinking it had terrified me. Finding out that he'd been thinking it, too... Hell, I couldn't even process that yet. It was still ricocheting around my brain, lighting up every nerve center. "Mason, I—"

"No, it's okay. I know. Anyway, this isn't the time."

"No, it's really not."

He glanced at the clock. "How long before the pie?"

I went almost limp with relief at his easy change of subject. "Half a round of Scrabble?"

"It's unfair. You're a writer."

"I don't think you're going to have any trouble. I've come to the conclusion that you're smarter than you look."

"Hey!"

"That was a compliment, dumbass."

"Oh."

"Good-looking men aren't always known for their brilliance."

"I got it, I got it."

"I'm losing my touch when I have to explain my lame-ass jokes," I muttered, walking past him into the living room. "So, are we on for that game, or what?"

We played Scrabble. And then we ate pie. And then we played rummy and ate some more pie. And then everyone went to bed, and we stayed up, drinking pots of coffee and playing the boys' video games. Every hour or so we'd go upstairs and check on the crew. Misty and Myrtle were in with Josh again, Myrt snoring like a chain saw. Jeremy was on his own, as was Marie.

It was relaxed and easy, even fun, spending the night trying to keep each other awake and protect ourselves from a killer. I mean, given that I had to do that at all, there was no one I would rather have done it with.

We didn't talk about anything heavy. And we didn't let things get romantic, both of us holding on to ourselves with nothing but sheer willpower. And, you know, the fear that getting distracted could mean we'd all wake up dead. That helped, too. We couldn't mess up now. Not tonight. Tonight might be the organ thief's best chance to succeed. Tomorrow we might not be so cut off. Hell, if things panned out with that cell phone, tomorrow we might know who the hell he was. So we stayed awake, and we played games. And we pretended that we didn't want to rip each other's clothes off.

Finnegan Smart didn't like sleeping in the fancy rooms of the lodge, and there wasn't a cabin available. So he did what he always did on such occasions. He pulled out the cot and bedding he kept in the storage room, and set up camp right in the Security Shack. He had heat, he had power, a coffeepot ready to go first thing in the morning and a shotgun close to hand. He was set for the night.

But then he heard something rattling around outside his door. In this storm? Something bad must be happening if someone was out in the dead of night in this weather.

He got up in his shorts and went to the door. He looked out the little glass panel first, of course, and then, frowning, opened it. "What can I do for you? Is something wrong?"

His visitor came inside, shaking off snow, and turning to face him. And then something jabbed him in the gut, and the next thing he knew, the room was swimming and he was fading fast. He dropped to his knees and looked down at his hands. His belly was gushing blood all over them.

Mason was looking in on the kids, and I eased open Marie's bedroom door to peek in at her. She was still lying in the bed, just as she had been every time I'd checked on her for the past several hours.

That's a little odd, isn't it? People move around in their sleep. But she's in the same position. Is she okay?

Cussing myself out for not doing so earlier, I tip-toed inside, put my hands on her shoulders and whispered, "Marie?"

She rolled onto her back, squinting up at me. "What? What's going on?"

I sighed in relief. I don't know what I'd thought, but it had suddenly occurred to me that she'd been pretty depressed lately. And had reason to be. "I was just checking on you. Everything okay?"

"Yeah. Fine."

I nodded. "All right. I'm sorry, I just…flaked."

"It's okay," she said, smiling. "It's nice that you care."

"Yeah, yeah, let's not get mushy here. Go back to sleep."

"Night," she said and I backed out of the room. I turned and bumped into Mason's chest. My nose was buried in his T-shirt, and I was awash in pure sensual pleasure. God, he smelled good.

I couldn't lift my head because if I did we were going to start making out right there in the hallway. And if we started making out, we'd be in bed in about two minutes, so we couldn't start making out. Maybe tomorrow.

I stepped back. "Sorry."

"Don't be."

I looked up, now that I was a safe two feet away from him. "You're exhausted. Why don't you take a nap? I can stay awake by myself for an hour."

"Not a good idea. I'll catch cat naps during the day. Night is when he's more likely to try something."

"Tonight in particular," I said.

He nodded in agreement.

I rolled my eyes. "Dammit, Mason, you could've lied."

"What would be the point? You already know."

I walked up to him and grabbed him by the T-shirt. "Keep me alive long enough to jump your bones, Mason Brown, or I swear to God, I'll come back and do it anyway." And then I leaned up and pressed my mouth to his. When he groaned and started kissing me back just as hungrily, I pulled away and headed back downstairs.

Saturday, December 23

Rachel had fallen asleep on the sofa, leaning over to one side, mouth slightly open, game controller still in her hand. She was still there as the sun rose, though Mason had draped a blanket over her and set the controller on the coffee table. She smelled good. She'd taken a shower last night, put on fresh clothes, not intending to sleep, then had fallen asleep anyway. He looked at her and grinned.

It was dawn on December 23. The day before Christmas Eve. They'd made it through the night without incident, and the storm had finally stopped. The sun was beaming through the windows, reflecting off the snow, blindingly bright. Within hours the roads would be cleared, the cell tower repaired, the state police here, and he could get his family the hell away. Last night had been the most dangerous point.

And they'd survived.

He was relieved as hell, and feeling more certain than ever that the killer had gotten out of there before the storm hit. Otherwise, he certainly would have tried something last night.

He heard a motor buzzing in the distance and realized it was coming closer. Going to the window, he squinted and saw rooster tails of snow flying behind a pair of speeding snowmobiles, and he knew without even thinking about it that something was wrong. His gut told him so. The speed of the sleds told him so, too, and his happiness over surviving the night waned.

"What's going on?" Rachel sounded sleepy, as she scuffed closer and looked past him at the approaching snowmobiles.

"I think we're about to find out."

The machines stopped, and their passengers jumped off and tugged off helmets while hurrying to the front door. Rosie and Cait Cole, shaking her blond hair and looking ragged.

He opened the door before they got to it. Cait didn't come in, just stood on the step in front of Rosie. "I need you to come with me," she said. "Fast. Now." She was shaking. Her voice trembled.

Mason shot a look at Rachel and she nodded, acknowledging that she heard it, too.

"I'll stay with the family, Mace." Rosie eased past Cait and up to the door. "You have to go with her."

"I'm coming, too," Rachel said. She dove into the closet, tossed him his coat, then went back for hers.

Mason pulled on his coat as Cait moved aside to let Rosie in. "You armed, partner?"

"To the teeth," Rosie said. "And some of the security guys are on their way to back me up. Everyone here will be safe, I promise."

"Okay, I won't be long." Mason had shoved on his boots by then, and pulled on his hat. Leaning close to Rosie, he said, "Don't let Jeremy out of your sight, okay?"

"Jeremy?" Rosie frowned. "Something happen I don't know about?"

"I'll explain later. Watch him, that's all."

"All right. Ain't nobody getting in or out of this cabin while I'm on duty, my friend. You better believe that."

Mason nodded, then glanced back to see Rachel dressed and ready. "Let's go."

I knew something bad had happened. But I didn't know how bad until we walked into the Security Shack and saw Finnegan Smart lying in a puddle of his own blood, his green eyes wide open, their light forever extinguished. The door closed behind us, and I jumped out of my skin when I turned around, but it was only Cait, pulling it shut, leaning back against it, staring at the body on the floor as her eyes welled.

"I didn't know what to do. I came in this morning and found him like this and—"

"Did you touch anything?" Mason asked, scanning the room, seeing everything. He was like a hawk. Me, I was feeling instead of looking, but there wasn't much to feel without a person nearby to give off signals. Cait was grieving and in shock. She was scared, too. And angry.

"I tried to help him, but as soon as I touched him, I knew…"

"Okay, okay, hang on, Cait," Mason said.

"He didn't deserve this. He was a good man, dammit. He didn't deserve this."

"I know he didn't." Mason moved closer, as close as he could without disturbing the blood on the floor, and bent low, lifting Finn's T-shirt. I turned my head away, and tried to block Cait's view, which was pointless, because she had her eyes closed.

"Stab wound, just one. Looks like it severed the abdominal aorta." Mason sighed heavily, and when I heard him move it felt safe to look again. "It was fast, Cait, if that's any consolation. I doubt he even felt the pain of it before…" He stopped there, and I watched his eyes tracking the blood across the floor to a spot just a few inches from where I stood.

"Someone came to the door. He went to open it, let them in. No sign of a struggle, no defensive injuries. My bet is, it was someone he knew and had no reason to mistrust."

"This isn't right," Cait muttered. She'd opened her eyes again, and they were fixed on the body. I tiptoed across the room, nodded toward the blanket from the rumpled cot and asked Mason with my eyes if I could cover poor Finnegan up.

He gave me a nod in return, so I did it as gently as I could without getting too close.

Having him covered freed his grip on Cait's eyes, which shot to Mason now. "Why? That's what I want to know? Why on earth would this murdering bastard target Finnegan?"

"Where's the cell phone?" I asked, because it was

the obvious answer. Once that phone dried out and we plugged it in—and if it worked—we would know who the killer was. We'd figured that was a possibility. If the killer had murdered Finn and taken the phone, then there was no longer any doubt. That phone was the key.

Mason looked at Cait. "Do you know where he would have put it? He said he would lock it up for the night."

"There's a locker in the back," she said. She wiped her eyes and pointed. The locker was metal and free-standing, with a padlock on the front. It was still locked. Mason walked over and stopped in front of it. "There's something on the floor." He bent low and came back up rubbing something between his thumb and forefinger. "Rice."

"He must have done what you said and put the phone in rice overnight to try to draw out the moisture," Cait said.

Mason still had his gloves on. He tugged the lock, which turned out not to be locked at all. It only looked as if it was. The hasp was free, and Mason opened the door.

A bowl sat inside, a set of keys on a chain lying beside it. "Here's the rice. I can see traces of blood in it, though." He pulled out his own phone and took a couple of pictures, then turned, pocketing it again as he turned to Cait. "Can you find me something to pour the rice into? I don't want to run my hands through it. There might be trace evidence in there."

Her eyes were back on the blanket-covered body. She'd checked out. I was going to have to step in. In two seconds I located a package of plastic waste-basket liner bags, took one out and held it up. "Will this work?"

"Yeah, perfect. Stay there, I'll come to you."

He crossed the room just as carefully as before, while I tried to open three sides of the bag before finally finding the right one. Then I held it open while Mason slowly poured in the rice. I grimaced at the bloody bits.

As we'd already guessed, the cell phone was gone.

Mason took the bag from me and set it aside. Then he showed me his cell phone. The photo he'd taken of the keys inside the cabinet. I frowned, and he made it bigger. "Is that—"

"A nice, crisp bloody fingerprint," he said softly. "My guess is that's the key that opened the padlock. Our killer must have taken the key chain from Finn."

"We've got him." I handed the phone back to him, and he pocketed it, set the rice bag and the bowl onto the desk, and nudged us back outside.

"We haven't got him yet. If he's in the system, yes. If we find a suspect to compare this print with, yes. But until then, we're no closer."

"But we can rule people out with this, can't we?"

"Eventually, yeah. Right now we have to lock up the shack, preserve the chain of evidence. I've got a good shot of the print, with enough detail to email it out once we get a signal again." He looked at Cait.

"How long before you think we can get some help out here?"

She was staring blankly at the closed door. I nudged her. "Cait?"

Blinking, she came back to the present. "I... What?"

"Now that the storm is over and the sun is shining," I asked her, "how long before the roads are passable again?"

"The sun is shining." She blinked and looked back at the lodge. It was a beautiful place, fitting into the landscape as if it were a part of it. "How am I going to keep the guests off the slopes now? With a killer on the loose? How am I going to keep anyone safe... without Finn?" Her eyes were growing wild when she turned to Mason. "We have to get them out of here. All of them. We have to send them home."

"Once the police get here, we can do that. They're going to want to clear the guests one at a time," he said.

That didn't help. She still looked panicky. So I took a swing at it. "For this morning, Cait, you can tell the guests that the lifts are down due to the storm, the power outage, whatever, and that they'll be up and running as soon as possible. Probably before the day is out. You can tell them the truth once the cavalry arrives. But we need to know how soon that will be."

I was reaching her. She was listening, nodding as I spoke. "Noon, at the latest. Probably. I sent a pair of Finn's boys out on sleds to try to get through to the village and let the police know how bad things are up here."

"Great. Once someone knows what's going on, they'll get to us as fast as humanly possible," I said, looking for something positive in this mess.

"Can you communicate with the people you sent out?" Mason asked.

She nodded, her gaze drifting back to the shack door. "Yeah, with the walkie-talkies, when they're in range." She licked her lips. "The base station is in there," she said, nodding at the door. "I have a handset in my office."

"Good," Mason said. "I need you to lock this door and make sure no one goes inside. Post someone here. I want it watched until the police arrive."

"All right."

"We'll try to reach your team from your office, and I'll give them the number to reach my people in Binghamton. They're familiar with the case and can fill the local guys in."

"Okay."

"Then I have to get back to my family."

Cait blinked at him. "You…what? No. I need you here, Detective. I can't keep all these people safe by myself. Not without Finn. I need your help."

He went silent, looked at me, and I looked right back at him. I didn't really see how he could refuse the poor woman when she was practically begging, clearly grieving, and terrified, to boot. I said, "We'll stay and help you, Cait."

Mason shot me a look, but I told him, "It'll be okay. Rosie can bring the family over to the lodge. It'll give us more eyes watching over everyone, your mom and the boys will be under the same roof, and Josh will have his water slides back again. Win-win, right?"

He looked worried. But he didn't say a word.

16

It was a waiting game, and a tense one. Mason and one of the security staff took the Abominable out to the cabin to gather the family. I told him to have them bring extra clothes, because we might not get back there tonight, though I had every intention of returning myself to pick up Myrtle just as soon as I knew where things were going, not to mention where in the lodge they found room for us. She was fine by herself for a few hours as long as her food dish was full and her bed was warm.

While we waited for everyone to get there, Mason went off with Cait to talk to her security staff, and I stayed with Mason's mother, who knew absolutely nothing about anything that had gone on, and Marlayna, who did. Marlayna looked pale and nervous, and Angela clearly knew something was being kept from her. I was kind of surprised she wasn't demanding to know what. I would've been. But then, she wasn't like me. She would rather be kept in the dark about the unpleasant stuff. She'd probably always been one of those "let the men handle it" sort of women.

Huh. No wonder she's not a fan. I'm her polar opposite.

The gang arrived in the nick of time, saving me from having to figure out how to go on keeping her in the dark while still managing to reassure Marlayna. And since all Josh cared about was the water park, that was where we wound up. Splashing and sliding seemed inappropriate with poor Finnegan lying in the Security Shack getting cold, so I didn't join in. Jeremy and Misty did, though, and it looked as if they were having the time of their lives in short order.

Good. It was doing them good to have a little fun. And I thought Jeremy was looking a bit better, too.

I ordered mounds of junk food for lunch, since Mason and I had missed breakfast thanks to our early morning wake-up call from Cait, and I was starving. Stacks of burgers and mounds of fries. The lodge served the ones with the coating on them, so they were extra fattening and extra delicious. Misty wrinkled her nose and asked for a salad. I told her a burger wouldn't hurt her and might help her with her skiing. You know, make her heavy enough to actually slide downhill. Ha ha, she said, then went and got a salad.

Pretending things were fine was wearing on me.

At twelve-thirty Cait found us. By then the table was devoid of everything but empty plates, Angela had gone off in search of a drink of something stronger than hot cocoa, and Marlayna and Rosie had gone with her. Frankly, I thought Marlayna had already tipped a few that morning, but I didn't blame her. She was trapped in the wilderness with a murderer, and she was scared.

It was just Marie and me at our little round table near the water slides, watching the kids splash and raise hell, when Cait and Mason joined us.

Cait didn't even sit down. "Our guys got through. The roads are still blocked, but the police are coming in by helicopter. Another hour and they should be here."

I sighed in relief. I don't know why. I'd had *police* with me all week long, and it wasn't like anyone who might be coming in was going to be better at his job than Mason Brown was. I guess the thought of backup, extra sets of eyes and hands and guns, was what felt so good. And knowing that this was almost over.

It was almost over, and we were all still alive.

Mason said, "They're going to want a complete list of the guests when they arrive. We can't have our guy avoiding them, if he's here."

"They'll probably want the evidence we collected too, Mason," I told him, thinking of my Secret Santa gift.

He met my eyes. "It's still at the cabin."

"Should we—"

"Not until they get here. We're too close," he said. "I'm not letting you or my family out of my sight until we have more hands on deck. Then we'll go get everything."

"Okay, so we have an hour to kill, then." I sat back down in my spot. One more hour. One more hour and we would be home free.

The helicopter landed a few hundred yards from the lodge, but it was fully visible from the giant windows of the dining room. We knew the cops were coming via Cait's men and their walkie-talkies, so we'd hustled the kids out of the water, gotten them dried off and dressed, and grabbed a table in the dining area off the lobby bar, instead of in the restaurant, because it was more centrally located.

Every guest who had been bitching about the lifts still being down at one in the afternoon on a sunny, bright December 23 was now at the window gaping at the band of men debarking from the chopper. Mason pulled on his coat, and he and Cait headed outside to meet them. Some of them wore overcoats that said POLICE across the back. Discreet they were not.

"What's going on, Aunt Rache?" Misty asked as we stared out the window like everyone else in the place.

"I've been wondering that for several days now," Angela said.

Marie looked scared. Maybe she was still afraid Jeremy was involved, and the sight of those cops would have been terrifying if that was the case. I put a hand on her arm and watched as Mason talked to the apparent head cop. And then two of the guys in the POLICE coats came trotting toward the lodge entrance. When they came in, they paused briefly at the desk, spoke to the girl on duty there, and then came straight to our table, near the windows. They were young. Barely out of braces, I thought, but rugged-looking, and deadly serious.

"Are you the Brown family?" one of them asked me. I guess I looked like the head of our little group.

"Sort of," I said. "I'm Rachel de Luca, and this is my niece Misty. The rest are Browns, Marie, Angela, Jeremy and Joshua." I didn't bother introducing Rosie, who'd walked Marlayna over to the bar for another drink. Poor woman was barely holding it together.

"Officer Bennett," he said. "This is Officer Johnson. We're here to protect you."

Just then the PA system carried the desk clerk's voice far and wide. I looked across the lobby at her, and I thought she looked as scared as she sounded. "All lodge guests please report to the lobby immediately. Again, everyone is asked to please report to the lobby immediately in a calm and orderly manner."

People were really muttering now, and we were

definitely the center of attention, with the two cops
flanking our table like we were A-list celebs and
they were our bodyguards. One brave fellow the size
of a linebacker got up from his table of seven and
started to approach us, but Bennett put his hand on
his gun, while Johnson strode right up to the guy to
cut off his progress.

"Whoa, whoa, I just wanted to ask what's going
on," the probably innocent guy said, backing away.

"Information will be forthcoming," said Johnson.
He might look young, but his uniform and his de-
meanor were clearly no-nonsense, and the other guy,
who was twice his size, backed down fast.

I saw Mason leading a handful of the other cops,
including the apparent boss, out to the Security
Shack, while Cait and the rest of them entered the
lodge. The elevators pinged, and more people came
out. They were obeying the announcement, and the
lobby, the lobby bar and the second-floor hallway
that looked down over the lobby were all soon filled
with guests waiting to hear what was going on.

Cait, with a cop in a trench coat that looked nowhere near warm enough, went to the front desk and
took the microphone the clerk had been using earlier. She looked at the cop, and he gave her a nod.

She started talking. "During the storm, we had
an incident here at the lodge. A crime was commit-
ted, and there is a chance that the perpetrator is still
here. The police are here to protect you all until the
road is cleared so that you can go home safely. Since

that isn't likely to be until later tonight, they will use the time to interview each of you."

Now the muttering took a turn for the louder, and someone shouted, "What kind of crime?"

"Screw this, I'm leaving right now," someone muttered from the depths of the crowd.

The trench coat cop, fifty-something and handsome enough to play a cop in a film, took the mike from Cait. "Quiet down, please," he said. "I'm Lieutenant Mendosa, and I'm in charge here. You're all perfectly safe, I can assure you of that. I'm also here to assure you that *no one* is going *anywhere* until the road is passable again and we've cleared you to leave. This is for your own protection."

Cait snatched the mike back, and the surprised look the cop sent her was priceless. "You're all going to get vouchers for a free stay to make up for this disastrous holiday. And no one will be billed for the past few days. I am so very sorry. And I promise, you'll be able to leave tonight."

"I'm calling my lawyer," someone muttered, pulling out his cell phone.

"Don't be a douchebag," I said, and I said it at full volume. "And good luck, since the storm knocked out the local cell tower."

He scowled at me, then quickly looked down at his phone. Then he did what everyone does when there are no bars showing—he held it up in the air and turned in a slow circle.

"Douchebag," I muttered.

Mason came back inside stomping snow off his boots, and went over to speak briefly to Lt. Mendosa, then came to our table, nodded at the cops and looked at me. "I have to get that Secret Santa gift evidence out of the cabin and get it to the cops."

"Not without me, you're not."

"I just want to lie down," Marie said softly. "This has been too much, just too much."

"You can use my room," Angela said. "I intend to stay here and make good use of the bar."

Marie stared at her boys. "I'm a little afraid to go up there alone."

Jeremy looked at his mother, and I saw him man up. He was a good kid. He really was. "I'll go up with you for a little while, Mom."

"Me, too," Josh said.

They all got up. The two cops looked to Mason for instructions, and Mason hesitated.

Rosie clapped him on the shoulder. "Have these two go on upstairs with Marie and the boys, Mace. I'll keep an eye on your mother, Marlayna and Misty down here."

That made sense, since Angela was even now at the bar with Marlayna, ordering more drinks. Misty was with them, drinking what I sincerely hoped was an ordinary soft drink.

"We won't be long," Mason said.

I grabbed my coat from the booth where we'd all been sitting. I'd stuffed my hat and gloves into the pockets, and my boots were still on my feet. On the way to the door, I veered left to the bar, swept Misty's glass to my lips for a taste, then nodded in approval.

"Hell, Aunt Rache. Suspicious much?"

"Just making sure."

Mason was looking grim, but that made him smile a little as his eyes met mine.

I zipped my coat, donned my hat and gloves, and we left. "We're bringing Myrtle back with us," I said. "And I don't care who likes it. I hate her being out there all alone with a killer on the loose."

I expected him to argue, but instead he said, "I don't like it, either. I don't think anyone will give you any trouble about it, though. This place is pet-friendly. Besides, with any luck we'll be on the road home by the end of the day." He stopped by a pair of snowmobiles, picked a helmet up from the seat of one of them and handed it to me.

"Can't be soon enough for me," I said, putting it on. Then I got on one machine, he got on the other and we were out of there.

"There's my long-suffering pup-dog. Poor baby, all alone all morning." I was on the floor, scratching Myrtle right in front of her ears, her favorite thing in all the world. "I'm gonna buy you a steak, princess. A big, extra-rare filet mignon. That's what I'm gonna do."

She wriggled her backside in delight, then whined a little and turned toward the door. "Yeah, I know. You must be about to burst. Come on." I took her leash off the hook by the door and snapped it onto her collar. "Be right back, Mason."

"Wait, I'll come with you."

"Just grab the stuff. We won't leave the backyard. Promise." He nodded, and we headed outside.

It was beautiful today. You never would have known how utterly miserable it had been only hours before. The trees were still coated in snow, so everything looked dusted in confectioner's sugar, but the brutal wind and dark skies had vanished. Nothing but baby blue now, and the sun as bright and yellow as I'd ever seen it, making the snow sparkle. Really sparkle, like a kindergarten class had been set loose with a few hundred tons of glitter.

Wow.

As was my habit, I didn't lead Myrtle but let her lead me so long as she felt comfortable. She was very particular about where she chose to do her business, and I'd figured out early on that there was no point in trying to choose for her, and even less point in trying to rush her. She was on Myrtle time, and this decision was as important as any being made in… oh, I don't know…say, the White House.

She sniffed and snuffled and pushed snow around with her head like a little plow, and eventually we wound up behind the cabin, near the edge of those woods in which we'd found poor Alan Douglas. I rubbed my arms and looked at Myrt. "Will you hurry up? I don't like it out here."

"Don't worry," Mason said from somewhere close but…high.

I looked up. He was looking down from one of the second-floor bedroom windows. "You haven't been out of my sight for more than a second, Rache."

I'm pretty sure I sent him the goofiest smile he'd ever seen, and I quickly lowered my head to hide it. I must've looked like a love-struck puppy, and that was just so not me.

Lately, girlfriend, it's precisely you.

I know it is, Inner Bitch. I know it is. So do I fight it or just give in to it?

Do what feels best. Isn't that what you preach to the masses?

Doesn't mean I believe it.

Maybe it's time to start. I mean, come on, Rachel. Don't you ever wonder why the bullshit you write appeals to so many people all over the world? Don't you ever wonder why so many of them write to you telling you how your books changed their lives? Saved their lives, sometimes? It's obviously working for them, or they wouldn't keep coming back for more.

I never really stopped to think about that.

Then think about it now. If it works for all of them, maybe it's not all bullshit after all.

I rolled my eyes.

Mason doesn't think it is.

Myrtle had finished her job and was kicking up snow with her hind legs with all the agility of a mule on crack. She did it every single time. I had no idea why. Then she bounded through the snow like a child, burying her face, shaking it back and forth in the white fluff, then looking up again toward me with snow all over her.

"You look like a miniature Yeti," I muttered, then looked up to see if Mason was catching this little display.

He was. His warm smile beamed down, and I went all goofy inside again. Hell. Had I forgotten there was a murderer after me?

I started to look away, but something fluttering two windows over from Mason caught my eye. I squinted and realized it was the edge of a curtain, caught in the window frame.

Part of my brain kicked into overdrive, while the other part kept telling me it was nothing. So someone had opened a window and shut the curtain in it. It was no big deal. Right?

"Come on, Myrt, let's go inside."

She trotted along beside me, right up to the back door, where Mason had appeared. I bent, unsnapped the leash, petted my dog and straightened again.

He took one look at me, and asked, "What's wrong?"

Too perceptive, this guy. "There's a window upstairs with a piece of the curtain shut in it."

His frown came fast and hard.

"You looked around out back yesterday, right?" I asked. " After we thought Jeremy had snuck out?"

"Yeah. I looked thoroughly. There was nothing like that."

"Unless you missed it."

He was already heading upstairs. I raced behind him.

"I didn't miss it."

"So that means someone opened a bedroom window since then. Which means during the storm."

"Uh-huh." He went straight to Jeremy's room, opened the door and strode to the window. But the curtains there were hanging normally.

I was still in the doorway, so I had a head start checking the next room. Marie's room. I opened her door and went straight to the window with the curtain caught in it.

"Why would Marie have had her window open during that storm?"

Mason came over to where I was standing and looked out the window at the smaller roof jutting out below it, where the kitchen was.

"Do you think that's how she snuck out to go meet Douglas?" I asked. "We never asked her." I looked past him. "It wouldn't be hard, with that lower roof to jump onto. From there to the ground isn't too tough a leap."

"She's a grown woman with two kids. Why would she be jumping out of windows and climbing over rooftops in the dead of night in a snowstorm? Besides, that would explain her sneaking out the night *before* last. This had to happen *last* night."

I glanced at the nightstand. Box of tissues. Magazine. Alarm clock slash radio. "She's been through a lot. I'm sure she had her— Wait a minute, what the hell is this?" I went to the nightstand and picked up the magazine, then turned to show it to Mason. *"Book Review Weekly."*

He frowned at me. "Why is that important?"

I was flipping pages rapidly. "It's a couple years old, for one thing. For another— Oh, my God." I'd stopped flipping pages, and my heart jumped into my throat. Mason came closer to look at what had me so dumbstruck and saw what I did. The page with the review of my book *Create Your Life*. It had a tiny rectangular bit cut out of it.

The bit that had called me "the archangel of new-age spirituality."

Mason pulled a plastic zipper bag from his pocket and held it up. The clipping from the Secret Santa gift was in it, nice and flat, and it was the same size and shape. It was also the missing phrase of my best review ever. It wasn't like I would forget it.

"This doesn't make any sense," Mason whispered. "*She* was attacked by this guy, too."

I was onto her now, though, and the pieces were falling into place for me as I paced. "No, no, it makes perfect sense. Mason. The person who attacked me in my car was there when I rolled it down that embankment. She would have been pretty banged up from the accident."

"She?"

"Then we got back to Marie's and found her all bruised and battered. She was never attacked, Mason. She made it up to account for the bruises she got when I rolled my car. It was her. It was her all along."

I walked as I talked, and my toe caught on something on the floor. Looking down, I saw a perfectly rolled-up blanket stuffed just under the edge of the bed. Bending, I swept it up and shook it at him. "*This* is how she fooled me when I was checking on her last night. She put this in the bed. The first few times I checked on her, this was taking up space. A freaking teenager's trick, and I fell for it. I thought she was lying there sleeping while she was out killing poor Finnegan and taking that phone so we wouldn't find out it was hers."

Mason's eyes met mine. "She tried to frame Jeremy. With the jackknife. Her own son!" Then his eyes went wider. "She's with the boys now!"

I turned and ran, and so did he. Poor Myrtle had to stay behind once more as we pulled on our coats, jumped onto the snowmobiles and sped back toward the lodge. I drove so fast I scared myself.

It wasn't far but it seemed to take forever. We killed the engines and raced inside, drawing the attention of Rosie and Lieutenant Mendosa as we ran past the front desk and through the crowded lobby toward the bar.

"Where are Marie and the boys?" Mason asked

before we even made it to where Marlayna, Angela and Misty were sitting.

"Still up in my room, resting," Angela replied.

"Do you have another key?" Mason asked her.

Nodding, Angela slid one from her handbag and handed it to him.

"What's going on? What's wrong?" Misty asked, jumping off her bar stool.

But Mason was already racing for the elevators.

"Just...just wait here," I said, and ran after him.

He pushed a button. I pushed it again.

"What's going on?" Mendosa asked.

Rosie was behind him, but kept looking back over his shoulder toward the bar where Marlayna was.

Mason told him to go stay with his wife, then stared impatiently at the elevator, which hadn't yet arrived.

"Stairs!" I pointed at the door with the familiar logo, yanked it open and started up.

"Room four-nineteen!" Mason shouted from behind me.

The place only had four stories. It figured Angela's room would be on the fourth one.

We ran, and I was faster than I thought I was capable of being. When we hit the fourth-floor landing I shoved the door open and lunged out into the hallway.

"Turn right, end of the hall!" Mason said, right beside me.

I sprinted so fast that as I rounded the corner the young cop standing guard outside the door reached for his gun. It had half cleared its holster by the time he recognized us and I skidded to a stumbling halt, holding up both hands to tell him not to shoot and almost falling over. Mason, who'd stopped faster, caught me from behind. "Easy, pal. We need to get in there." He started forward with the key card just as Mendosa caught up to us, gun drawn.

From a distance I heard the elevator ding open, and then Misty ran up—alone, thank God. "What the hell, Aunt Rache?"

I just held up a hand. Mason opened the door, and he and Mendosa burst into the room, guns drawn. The young cop followed them in, his own gun at the ready, too.

I ventured closer when I didn't hear anything, holding Misty behind me with one outstretched arm. She was crying softly now. Inching into the room, I saw that no one was there. No Jeremy. No Joshua. No Marie. Only the cops.

I half registered that Mendosa was on the phone as I took in the fact that the French doors were ajar. I went over and opened them fully, then stepped out onto the small balcony, where I saw that a pre-attached rope ladder, obviously designed to serve as a fire escape, had been deployed and was swaying in the wind.

"Dammit, she's got the boys," I said. "Both of them."

"Of course she does. She's their mother. But... why did they leave?" Misty whispered.

I saw her eyes searching mine, begging me to say anything other than what I did.

"She's the killer," I told her.

Misty clapped a hand to her mouth, her eyes going huge. Then she raced to the railing and leaned over. "Jeremy! Josh! Where are you?"

I put an arm around her and drew her back inside. She was still crying.

Mendosa looked from me to Mason, his questions in his eyes.

Mason handed him the zipper bag with the clipping inside it. "This was the clipping in that Secret Santa gift, the angel with the missing eyes. We found the magazine it was cut from in Marie's room."

"And a rolled-up blanket by the bed that she probably used to make us think she was sleeping when we checked on her last night."

Mason climbed over the railing onto the rope ladder, then paused and looked back at us. "Mendosa, get your men to organize a search. I'll start from here, and your men can start from the lobby. There's no way she didn't leave tracks."

"I'm coming with you," I said. "Misty, go back to the lobby bar and stay there with Angela, okay?"

"Do you think she'd hurt them? She wouldn't, would she? She's their mother."

"They're going to be okay. You just keep believing that, all right?" Mason was already halfway down the ladder. "I've gotta go, honey. We'll bring them back, I promise."

Mendosa put a hand on her shoulder, assuring me with his eyes that he would watch over her, then keyed his walkie on to update his men down in the lobby. Reassured, I headed down the ladder after Mason.

When we reached the bottom, I saw the tracks in the snow as clearly as he did. Three sets, one really big that had to be Jeremy's. Mason warned me to stay next to the footprints and not obliterate them as we followed the trail around the building, but they ended at the freshly plowed parking lot.

"The Jeep's gone," Mason said, cussing under his breath as he ran to the empty spot where it had been. "She must have taken my keys from the cabin."

He was looking toward the road when I heard running feet on blacktop. Mendosa called, "She's not going to get far. The grounds staff may have cleared the lot, but it's going to take a lot longer for the roads to be plowed."

"My mother leaves her keys in the car," Mason said. "Never takes them out, because there's a keypad on the door. Come on, Mendosa. Rachel, I want you to stay here."

"What? No!"

Mendosa caught up to us, looking around the lot. "Which car?"

"The Escalade," I said, pointing. "But—"

"No buts, Ms. de Luca. We're cops. You're not. Stay here," Mendosa said as Mason hit the numbered buttons on the door.

"I'll drive," Mason said. "You can radio in to get that chopper back in the air." Mendosa pulled out his walkie and was speaking into it while he got in the passenger side of Angela's Escalade.

Mason came straight to me, gripped my shoulders in both hands and kissed me hard on the mouth. "I have to go. Please go back inside and be safe. I can't lose anyone else I love right now."

"You...huh?"

But he'd already let me go and was diving behind the wheel. Then the SUV roared, lurched and was speeding across the parking lot and out of sight onto the narrow gravel road.

And then an arm came around me from behind and I felt a needle sink into my neck.

17

Saturday, December 23

Mason was stunned when they were only about two miles from the lodge and he saw the Jeep heading back toward them. With Jeremy at the wheel.

He braked fast, and so did the Jeep, skidding sideways a little, then coming to a stop at a cockeyed angle in the middle of the still-snowy road.

"We've got them," Mendosa said into his walkie. "Get backup out here. Two miles north on the lodge road. Cancel the chopper."

Something in Mason's gut was telling him this wasn't right. He got out of the car, gun drawn but barrel down, quickly moving to the Jeep and scanning the interior for Marie.

Jeremy opened his door and got out, looking pale and wide-eyed at his uncle. "Uncle Mace, what the *hell?*"

"Move away from the car, Jer." He took Jeremy

by the shoulder with his free hand, moving him to one side. "Where's your mother?"

Jeremy shook his head in anger and confusion, taking a few halting steps toward the Caddy and Mendosa. Mason swooped around the open driver's door, gun first, looking inside. Joshua was looking back at him, eyes huge.

"It's all right, Josh. I'm here. It's okay. Where's your mother?" Leaning into the vehicle, Mason checked the backseat. "Where's your mother, Josh?" He looked into the cargo area in the back. Mendosa was already back there, opening the hatch and looking around inside. He met Mason's eyes over the backseat and shook his head.

Josh was crying. "Uncle Mace, you're scaring me! What's going on?"

"Come on, Josh, come on out of the car." Josh did, and Mason put an arm around his shoulders, leading him to the Caddy, where Jeremy was standing, glaring at him.

"I'm not gonna ask you again, Jer. Where is your mother?"

"She's at the lodge."

Mason shoved his gun into his jeans. "Tell me everything," he said, then, "No, get in the car. *Then* tell me everything." He kept his arm around Josh, leading him, then opened the back door of the Escalade and picked Josh right up and set him on the seat. "Jer, move it, okay?"

"But the Jeep—" Jeremy said.

"Leave the fucking Jeep. Get in. Now." Mason held the door open while Joshua scooted to the other side to make room for Jeremy.

Mendosa took the wheel, so Mason got into the front passenger seat. He leaned over the backseat to talk to the boys while Mendosa turned the SUV around and gunned it for the lodge. "Tell me everything, Jer. And don't leave anything out."

Nodding, Jeremy started talking. "Mom said she thought the cop guarding our door might be getting ready to arrest me. But she said she'd heard the roads were open, so she wanted me to take Josh into the village, where we'd be safe until she could get me a good lawyer. We went down the rope ladder, sneaked out to the parking lot, and she gave me the keys to your Jeep, Uncle Mason. I'm sorry, but I was scared. I don't want to go to jail. I didn't do anything."

"I know you didn't. I know. We all know. It's all right. You were just doing what she told you."

"Something's wrong with her," Josh said softly. "She wasn't acting right."

Jeremy put an arm around his brother's shoulders and told Mason with his eyes that he agreed. "Mom was wrong about the road. It was plowed for a little ways, but a couple miles out it was still blocked with, like, a mountain of snow. So we turned around to head back to the lodge, and then you were there."

"Where was the last place you saw your mother?" Mason asked.

"In the parking lot."

Mendosa shot Mason a look, and he knew they were thinking the same thing. *That's right where we left Rachel.* Though he doubted the lieutenant was experiencing the same gut-wrenching dread that he was.

I have never thought of myself as having the reactions of a ninja, but when I felt that fucking needle sink into my neck I channeled one. That was the only way to describe what happened. There was no wondering what the hell was happening, no mistaking the jab for a bee sting. Nothing like that. I knew—instantly, I *knew*—that it was a needle full of succinyl-nowyou'redead, that it would paralyze me, leaving me to suffocate slowly to death while Marie cut out my eyes.

I knew all of that in the nanosecond it took to feel the jab, and my hand shot up fast in an instinctive act of self-preservation. I wedged my thumb under the plunger, hitting a target I couldn't see—no great task for me, right?—and kept it from depressing any farther. I clenched my fingers around the rest of the syringe and I twisted hard, wrenching it away from Marie. There was a snapping sound, and the syringe flew. It landed on the freshly plowed blacktop, almost at my feet, the needle broken off. Was the tip still in my neck?

"Bitch!" Marie shouted, jumping at me with her hands going for my throat. I punched her in the face with everything in me, knocking her backward into a snowbank, and then I spun around and ran. One lunging step forward, then two, and then I was moving in slow motion. It felt like I was wading through mud. No, something thicker. Quicksand, maybe, or fast-drying concrete.

Oh, no. Oh no no no no, the sux got in, my muscles are shutting down.

My body wasn't responding to my commands. It was exactly like one of those nightmares when you have to run very fast, but your body refuses to do what your brain tells it, and you can barely move at all. I was running for the lodge mentally, but my body was barely moving. Barely responding.

And then I went down, face-first in the snow along the edge of the parking lot.

How much did that bitch manage to get into me? Enough so I'll suffocate? Enough to kill me? Or will I live through this nightmare right to the end? I wonder which is worse?

Her hands were on my shoulders, rolling me onto my back. And I felt it. I felt everything. I tried to will my legs to move. My arms to move. God, I was getting dizzy. Had my lungs already stopped functioning? I told myself to breathe. Inhale. Exhale. Yes, it seemed to be working, not easily, but a little, despite the black spots starting to pop in and out of existence in front of my eyes.

Marie's little red caboose had definitely gone chugging around the bend, I thought. She'd lost it. She vanished for a few seconds. Maybe a few minutes. I don't know. I tried to call for help, but there wasn't enough air in my lungs to make more than a whimper.

This isn't happening. It can't be happening.

I heard a motor, the familiar roar of a snowmobile, and shifted my eyes in its direction, praying I could somehow get the driver's attention. But Marie was the one driving it, speeding right up to where I lay between two cars in the parking lot. She drove it right up beside me, then past me, and I saw the red plastic toboggan she was towing. She rolled me onto the sled, wrapped a rope around me to hold me on board and then jumped back on the snowmobile and gunned it. My body bounced and bumped as I was pulled farther and farther from the lodge and out into the woods. The cheap plastic toboggan tried to buck me off at every bump and fling me over the side at every turn. There was nothing I could do to hold on. I couldn't move.

She won't take me far, I told myself as my back took a pounding from the terrain. *The sux won't last long enough for her to take me far. I'll either be dead or it'll wear off. Which reminds me...*

Inhale.

Exhale.

Repeat.

I'm still breathing. Just a little. Tiny, tantalizing tastes of air, not even enough to blow the seeds off a dandelion. But maybe enough to keep me alive.

But do I want that? Do I really want to keep my-

*self alive? Because I know what's coming next. Do
I really want to be present for that?*

Where the hell is Mason?

Mendosa had radioed his second-in-command to
send men into the parking lot to look for Marie and
Rachel, but the black Escalade was skidding to a
halt in the parking lot before his men even had time
to report back.

Mason jumped out of the SUV and ran to where
Mendosa's men had gathered. As he shoved his way
through them, he saw the syringe lying in the snow,
along with a few drops of blood and signs of a struggle. He swore softly, bending down for a closer look
at the needle. The tip was broken off. Probably happened when it landed on the pavement. But it looked
as if there was still quite a bit of the drug inside.
Maybc there was hope.

There had damn well better be hope. God, what
the hell had happened to Marie to turn her into a
stone-cold killer?

He saw snowmobile tracks leading out of the
parking lot and into the woods west of the lodge.
He looked at the men. "I need a snowmobile. Hurry."

"Bring two!" Mendosa shouted.

Mendosa's men raced to where the machines were
lined up, only yards away.

"What's going on, Uncle Mason?" Jeremy called
from inside the Escalade.

"I don't know."

"It's Mom, isn't it? She's lost it, just like Dad did. Hasn't she?"

Mason looked at the boy, and Jeremy tipped his head back and turned away. "I knew it. I should have said something. I knew she was slipping. Talking to herself, sometimes to Dad, late at night. Dammit, I knew. I just thought she'd get better, you know? I just thought..."

"It's not your fault, Jeremy. None of this is."

"She took Rachel, didn't she? Is she going to hurt her?"

"Jeremy, we don't know anything for sure, but I'm going to find them both, I promise you that. Right now, though, I need you here. I need you to take care of your brother. And I need you to send someone out to the cabin to get Myrtle."

Snowmobiles skidded to a halt, more than just two of them. Misty jumped off the back of one driven by Rosie and flung herself into Jeremy's arms. "Are you okay? I was so scared when you weren't in the room!"

"Rosie, get Misty and the boys back to the lodge."

Rosie nodded and dismounted, and Mason jumped on the vacated snowmobile and took off, following the trail Marie had left. As he sped through the snow, Rachel's words about death came back to him. About how your flaws were erased, how you got better on the other side. And he started praying with everything in him. *Eric, if you can hear me, and if there's any way you can help here, you've got to step up,*

*bro. You've gotta stop her. Stop her, Eric. Redeem
yourself. You fucking owe me. And God knows you
owe Rachel.*

Marie stopped the snowmobile, untied the tow
rope and pulled me through the woods on the plastic sled. It shouldn't have been easy for her, but
she seemed to have developed some kind of super
strength or something. I guess she figured the
snowmobile tracks would be too easy to follow, or
maybe she was taking me somewhere the snowmobile couldn't go. I couldn't see what was ahead of
us, only behind, lying face up on the sled, unable to
move my head. Dizziness swamped me again.

*Breathe in. Breathe out. You dumbass, if you keep
forgetting, you're gonna die.*

So I did. I breathed those almost-worthless whiffs
of not nearly enough air, and I tried to breathe them
faster, to make up in frequency for what they lacked
in size.

But then I couldn't anymore, because Marie sat
on my chest and used her legs to propel the sled forward. It tilted sharply down, and I realized we were
at the top of a hill, a steep one, and before I even
had time to panic we were flying downward at dizzying speed. The dark spots returned, expanding
to fill up more space in my eyes. I tried to inhale,
but my lungs couldn't fight her weight. I was going
to die right there. My lungs screamed for air, but I
couldn't give them any.

We finally stopped and she rolled off me.

Breathe in! Quick!

I did, inhaling for all I was worth, but it amounted to a breath so small and so shallow that it didn't even make a sound. I did it again and again and again, all the while wondering why I was fighting so hard to stay alive.

Because I fucking believe, that's why! I believe! This is not the way my life is supposed to end. I did not get my eyesight back after twenty years only to die a few months later. And I did not meet Mason Brown just to put off being with him until it was too late. This isn't how it's supposed to work.

My own platitudes, all the words I'd ever written, played through my mind. You create your own experience according to what you believe. Okay, then, what do I believe?

I believe that I am not going out like this. I'm going to have a happy ending, dammit, and this isn't it.

Do you really believe that, Rache, or are you just trying real hard to?

I mentally cussed out my inner bitch, but while I was at it I searched my soul, and I knew that I honestly did not believe Marie was going to cut out my eyes. I didn't. That's why I was fighting so hard to breathe. Because somewhere inside me I knew it wasn't going to end this way.

And what about Marie, Pollyanna? What did she believe that led her to this?

Marie dragged me a little farther into the cover of some nearby pines. And then she finally stopped and sank to the ground, panting.

God, I wish I could pant like that. My lungs are starving. Breathe in, breathe in, breathe in, dammit!

"I have to put my family back together," she said softly. It startled me, when I realized she was speaking to me. "Everything was taken away. Everything. And I know it was punishment."

She moved closer, kneeling in the snow beside me, taking a backpack from her shoulders. "I knew what my husband was. What he was doing. I knew it. And I didn't tell. I just... I kept his secrets. I let him do what he needed to do. I could see how it was with him. How tense and tight he'd get just before... And how relaxed and easy he'd be right after. He couldn't help it. He wasn't a monster."

Not a monster? I would have laughed if I could have. *He was a sick, twisted fuck, and apparently you two were a perfect match.*

Breathe in. Breathe out.

"He took his own life. He wanted to stop so badly that he killed himself. And still the killing went on. I knew, you see. Mason didn't tell me, but I knew. The people who got Eric's organs went on killing."

Not all of them. Only Terry Skullbones and Dr. Vosberg. No one else.

"I knew when I lost the baby that I was being punished. Eric wanted the killing to stop, and I could have turned him in, stopped him when he was alive, but I didn't. He'd still be alive if I had, but I didn't. He wanted me to stop the killing. And I knew...I knew the only way to do that was to take back the organs. Take them all back. And then I could join him in the afterlife."

That is one warped and twisted theory, Marie.
Breathe, breathe, breathe.

She unzipped her backpack and took out a tiny blade, a glass jar with a lid and a bottle of what I thought was alcohol. Everything was surreal, fading in and out. I had the distinct impression that I kept leaving my body, floating above it and looking down at myself there on the sled under those strong-scented pines. I heard the way their needles whispered against each other in every breeze. Marie leaned closer to my face, kneeling beside me in the snow. "I might not be able to get them all, now that Mason is so close to figuring it out. But I can get his eyes, and maybe, if I'm smart and clever, a few more before they catch me. I'm sorry about this, Rachel. I like you. But I can't take the risk that you'll start murdering people like Eric did."

I'm the one who stopped him, you crazy bitch!

I told my body to breathe, then tried to drag my focus away from the me on the ground. That me was looking pretty rough right now, eyes open but blank and dull, mouth open, still trying to grasp those tiny insignificant bits of air, nothing moving except my hair, and that only because the wind kept blowing it.

I tried to look away from Marie and what she was

about to do, and realized that I was expanding, floating higher. I knew then that it was over, because there was no possible way I could fit back inside my body now. No way. I couldn't believe I'd been wrong. That I really *was* going to die. It still didn't seem possible.

And then I saw him. Eric Conroy Brown. Mason's brother.

He was standing there, reaching out to me. The serial killer responsible for all of this. The one who'd killed my brother. That *bastard*.

But then I saw someone else, a little farther away. I frowned and inwardly whispered, *Tommy?*

Not the gaunt, addicted version in the photos we'd shown the police when he'd gone missing. But healthy, strong, and also utterly serene. He looked at Eric's outstretched hands, and then he looked at me and nodded.

So I let the murderer take hold of my hands, although I didn't really have hands anymore. I told myself this was just how I was experiencing this oxygen-deprived hallucination.

It's real and you know it.

Yeah. I guess I do.

Then I looked down again at what I did not want to see. Marie was straddling my body now, holding the blade near my eyes. My eyes had fallen closed. I wondered if I was dead. But right at that instant I felt Eric's nonexistent hands squeeze mine, and my eyes, the real ones, popped open. They were wide, and they were unfamiliar to me. Brown, not blue.

Marie shot off my body as if she'd taken a bullet in the chest, landing on her ass in the snow, the blade flying from her hand. Then she blinked wide-eyed at my dying body, and whispered, "Eric?"

I looked around for him, but he wasn't there anymore. I saw my brother in the distance. He smiled and looked down again, so I did, too, and saw Mason's snowmobile diving over the lip of that hill and speeding recklessly down it. At the bottom he simply let go and dove off the thing, lunging through the snow toward Marie and my body, following the trail the sled had left.

It wasn't far. Way closer than it had felt when she'd been pulling me. And then he was there, leaning over my body, and I saw the way his shoulders were heaving, heard him saying my name. Then he pressed his mouth to mine and breathed air into my hungry lungs.

My brother waved goodbye, and *whoosh!* I felt as if I'd been sucked into a powerful vacuum. I opened my eyes. I was back in my body again.

Mason lifted his head. I looked out at him through my own eyes, which were still intact, still in my head and, I guessed, still blue. I reminded myself again to breathe, and it was a little bit easier this time. I needed more, but this was better.

Then something dark rose up behind him. Marie, with the scalpel poised above his back. I widened my eyes, and Mason read me, spun and caught her in the chest with an elbow. She doubled over, and he clocked her in the chin and knocked her on her ass.

He scooped me up off the sled and carried me back to the bottom of the hill where he'd left his snowmobile. We passed Lieutenant Mendosa on the way, and Mason said, "I've got to get her to a hospital. Marie's back there. She has a scalpel. Use your weapon if you need to."

"I'll radio the chopper," Mendosa said. Then he pointed. "Get her to the clearing—twenty yards that way."

I rested my head against Mason's chest and closed my eyes.

See? I was right. This wasn't how it was supposed to end.

18

Sunday, December 24

When I opened my eyes, Mason was sitting close to me, head down, eyes closed, holding my hand. I loved the way that felt, his big hand all wrapped around my smaller one. I know, that's pretty sappy, but since I almost died I'm going to allow it, just this once. I told myself to squeeze his hand so he'd know I was okay and was a little surprised—and a whole lot relieved—when my body did what I told it to.

He looked up fast, right into my eyes. "Rachel?"

I wasn't sure I'd be able to talk, but I tried it. Gave him what I hoped was a spunky smile and asked, "Who the hell else would it be?" Yikes. I sounded like a bullfrog with a cold. "So am I okay? How long have I been out? And where's my dog?"

He relaxed just like I knew he would if I mouthed off at him. "Myrtle's fine. She's with the boys. You've been out overnight. And yes, you're okay. You managed to snap the needle off in your neck. Didn't get much of the drug into your body."

"It was close, Mason. Way too close. Frankly, your family is getting to be a real pain in my ass." I stopped kidding, went serious. "Where is she? And the boys, where are they, and——"

"Easy. Here, have a drink." He was out of his chair, nervous and not knowing what to do with himself, how to act. But he held a big plastic tumbler with a straw in the top so I could take a sip.

I did. Water. Shit, I was hoping for vodka.

"Marie can't hurt anyone else. She's in jail, and she's not getting out anytime soon. Not with what she's done."

"She's sick, Mason. She needs a mental ward, not a prison sentence."

I saw the surprise in his face when I said that. "What? You're surprised I have a heart?"

"I know you have a heart," he said. "I just figured you'd be leading the lynch mob."

"Well, I'm not. So where are the boys?" I asked.

"They're asleep in the waiting room with Angela. They…they don't know everything yet. I couldn't tell them yet that their mother murdered five people." He closed his eyes.

Hell, he'd been through as much as I had. "Five?" I asked.

"The vet. She confessed to everything once we had her in custody. Even planting Jeremy's jackknife at the scene. Said she didn't really want to frame him.

Just to distract me long enough to let her complete her...mission."

Those kids. Those poor freaking kids.

"She was already falling apart by the time she killed Alan Douglas," Mason went on. "I think there was a part of her that really did like the guy. She was torn, and that made her sloppy." He looked anguished. "So how the hell do I tell Josh and Jeremy all that?"

I said, "Would it help if we told them together?"

He opened his eyes and nodded. "It would. I just don't know what I *can* tell them. How much I *should* tell them."

I scootched higher in the bed, sitting up a little, and he reached down to adjust the pillows behind me. "Tell them that their father's death and then the baby being stillborn was too much for Marie. It broke her mind. She did some bad things, hurt people. But she's not a bad person. She's just going to have to stay in a hospital where she can get some help to get better, maybe for a very long time." Because I didn't think a woman who'd murdered five people and cut the organs out of three of them would ever be pronounced sane and turned loose on society. Then again, with our system, you never know.

"And tell them that in the meantime..." I tilted my head, watching his face, and I knew what he'd decided, just like that. "In the meantime, they get to move in with their uncle Mason. Right?"

He nodded at me, and I knew I was right. He'd already made that decision. "Yeah. I'm all they have, Rachel. And that means another delay for us. For our...relationship."

"Our relationship, huh? You're not overconfident or anything, are you?"

He smiled sadly at me, and I hated to see him looking so morose. "Look, neither of us was ready for anything serious before. I had to adjust to being a sighted, independent adult, and you were just an idiot."

"Hey!"

"Don't interrupt me, I'm on a roll. Now I'm getting adjusted. I may not be all the way there yet, but I'm getting there. You, however, are a brand-new father to two bouncing half-grown motherless boys. Your life is about to change radically. You need time to settle in. See how life is gonna play out. Find your new normal."

He lowered his head. He looked so damn serious. Maybe even choked up.

"Mason, I'm not going anywhere."

His head came up. "You're not?"

"Hell, no, I'm not. What do you think? That I'd trust you to figure this out on your own? No way. At the very least you need me around to convey tips from Sandra and Jim, the best parents I know."

"So...?"

"So...we try the whole relationship thing. We

date. God, I hate that word. I help you out with the boys. You help me out with the dog. There's no reason Myrt and I can't be part of your new normal, is there?"

"No reason I can come up with."

"Good." I looked at him. He looked back at me. I said, "So are we going to kiss on it or something?"

His grin was broad, and I had a second to admire those damned killer dimples of his as he leaned in for a long, wet kiss.

When he sat up again he said, "Did you ever stop to think that we might never have found each other if all of this hadn't happened the way it did? Your brother, my brother..."

"Me being blind so you could run me over with your car."

"Yeah."

I looked him square in the eye and said, "Yes. I've thought about it."

"Think there's anything to it? Fate? Predestination? Everything happening for a reason?"

I tipped my head slightly, thinking. "I think maybe the bullshit I write isn't quite 100 percent bullshit after all."

He nodded, then got up and went over to the door, where he waved at someone out in the hall. A second later I heard running feet as Joshua came thundering into my room with Myrtle in his arms like an oversized baby. He brought her right to my bed, and she wriggled up beside me and licked my face, her whole butt wagging in joy.

I hugged her neck, basking in doggy love as Jeremy and Misty came in, arm in arm. I looked around the room, realizing the boys had become important to me. They'd become family to me. I might even love them a little.

Angela came in last of all, taking her time. When she got there, she met my eyes, came to my bedside and clasped my hand. "I'm very glad you're all right, Rachel. In the past several hours I've seen firsthand how important you've become to this family."

"Thanks, Angela. That means a lot to me."

Myrtle patted Angela's hand, her way of asking for some petting, and Angela complied. "How did you guys ever get a bulldog into a hospital?" I asked as I watched them.

"We threw your name around," Misty confessed. "She's not an official therapy dog, but in the end, they said they'd make an exception because it's Christmas Eve."

"It is, isn't it?" I looked at the boys. They looked tired, haggard, worried, heartbroken. Then I looked at Mason. "I have to get out of here, Mason. We need to have Christmas. All of us together. It's important."

"I agree," he said.

"Me, too," Jeremy put in. Joshua sat on the edge of my bed, leaning in to hug Myrtle and me all at once.

I met Mason's eyes, and I knew one thing for sure.

Everything in life, even the bad stuff, happens for a reason. And that ragtag band of misfits around me in the room right then...they were one of the best reasons there could ever be.

* * * * *

MILLS & BOON®

Mills & Boon have been at the heart of romance since 1908... and while the fashions may have changed, one thing remains the same: from pulse-pounding passion to the gentlest caress, we're always known how to bring romance alive.

Now, we're delighted to present you with these irresistible illustrations, inspired by the vintage glamour of our covers. So indulge your wildest dreams and unleash your imagination as we present the most iconic Mills & Boon moments of the last century.

Visit **www.millsandboon.co.uk/ArtofRomance** to order yours!

Bound by blood.
Separated by scandal.

Twins Calida and Terisita Santiago have never known a
world without each other… until Terisita is wrenched
from their Argentinian home to be adopted by world-
famous actress Simone Geddes.

Now, while Terisita is provided with all that money can
buy, Calida must fight her way to the top – her only
chance of reuniting with her twin.

But no-one could have predicted the explosive events
which finally bring the Santiago sisters into the
spotlight together.

M451_TSS

Loved this book?
Let us know!

Find us on **Twitter @Mira_BooksUK**
where you can share your thoughts, stay up
to date on all the news about our upcoming
releases and even be in with the chance of
winning copies of our wonderful books!

Bringing you the best voices in fiction

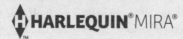